HEAT
TRAP

THE
PLUMBER'S MATE
MYSTERIES
THREE

JL MERROW

RIPTIDE
PUBLISHING

Riptide Publishing
PO Box 1537
Burnsville, NC 28714
www.riptidepublishing.com

Heat Trap

Cover art: Christine Coffee, coffeecreatescovers.com
Editor: Carole-ann Galloway
Layout: L.C. Chase, lcchase.com/design.htm

ISBN: 978-1-62649-724-5

Second edition
March, 2018

Also available in ebook:
ISBN: 978-1-62649-723-8

HEAT
TRAP

THE PLUMBER'S MATE MYSTERIES THREE

JL MERROW

RIPTIDE PUBLISHING

To all the lovely people who helped me with this book: Susan Sorrentino, SC Wynne, Pender Mackie, Lou Harper, Blaine Arden, Josephine Myles and, as ever, the stalwart members of Verulam Writers' Circle and my editor, Linda Ingmanson. I couldn't have done it without you. And to all the readers who've travelled on this journey with Tom and Phil that started with Pressure Head *and* Relief Valve—*thank you!*

TABLE OF
CONTENTS

PROLOGUE

I'd never gone into a pub cellar before—I might be a plumber, but the sort of liquids they have piped in down there aren't really my area of expertise. Then again, I suppose I've downed a few pints in my time. I'd expected it to be fairly small, just room for a few barrels and pipelines. Maybe another room where they stored the spares, and the bottles of wine and bags of crisps and stuff.

It was actually pretty massive, with four or five separate rooms leading off from the narrow stone stairway. It didn't stretch as far as the whole upstairs floor space, owing to the medieval well in the public bar which must still have been in use when the cellar was dug, but it couldn't be far off. If trade at the Devil's Dyke ever took off in a big way, landlady Harry could put in a whole separate bar down here if she wanted to. The walls were whitewashed brick, with those low, curving ceilings you always seemed to get in cellars built during Ye Olde Tymes.

It was as if I'd dropped in on a hobbit with a drinking problem.

And a housekeeping problem, come to that. It smelt pretty rank down here. There was something about the odour that made the hairs on the back of my neck stand up, although maybe it was just down to the chill in the air here after the oven-like conditions back upstairs in the land of the living. I stood stock-still, opened up the spidey-senses and *listened*.

I practically fell over with the force of the vibes buffeting me in the chest.

I couldn't believe I'd been sitting in the bar having a pint, oblivious. How could I have blocked out something that strong? There was guilt and anger—and fear too. My stomach went cold as I realised just what I was likely to find down here.

I turned to Marianne. "I reckon you've got more to worry about than a burst drain, love." My face must have looked as iffy as I felt, as she wrapped skinny arms around herself, her pretty face a picture of worry.

I followed the thick, sickly vibes out of the main cellar with its shiny metal barrels and high-tech pump lines, the hum of the chiller unit fading behind me. They took me down the dimly lit passageway that led to the farthest cellar room. It was clearly used as a dumping ground for any old rubbish Harry hadn't got around to chucking away yet.

Among other things.

It was warmer in here, although still nowhere near as hot as upstairs, and close up, the stench was sickening. Let's face it, in my profession you get used to the odd nasty niff, from blocked drains and bunged-up loos and that, but the stink of death? That's something else. I think it's the sweetness that gets to me most. Like, what the hell is something so awful doing smelling sweet? I gagged and clapped a hand over my nose and mouth. It didn't help. The reek of decay seemed to seep inside my lungs even when I wasn't inhaling. I had to force myself to go on looking.

Didn't take me long to find it. Talk about following your nose. It was wedged behind some barrels—actual old wooden ones, covered in cobwebs. God knows why they were down here. Maybe they'd been left by the original owner of the place. Any beer they'd ever held had long since been drunk, or maybe just evaporated over the centuries.

The body didn't actually look as far gone as you'd think, given the smell. The features were swollen, grotesque, but still recognisable.

At least, I recognised them.

CHAPTER ONE

Sometimes, even getting out of the house and switching your phone off won't save you. This time, it started with a quiet Saturday lunchtime pint up at the Devil's Dyke pub in Brock's Hollow. It was one of those blistering-hot days you occasionally get in May that lull you into thinking Britain's going to have a proper summer for once, and generally mean it'll rain for the next three months solid. Not that I'm cynical or anything. I was sitting out in the beer garden with my mate Gary, listening to bees buzzing around the flowers, kiddies playing football on the grassy bit by the car park, and a bloke at the next table having a rant about global warming. A half-hearted breeze wafted listlessly, weighed down by the scents of lilacs, cheese and onion crisps, and beer.

We were under the shade of an umbrella so Gary wouldn't risk getting a freckle and ruining his wedding photos the following month. I'd have told him not to be so daft, except I knew that as his best man, I'd be the one getting all the grief about it on the day. And anyway, it *was* pretty hot. I had my sleeves rolled up even in the shade, and you had to feel sorry for Julian, Gary's Saint Bernard. Between the fur coat and the sheer bulk of him, he had to be only a couple of degrees away from turning into a big doggy puddle on the grass.

I was just contemplating getting another round in (something soft for me, with a shedload of ice in it; I had work this afternoon), when the Devil's Dyke herself, pub landlady Harry Shire, hove into view, her border collie Flossie panting at her heels.

"Tom. Gary," she greeted us gruffly. I leaned back in my seat to look up at her—Harry's six foot tall if she's an inch, so there was a long way to look. "Your bloke joining you?"

"Not as far as I know." Phil got on fine with Gary's fiancé, Darren. He got on a lot less fine with the man himself, so if I knew my bloke, he'd be giving the Dyke a wide berth this lunchtime. "Any reason?"

She nodded. "Got a job for him."

"Ooh, this sounds thrilling." Gary leaned forward on the table while Flossie and Julian sniffed each other's arses politely. "What is it? Light-fingered barmaids lifting money from the tills? The case of the disappearing beer barrels?"

"It's private." Harry folded her arms. When most women do that, it makes their boobs look bigger. Harry, though, it just made her biceps stand out. I couldn't help noticing they were a lot more impressive than mine. Come to that, her boobs were and all, but I didn't have a problem with that.

Gary pouted. He hates being left out of any juicy secrets going around.

"Want me to ask Phil to pop round?" I asked. "I'm seeing him tonight."

"If you would. Soon as he can."

I didn't like the sound of that. "Tell you what, you got your mobile on you? I'll give him a bell."

Harry looked down at me for a moment, then handed over a scratched-up phone that looked older than her latest barmaid. It took me a mo to remember how to use the ones with actual buttons, but I managed to get Phil's number into it.

"Alban Investigations," he answered promptly.

"Hi, it's me. Tom," I added, in case the line was a bit crackly his end. "I'm up at the Dyke, ringing on Harry's phone—she wants a word, okay? Work stuff. Your work, I mean. Not hers."

"Pub lunch again? All right for some. Yeah, put her on. See you about six?"

"Yeah, see you then." I handed the phone back to Harry—then noticed Gary smirking at me and hastily wiped the soppy smile off my face.

Phone to her ear, Harry nodded her thanks and strode off, clicking her fingers for Flossie to follow. I watched her for a minute, then turned back to frown at the dregs of my pint. Whatever the problem was, I hoped it wasn't serious. Harry might not be full of the traditional mine-host pub landlord's hearty bonhomie, but she was a good friend to have. And she knew her beer.

"I don't see why she couldn't have told us what it was about," Gary muttered, giving the olive in his martini a petulant swirl. "You know me. Are my lips ever loose?"

"Sorry—don't think I'm qualified to answer that one. You'll have to ask Darren." Gary's and my friendship has always been strictly *without* benefits, seeing as how I tend to go for the mean, moody, and macho type, not the cuddly, kinky, and camp sort, and for his part, Gary reckons vanilla's only fit for flavouring ice cream. Which was why he was about to marry a dwarf ex-porn star, and I was currently walking out with the owner, manager, and sole staff member of Alban Investigations, otherwise known as Phil Morrison.

"Well, if Phil should happen to let any little details slip, you will share, won't you?" Two sets of puppy eyes turned my way in an eerie joint attack from Gary and Julian.

"Course," I lied cheerfully, and Gary brightened. He's never really *got* the concept of client confidentiality. He's got his own IT firm, and some of the things he's told me he's "stumbled across" on his customers' hard drives would make your hair curl.

Nothing illegal, mind. He might be the world's worst gossip, but he's got standards. Or at least, he's worked out that I have.

"It's odd, though," Gary was saying. "Harry, needing a man? When has *that* ever happened?"

"Well, she called *you* in to install the business software. Or don't you count?" I laughed as Gary treated me to a view of a slowly swivelling finger. In principle, though, he wasn't wrong. Harry was one of the most self-sufficient people I knew. Come the zombie apocalypse, I'd be heading straight for the Dyke and hiding behind the bar. "Maybe it's just a know-how thing? She wants someone found, maybe, or some information, and she doesn't know how to get hold of it?"

"Ooh, do you think she's got a long-lost love child she was tragically forced to give up for adoption? The product of an illicit heterosexual affair, perhaps?"

I think I must have winced or something. Although it wasn't because Gary made the word *heterosexual* sound like something out of

The Joy of Extreme Sex. Love children produced by illicit affairs were still a bit of a sore topic with me.

Seeing as I'd found out only a few months ago I was one.

Gary cleared his throat, straightened his face out from lascivious to sympathetic, and patted my knee. "Sorry, darling. Didn't mean to poke a raw nerve. But while we're on the subject, have you found out anything more . . . ?"

"Nope," I said flatly.

Apparently not flatly enough to deter further poking. Or patting, for that matter. "What, *nothing*? Are you sure that man of yours is doing a proper job?" Julian pricked up his ears, decided he needed to get in on the action, and plonked his jowls down on the knee not receiving his master's attention. His head felt like a hot water bottle, but at least his drool would evaporate quickly in the heat.

"Phil's not doing anything about finding my real dad. I haven't asked him to."

Gary stared at me, blank incomprehension all over his soft, round face. "But don't you want to know? I mean, it's *so* exciting! You could *literally* be anyone."

"Yeah, well, sorry to disappoint you, but I'm pretty sure I'm not Princess Diana and Dodi Fayed's love child."

"Well, of course not, darling. You're not dark enough, and anyway the timing would be all wrong. Still, maybe some dashing young guardsman . . ."

"No. My mum's still my mum, okay?"

Gary nodded thoughtfully. "Although I have to say, I find her *much* more interesting now."

"You would." There was a loud bang as one of the kiddies punted the football straight into my van's windscreen. I cringed, and the lad, who must have been all of seven or eight, froze for a moment, visibly worried he was going to cop it. Luckily he was never going to be the next David Beckham and the ball bounced off harmlessly. Play resumed as though nothing had happened, but I noticed one or two blokes giving their cars nervous glances.

"Well, of course. She's a lady with a dark, hidden past." Gary sighed wistfully. "We have so much in common."

"Hint all you like, I'm still not going there." Mainly because I was one hundred percent sure it was utter bullshit. On Gary's part, at least. The matter of my mum's dark, hidden past had been made painfully clear to me by Auntie Lol's cache of old letters.

Gary sighed again. Actually, this time it was more like a huff of exasperation. "I just think you should do something about it, before it's too late. People don't live forever." He shot me a significant look. "You of all people should know that."

"Oi, what am I—the angel of death?"

He pursed his lips. "Nooo . . . You're more like a harbinger."

"Whatever one of those is." I had a feeling I wasn't going to like it.

"A portent. A deadly warning." Gary beamed. "You're a banshee!"

"*Oi.* I'm not a bloody banshee. I turn up *after* the fact and find stuff, that's all. And there's no wailing involved either."

Gary shrugged. "I'm just saying, you seem to spend a lot of time in the company of corpses, that's all."

"Trust me, mate, I spend as little time as possible with 'em. So how's the wedding plans going?" Okay, as attempts to change the subject go, it was less than subtle, but Gary's never been able to resist talking about his love life.

"Famously, darling. I'm meeting up with Darren's parents tomorrow to discuss things."

"Yeah? This the first time you've met them?"

"Of course not. They see me as a surrogate child."

"So what're they like? Are they, you know . . ." I'd been about to say *dwarves*, but I bottled it. "A lot like him?"

"Oh, absolutely. Darren comes from a long line of market traders. He was selling fruit and veg before he was knee-high to a proverbial."

I wasn't going to touch the issue of Darren's height with a bargepole, proverbial or otherwise. "Let me guess, his first words were 'two fer a pahnd'?"

"Something more along the lines of 'firm and juicy,' I believe." Gary tossed down the last of his martini, then sucked the olive off his cocktail stick with a suggestive slurping sound.

"Want another?" I asked.

Gary pouted at his glass. "Just a Diet Coke, darling. Putting on weight now would be a *disaster*. And the same goes for you. A man of your height shows every extra ounce." He wagged a finger at me and chortled.

Bloody hell. It was bad enough when it was only Darren making the short-arse jokes.

After finding out about my real dad from my late Auntie Lol, I'd meant to get right on the case—well, get Phil on the case—of finding out who I really was. But I'd had a run of jobs to catch up on, and what with one thing and another, I just . . . hadn't.

It hadn't helped that I'd had a pretty good idea how my sister, Cherry, would react if I started trying to rake up the past. We'd been getting on a lot better lately, Cherry and me. Seeing a lot more of each other—Sunday roasts with Phil and her reverend fiancé, the occasional weekday lunch in St. Albans for the two of us, that sort of thing. Seemed a shame to upset the apple cart. And, well . . . Dad wasn't such a bad sort. I mean, he'd been fine about me being gay and not having a high-flying career or anything.

Although now I was wondering if he just didn't care, seeing as I wasn't his.

But he'd been the one who'd been, well, a dad to me. It hadn't been his fault he'd been a bit past it by the time I came along and wanted someone to take me playing footie in the park. He'd been the one who'd taught me how to ride a bike—not that I could remember it, exactly, but it must have been him. God knows my big brother, Richard, wouldn't have bothered. And Dad was the one who'd given me my pocket money and paid for my driving lessons. Not to mention, given me the disappointed look when I pranged the car my first time flying solo.

It didn't seem right. Like trying to find my real dad would be ungrateful or something. And, well. It wasn't like he'd ever bothered to find me, was it?

So I'd let it slide.

Now, though . . . Gary had got me wondering again.

I brought it up with Phil that night, when we were sitting on the sofa, me still picking at my dinner and him flicking through the channels on the telly with Merlin purring away like a buzz saw on his lap.

"Gary reckons I ought to do something about finding my real dad."

"So? Not up to him, is it?"

I sighed and bunged my plate on top of Phil's on the coffee table, where it was just far enough out of reach to be a barrier against temptation. I was stuffed, really. Arthur came and gave the plates a sniff, then backed off quickly, furry tail twitching. Apparently, lamb biryani wasn't his thing. Who knew? Then again, I had pretty comprehensively picked out all the meat already.

"Yeah, but... he's got a point. I mean, my dad's got to be, what, at least in his sixties? If he's even still alive. If I don't do something now, maybe I'll never get the chance."

Phil pursed his lips. "Not going to be easy, finding the bloke with only a first name and a photo. Have you thought about talking to your mum?"

"Yeah. A bit too much. Christ, I don't know." I closed my eyes and scrubbed my hands over my face. A warm, solid arm slid around my shoulders, and Phil gave me a comforting squeeze. "How am I supposed to even bring the subject up? 'Oi, Mum, remember the old days when you used to be a bit of a slapper?' Ow!" Phil had flicked my ear. I opened my eyes and glared at him.

"Don't talk about your mum that way. And you've simply got to decide, haven't you? Whether finding your real dad is that important to you."

"*Important*? Of course it's important. Bloody hell, wouldn't you want to know where you'd come from?"

He shrugged. "Some people would say it's more important where you end up."

"Yeah, but . . . it's blood, innit? Thicker than water and all that crap."

"So's a lot of things. What if he turns out to be a right bastard?"

There was a split second before he realised what he'd said and tensed. I laughed. "That's me, remember? Ah, shit. I dunno. Look, I know it's not fair to ask, but is there anything you can do without talking to Mum?"

Phil nodded slowly. "Maybe. I can pay a visit to North London, see if I can track down anyone who knew your family when you were living there. Flash your old man's photo around, see if it jogs any memories." He half laughed.

"What?"

"Bet I can find someone who remembers you, at any rate. Can't have been too many primary schoolkids stumbling over bodies in the park. Least not back in those days."

Thanks for the memory, Phil. "What, like it happens every week now? Yeah, you're probably right. I blame video games. They're whatsit, desensitising everyone to violence."

"Don't know about that." Phil leaned back in the sofa. As he still had an arm around me, so did I. Not that I was complaining. Merlin, on the other hand, gave a peed-off miaow at all the shifting around, but he could lump it. "Think about it. If everyone's indoors on the video games, who's finding the bodies? Or leaving 'em there, for that matter?"

I let my head rest against his shoulder. "Stop trying to blind me with logic."

"Why, is it working too well?"

"Git. Hey, what happened with Harry?" I asked as a thought struck me. "You sort something out with her?"

I wasn't digging for info.

Honest.

Phil nodded. "She's coming round here tomorrow morning. You're not working, are you?"

I did work the occasional Sunday, but generally I tried to avoid them. For one thing, husbands were usually around. I prefer dealing with the wives—and in an area like this, posh commuter belt for the most part, you get an awful lot of stay-at-home wives. They're usually pretty friendly, only too glad to have someone round to chat to. The husbands, on the other hand, tend to fall into one of two camps. Either they want to keep it all strictly business, no idle chitchat with the help, or alternatively they're in my face the whole bloody time talking bollocks about how they'd be doing the job themselves, if only the wife hadn't called me in. I s'pose they feel their masculinity's threatened or something, just because I know my way around a wrench and they don't. At any rate, it makes for a less relaxed working environment.

Anyway, Sundays aren't supposed to be for working. Not unless you have to. Day of rest, innit? Sundays are for stodgy roast dinners with the family, or if you can think up a good enough excuse to steer clear of your nearest and dearest, slobbing on the sofa watching sport on the telly.

"No, but I can clear out if you need me to." Then again, if he didn't want me around, why bring her to my house? He had a perfectly good flat of his own, not to mention an actual office. "You planning on having me sit in? Harry didn't seem too keen on me knowing her business back up at the Dyke."

"Nah, that was because of your mate Gary. She reckons he can't keep his trap shut." Phil's eye roll made it clear he thought that one was a bit of a no-brainer. "She's fine with you knowing about it. Her idea, in fact. Think she's hoping you might be able to put that talent of yours to use."

I grinned. "What, that thing I do with my tongue? Thought she wasn't into blokes."

Phil grunted. "Don't flatter yourself. You know what I mean. Anyway, they'll be here at ten."

"'They'?"

"Her and Marianne."

"Her and *Marianne*?"

"Yeah, you know. New one at the Dyke. West Country girl. Her with the cartoon tattoo."

It was a My Little Unicorn in rainbow colours. If she'd got it done to make her look harder, she'd seriously missed the mark.

"I know who she *is*. I wasn't expecting it to be about her, that's all." God help me, I was starting to wonder if *she* was Harry's long-lost love child.

"Maybe it isn't. Maybe she's just the moral support."

"What, her? If Harry leans on her, she'll snap."

"I said *moral* support, not a bloody crutch." He looked down at me smugly from his six foot two. "Wouldn't have thought you'd be one to judge a book by its cover. Small doesn't *have* to mean weak."

"Yeah, but if she weighs more than seven stone soaking wet, I'm a sumo wrestler."

"Wouldn't advise it. Those nappies aren't a good look on anyone."

See, this is how I knew he loved me. Because he *didn't* add, *especially on skinny short-arses like you.*

"So what is a good look on me?" I put on my best flirty smile.

"Me," Phil said. And went on to prove it.

CHAPTER TWO

Harry and Marianne turned up on my doorstep dead on ten o'clock Sunday morning, so it was just as well me and Phil had gone for mutual blowjobs and not a full-on shag.

Harry was in her usual summer gear of khaki cargo trousers and a man's shirt worn loose over a tank top that would have been at home in an actual army tank—all that was missing was the dog tags. Marianne was all fresh and perky in a pair of denim cutoffs and a tight white T-shirt with *The Devil's Dyke* scrawled across her boobs. The boobs I could take or leave, but the shirt covered up the tattoo on her shoulder, which was a definite bonus.

"Come on in," I said, standing back so they could get past. It felt a bit weird having Harry in my space rather than me in hers. I wasn't sure I'd ever seen her outside the pub, although I guessed she must leave it all the time, really. Well, at least once a week or so. Probably. "Phil's in the living room."

I ushered them in, and Phil stood up to shake hands. Him and Harry were much of a size, but I reckoned she probably had the firmer grip. Marianne's handshake looked limp and came with added giggles, like she wasn't used to all this grown-up stuff.

That made two of us. I hadn't even thought of offering a handshake. Then again, I'd known Harry a lot longer than Phil had. Nah, shaking hands would have been weird.

Phil invited them to make themselves at home on my sofa, which they did, Harry looming protectively over Marianne even when they were sitting down. Merlin stuck his furry nose into the room, took one look at Harry, and made a strategic retreat. Arthur, being made of sterner stuff—not to mention, twice as much of it—padded in fearlessly and jumped onto Marianne's lap. She winced.

I gave her bare legs a sympathetic look. "Claws? Just shove him off if he's a bother."

Marianne's big blue eyes gazed up at me, only the faintest hint of pain in those innocent depths. "Oh no, he's lovely, he is. I love cats." Her West Country burr was warmer than the weather as she stroked Arthur with both hands at once. If it hadn't been for the boobs, I'd have put her age at nearer ten today.

"Coffee?" I offered, to show I wasn't totally useless at the old mine-host bit.

Harry nodded. "Black, two sugars for me."

"Plenty of milk in mine, please. No sugar," Marianne said.

"Sweet enough already, are you, love?" I teased, which made her giggle again.

Harry didn't seem all that amused. Which *could* have fitted in with the love-child theory, but . . .

"Do you think they're . . . you know?" I whispered to Phil, who'd followed me into the kitchen and was frowning into the biscuit tin. "There's another packet in the cupboard."

"Right. And I don't know, do I?"

"You're the private investigator. I thought you could tell things about people. Body language and stuff."

"Not stuck out here, I can't. Just make the coffee, all right? And then maybe we'll get to hear what it's all about." His tone was exasperated, but he gave my arse a squeeze on his way past with the biscuits.

It felt well weird, bringing out drinks for a pub landlady and a barmaid. I managed without spilling any of them, resisted the temptation to ask for four pound fifty, and we all sat down and sipped our coffee. Marianne carried on stroking Arthur with one hand. Nobody had a biscuit.

Phil broke the silence. "So what is it you think you might need my help with?"

Harry put down her mug on the coffee table, and Marianne shot her a wary glance. Arthur stuck out a paw, his claws showing just enough to remind her she was supposed to be stroking him.

"Marianne's ex," Harry growled. "Little shit by the name of Grant Carey." She tossed a photo on the table. It showed Marianne in a strappy dress with a bloke not much taller than she was. He was around his midtwenties, dark haired, lean and, all right, pretty good-looking, if you liked that sort of thing. Nice taste in suits, not that I'd know, really.

Phil leaned over, picked it up, and gave it a good, hard stare.

"Grant, eh? Bet he thinks he's God's gift." I smiled at Marianne. She managed a wan little smile back, but Harry gave me a granite glare.

Phil muttered, "Christ, you slay me."

I straightened my face. "What's he been up to, then?"

Marianne made a fuss of Arthur, chucking him under the chin and scratching behind his ears. He gazed up at her in self-centred, slitty-eyed adoration. "It's not . . . See, he ain't done nothing. Not really, he ain't. It's just he won't leave me alone. Says I ought to go back home with him."

Phil looked up from the photo and voiced what I was thinking. "And you've tried asking him to stop pestering her?" His question was clearly aimed at Harry. Put it this way, if Harry asked me to stop doing something, I'd stop it. Grant didn't look like he'd be able to put up much of a fight either.

Harry glowered at us. "I tried. Next day I had the coppers turn up and give me a caution for threatening behaviour."

Ouch.

"And after they'd gone, he was back, the little turd. Told me I'd better hope he didn't even break a nail in future, or he'd have me up on assault charges before you could say 'lost licence.'"

"Shit. Could they really take your licence away?" I asked.

Harry and Phil nodded in unison. Well, he'd been a copper for six years; I supposed he'd know the law. It was Harry who answered, though. "Conviction for assault—it's like a bloody red rag to the Licensing Committee. Not that they need one. Bloke in Kent lost his licence a few years ago for letting a horse walk into his pub."

I stared. "Bloody hell, I bet no one was asking 'Why the long face?' that day."

Marianne giggled, then went pink and busied herself appeasing her lord and master, otherwise known as Arthur.

It wasn't funny, though. If Harry lost her pub licence, she lost her home and her livelihood with it.

Phil leaned forwards again. "Those were his words, were they? About losing you your licence?"

Harry nodded, her face stony. "Oh yeah. That bastard knows *exactly* what he's doing."

"Yeah, but," I put in, leaning forwards in my chair, "can't Marianne make a complaint about him? I mean, if he wants to make it police business, why don't you play him at his own game? Get a restraining order to stop him coming near her, that sort of stuff?"

Harry and Phil exchanged glances. There was a general undercurrent of *some-mothers-do-'ave-'em* in the air. Even Marianne sent me a pitying look, and Arthur flicked a contemptuous tail.

"What?" I asked, narked.

It was Marianne who answered. "He wouldn't like that, see." She seemed to hunch in on herself. "He don't like it when people tell him what to do. Gets real nasty about it, he does."

"Nasty, as in . . .?" I prompted.

Harry made a disgusted sound. "Come on, there's plenty of ways he could get back at Marianne through me. Setting me up for allowing underage drinking. Letting loose a box of cockroaches in the kitchen and calling Environmental Health. From what she's told me, I wouldn't put it past the little shit to get someone to punch him so he can claim it was me."

Did people actually do that? "Seriously?" I turned to Marianne. "You know him best. You really think he'd do something like that, just for revenge?"

She wasn't stroking Arthur so much now as cuddling him like a teddy bear. He kneaded her legs with his paws, clearly not entirely certain he approved. "He would too," she said, her voice a whisper.

Crap.

"So what do you want me to do?" Phil asked.

Harry leaned in, her fists balled on her knees. Her scarred knuckles didn't actually have *LOVE* and *HATE* tattooed on them, but they looked like they ought to. "I want you to find something on him. Anything. Little shit like that, there's bound to be something we can hold over him." She barked an angry laugh. "Or send him down with. Nice long stretch in prison'd do wonders for his manners."

Not to mention his social life, I thought grimly. Small, slim, and pretty in prison? I was starting to feel a bit sorry for the bloke.

"Got any pointers for me?" Phil asked. He'd taken out his notebook and pen. "Any dodgy business you know he's mixed up in? Ex-girlfriends who might have something on him?"

Marianne bit her lip. "I only know about his last girlfriend before me."

Phil nodded encouragingly. "Name? Any contact details so I can have a word with her?"

"Well, I got 'em. But it won't help you." Marianne looked unhappy. "She killed herself, see. That's how I met him—at Keri's funeral."

Bloody hell. My budding sympathy for Grant Carey was rapidly getting napalmed into extinction.

"She was a friend of yours?" Phil asked.

"We weren't *best* friends or nothing, but yeah, I knew her. We worked together, see? At this café in Docklands."

Marianne's little pink lips turned downwards. "Keri used to say some stuff about him, sometimes . . . But he seemed so nice when I met him, you see? And he was ever so sad about her. I thought maybe it'd all been in her head. It weren't till it started with me and all—that was when I knew it hadn't been just her."

Phil frowned. "Could you be a bit more explicit about his behaviour? Was he violent towards you?"

"Yes," Harry growled, right as Marianne said, "No, not really."

Phil's frown turned on Harry. She frowned back. For a moment, I thought they were about to start pawing the ground as a prelude to charging each other, but then Harry looked away. "You tell 'im. But no making excuses for the bastard."

"Well, he never hit me or nothing, see? It was just stuff he said." She hugged herself. Arthur flicked an ear at her and stretched out a paw, clearly annoyed the pampering had stopped. Despite the obvious lack of instincts about violent blokes, Marianne must have had a sixth sense about cats, as she went back to stroking him an instant before claws met flesh.

Something about the way she'd been rubbing her hands on her shoulders bothered me, though. I leaned forward. "Did he sometimes grab you a bit too hard, though? Maybe give a little shake? Sometimes leave bruises?"

Marianne blinked a few times, a bit too quickly. "He never meant to, see."

Harry snorted like a bull. "Day that little shit doesn't know exactly what he's doing is the day I take up ballet dancing."

Now *that* was an image to frighten the horses. Although maybe not, when I thought about it—Harry might be big and butch, but there was a sort of grace about the way she moved. After all, if Ali could float like a butterfly . . .

"Did he threaten you?" Phil put in, obviously not as taken as I was with the image of Harry in a tutu.

Marianne shrugged her skinny shoulders, her boobs rising several inches and nearly walloping a curious Arthur on the head when they came back down. "He never said stuff like, I don't know, like, 'If you talk to that bloke, I'll hit you.' It was more like, he'd go on about these awful things that happened to girls who didn't stick with their men, who went about like tarts, that kind of stuff." She took a deep breath, and the boobs bobbed again. "And there was this one time, see, there was this bloke he used to do business with who got on the wrong side of him. Alan, his name was. I don't know what he done, but Grant got that mad at him, and he said he'd have him. I never thought nothing of it, but next thing I know, Alan's been done for intent to supply. Cocaine, it was. He got ten years."

Phil raised an eyebrow about half a millimetre. "Are you sure it was related? Could have been a coincidence."

"That's what I thought. I mean, I never knew he was into drugs, but he weren't a saint, Alan weren't. I thought, well, he could have done it. Then Grant started saying stuff. It was when . . ." She broke off and gave Arthur some really intensive stroking. "I met this girl, see? In the Last Lick. I'd moved jobs when I turned eighteen, 'cos the pay was better there."

"What sort of place was that?" Phil interrupted.

"The Last Lick? Oh, it's a pub." That was a relief. For one mind-boggling moment I thought it might have been some seedy sex club. Don't get me wrong, if a girl wants to do that sort of thing for a living, it's her business, but I didn't like to think of someone as young and innocent as Marianne getting mixed up with all the slimy bastards you get hanging around those places.

Not that I've got any personal experience, of course. But I've read the *Daily Mail*.

"Anyway," she went on, "Cas used to drink there regular, and we got talking one night. And she was lovely, and I saw her again when I wasn't working, and we had loads of fun together. Like it was with Grant, back when I first met him?"

Right. Back when he'd been supposedly in mourning for his dead girlfriend. Lovely.

"And we was just friends, first off, and then, well, we weren't, you know?" She looked up. "I never meant it to happen; it just did, see? So I told Grant I couldn't see him no more."

Phil huffed. "Flipped his shit, did he?"

"He went really quiet. He didn't get angry at me, just sort of sad. Said he didn't know how he was going to go on without me. And I felt proper bad about it, so when he asked me to give 'im another chance, I did, see?" She picked up her mug with two hands. Neither of them was quite steady. "And he was *so nice* to me, after. Least for a bit. He asked me to move in with him, and I thought, well, if it makes him happy, see? So I did." She took a sip from her mug. "It was later he started saying stuff. See, Cas was still coming into the pub with her friends, even though we weren't together no more. So Grant said I ought to give up my job. But I didn't want to. I like working in pubs. Talking to people, all that stuff. I wouldn't know what to do with myself if I didn't have a job to go to. But then he started saying this stuff, like, how a dyke bitch like her would probably love it in prison, and how it was so easy for stuff to fall into someone's bag."

"Shit—did he do anything to her?"

"No. I never went out with her again, and I didn't dare let him see me talking to her no more." She took a sip from her mug, her eyes sad, and gave a little sniff. "She didn't want to talk to me anyway. Not after that. But I didn't give up my job," she added defiantly.

Good for her.

"What about this bloke? Alan?" Phil must have scented blood. "Did Grant talk about planting stuff on him?"

"I should've gone to the police, shouldn't I? But you don't know what he's like. He twists stuff. Makes it sound like you're the one who's lying, not him. And he never said nothing outright."

Harry was nodding. "He's a plausible little shit, all right. Almost had me convinced he was only looking out for Marianne when he came round."

Phil nodded. "Right. Well, that's something I can work with. See what I can find out about the case, and if there's any evidence linking Carey with the drugs."

He got Marianne to tell him everything she could remember, which pretty much boiled down to a name, Alan Mortimer; the name and rough location of the business he'd run before he'd gone on an enforced holiday at Her Majesty's expense—something to do with importing electronic goods, which was what Marianne reckoned Carey's business was all about too, although she was hazy on the details—and a few dates.

She'd been sixteen when she'd started going out with Carey. Sixteen, and living on her own in some London dump, slaving away in a café to make ends meet. Christ.

The last thing she did before she left was hand over a few more photos of Carey. I didn't get a good look until after Harry and Marianne had said their goodbyes, shaken hands again—this time with me as well, except for Marianne, who gave me a cherry-ChapStick-scented kiss on the cheek—and gone. Then I sat down on the sofa with Phil to have a proper butcher's.

Carey, like I said, was a slightly built bloke about my height. He had dark hair that was starting to recede at the temples, devil-style, and the sort of big brown eyes a teenage girl would probably think were soulful. He came across as a bit older on closer examination—at least my age. Which, by my reckoning, made him around a decade too old for Marianne—I mean, seriously, with her rocking the schoolgirl look, people must have wondered if he was her dad. Like I said, not my type, but Phil probably wouldn't kick him out of bed. I sent a sidelong glance at my so-called better half, who was studying the photos like he wanted to be able to remember them in private later.

Not that I was, you know, feeling insecure or anything.

Most of the pics were of Carey on his lonesome, with him gazing straight at the camera and smiling like he didn't have a care in the world. They were a bit less obviously posed than a lot of people's snaps tend to be, with him all friendly and relaxed looking. You wouldn't have believed this bloke would get up to the sort of stuff Marianne had told us about, if you hadn't heard her firsthand.

Maybe it was just all that practice he'd had at getting people to let their guard down around him. But there was one with Marianne in it too, and that one was a bit more revealing. Carey hadn't been expecting it, I reckoned. There was a cold gleam in those eyes of his, and his arm around Marianne's shoulders looked a bit tighter than could have been comfortable.

I don't like bullies. Never have. "Course, maybe it's not his fault," I mused. "Maybe he had a bad childhood. I mean, who calls their kid Grant Carey?"

"Forties film fans?" Phil suggested without glancing up.

"S'pose. Hey, he was one of our lot, wasn't he? Queer, I mean. Cary Grant."

"No. Cary Grant was straight. You're thinking of Archie Leach."

I frowned at Phil, but the tiny smirk on his face decided me against asking who the bloody hell Archie Leach was, and what he had to do with the price of fish. "So what do you think about Carey?" I asked instead.

Phil *hmm*'ed. "I think I've seen him around, somewhere. Which is interesting. For a bloke with a business to run in London, he seems to be spending a lot of time around here."

"Maybe he's expanding his operations. Taking advantage of the lucrative Hertfordshire market for knockoff iPods."

Phil shrugged. "Even dodgy businessmen take holidays now and again."

"In Hertfordshire? Costa del Sol all booked up, was it?"

"I didn't say it was his main holiday. Anyway, not everyone likes baking their brains on a beach." Phil gave me a pointed look. We were in the middle of a bit of a debate about where we'd be heading off to for our summer hols, once the gay wedding of the year was all done and dusted. I came down firmly on the side of sun, sea, and sand, but Phil was holding out for a bit of culture, which, as far as I could tell, meant trekking miles around dusty old ruins.

If I'd wanted to spend my time off doing that sort of thing, I could go and visit Mum and Dad.

"Maybe it's one of those activity holidays some people go on," I suggested, hoping we weren't about to rehash the whole bloody argument. "You know. Cooking holidays. Painting retreats. Countryside stalking escapes. Take a break in idyllic rural surroundings and indulge your creepy obsession at the same time."

Phil looked thoughtful. "There's an idea. You ever think of doing something like that?"

Bugger. So much for keeping this about Carey. "What, stalking my exes?"

"Activity holidays, as if you didn't know." He gave me a grumpy glare, which was the Morrison equivalent of an eye roll.

"See, this is where we have the problem. If you ask me—"

"*Which* I didn't."

"—activity holidays are a whatsit. Contradiction in terms."

"Oxymoron."

I flipped him a finger. "Same to you with knobs on. Nah, the whole point of a holiday is that you don't have to bloody well do anything. That's why they call it a holiday and not, you know, *work*."

Phil huffed. "I'm not asking you to go on a bloody plumbing holiday. Ever thought it might be fun, trying something a bit different? Doesn't have to be sodding intellectual."

I shifted uneasily in my seat. "So what's it going to be, then? Pottery in the Cotswolds? Circumnavigating the country on a bloody canal boat?"

"What are you, seventy? We could have a go at rock climbing, maybe. Or, if you're so desperate to get sand up your crack, we could go somewhere that does water sports."

"My mum wouldn't like it if I got up to any kinky stuff," I said primly.

My turn to get the finger. But at least he didn't come back at me with *Your mum hasn't got a leg to stand on*. Which was fair enough, really. I mean, a bit of adultery is hardly on a par with becoming an enthusiastic member of your local fetish club.

And, ye gods, I was giving myself mental images I *really* didn't need. I sighed. "Look, we're getting off track here."

"Noticed, did you?"

"Shut it. So where do you s'pose Carey's hanging out? Reckon he's got a mate around here he's dossing with? Or is he taking a lot of day trips?"

"Either's possible, but my money's on him getting a hotel room. Be a pain if he was out stalking and missed the last train home. And Marianne wouldn't run away somewhere she knew he had connections, would she?"

"Well, I'd hope not. She's not *that* dizzy. Hang about, though, she never said she'd run away from him."

"No. Harry did when we spoke on the phone. Marianne was too scared to tell the bloke it was all over—again—so she packed her bags and did a runner while he was out doing one of his dodgy business deals."

"Yeah? If I was her, I'd have run a bloody sight further than Hertfordshire. Gets tired easy, does she? Or was it some kind of reverse-psychology thing—*he'll never look for me only twenty-five miles away*, that sort of thing?"

"Had to have somewhere to run to, didn't she?" Phil huffed a laugh. "Seems Harry's got a bit of a reputation for taking in waifs and strays. That so-called bloody harem of hers?" He was referring to the parade of pretty girls who worked at the Dyke for a bit and then moved on to pastures new—local wisdom being that Harry's relationships never lasted long. "It's a load of bollocks. It's just a bunch of girls who need a safe place to stay for a bit. LGBT organisations put 'em in touch."

"Huh. I always knew Harry was all right." I scowled down at the table. "Makes me mad, that bastard threatening her."

"Oi, no coming over all chivalrous. Harry'll have your bollocks if she catches you."

"Miss 'em, would you?"

"Too right." Phil gave me a gentle squeeze in a relevant area, and the discussion sort of degenerated after that.

Not that I was complaining, mind.

Monday was another scorcher of a day, despite it being a bank holiday and therefore legally required to be wet and miserable. If we'd known it was going to be like that, we might have bothered with planning something—maybe hop on a train down to Brighton, something like that.

Then again, maybe not. Being stuck on a baking-hot train full of kiddies all hyper from the half-term holidays for the best part of two hours was probably even less fun than it sounded. At any rate, by the time the heat had forced us out of bed, it was too late to bother, so we had a lazy day at home. Well, I had a lazy day at home. Phil got out his laptop to do a few of the preliminaries on Marianne's case. Luckily for me, he did it with his shirt off so I had something to look at too.

Arthur came padding into the room while Phil was stalking Carey's Facebook page (status: in a relationship with Marianne Drinkwater. Seriously? *Drinkwater*? And her a barmaid?). He— Arthur, that was—eyed my lap speculatively.

"Not a chance, sunshine," I told him. "Last thing I want in this weather is *your* furry arse parked on top of me."

Phil looked up from his computer, which was one of those posh silver ones that are so thin you could get paper cuts from the edges, unlike my trusty old laptop that needed a six-inch-thick case to fit all the cogs in. "I hope it's the cat you're talking to."

"I would say you can park your arse on top of me anytime, but right now I'd be lying. Jesus, when did England move to the tropics?" I fanned myself weakly with the culture section of yesterday's Sunday paper—well, I had to get my money's worth out of it somehow.

"I blame gay marriage," Phil said absentmindedly, still tapping away at his keyboard. Then he shut the lid with a sigh. "God, I need some fresh air."

"You're in the wrong county for that. Try Sussex, or Norfolk, or pretty much any other bloody county. Somewhere with a sea coast."

"What is it with you and beaches? Reckon you're going to find one with buried treasure one day?"

"I dunno, do I?" I leaned back in the sofa and closed my eyes, wondering if a cool drink would be worth the effort of actually moving. "Maybe it's genetic. I could come from a long line of seafaring folk, couldn't I? What?" I added, miffed.

Phil was giving me a smug look. "I knew you hadn't forgotten about your dad."

"Course I haven't bloody forgotten. Not exactly the sort of thing that slips your mind, is it?"

"Poor choice of words. I mean, you've been thinking about it all bloody day, haven't you?"

"Well, not *all* day. I seem to remember someone taking my mind off it pretty well this morning. But yeah, I guess. Um. You mind not coming round tomorrow evening? Thought I might give Cherry a bell and invite her over. You know, to talk about stuff."

He nodded. "About time. And I meant what I said before. I'll have a dig around, see what I can come up with, all right?"

CHAPTER THREE

Tuesday was a mare of a day. I blamed the weather—tempers rising with the mercury, that sort of thing. And, all right, maybe I was a bit on edge about the coming evening. Not that I'd spoken to Cherry yet about popping round, but, well. I'd made the decision—finally. It was going to happen.

At any rate, I had a particularly bolshie lot of customers, and by the time four o'clock rolled round, I was hot, bothered, and ready to call it a day.

Mr. H. over in Fallow's Wood—the posh bit near Brock's Hollow—was the worst. A retired director of something-or-other important, he insisted on breathing down my neck the entire time I was installing his new Regency bath taps. It was like he was worried I was going to chip off some of the gold plating and run off with it.

"I hope you're taking good care of those. They cost a lot more than I'm paying you to put them in," he said, and then gave a little laugh so I'd think he was joking. Which I didn't, because I'm not daft.

"Don't worry, mate. I'll handle 'em like they're my own." I didn't tell him my own *what*.

"Hmph." He was quiet for a blessed thirty seconds or so, but the hairs on the back of my neck were still prickling, so I managed not to jump when he spoke again. "You sound very British. Second-generation immigrants?"

"Nah," I said, freeing the old taps carefully. They were still in perfect nick—but apparently not flashy enough. Well, if he didn't want 'em, I could probably find someone else who would. "It's just a name. We're not Polish. Not even a little bit."

"Names have to come from somewhere," he said snippily. "You must have at least one Polish forebear."

"Yeah, well. Long story. Right, best not talk during this bit, all right? Wouldn't want to damage the taps, would we?"

He finally backed off, thank God. Only to rally when I gave him the bill, and to argue till he was blue in the face—well, bluer; he had a sort of permanent purple tinge going on—that every tradesman he knew gave a twenty percent discount for cash in hand. Then he got his knickers in a twist when I told him I wasn't up for defrauding the government, so I'd like the full amount, please.

All in all, it was a gift from the gods when I got to the last job in Southdown and realised I wasn't going to be able to do it today. I'd have to order a new pump in, seeing as the one I had in the van turned out to be faulty.

Mrs. L. was pretty understanding about it, in the circs. Like she said, who needs hot water in this weather?

I swung by the supermarket on the way home, then had a shower. Lukewarm to show solidarity with Mrs. L., not that she'd know anything about it. It was still a bit early to ring Cherry—she might be in a meeting or something—so I grabbed a bottle of beer from the fridge and switched the telly on, but the sofa just wasn't comfy this evening. Too hot or something. I put my beer down on the coffee table, got up and stretched my legs a bit, then wandered into the kitchen. I stared out of the window (waste of time: the view hadn't got any more interesting since the last time I'd looked), gazed blankly at the calendar on the wall (the Chippendales: a present from Gary; Mr. May was rocking the oiled pecs and leopard-skin posing pouch look), and tapped my fingers on the kitchen counter. Merlin pricked up his furry little ears at the sound, but Arthur carried on ignoring me in favour of scarfing down his dinner like there was no tomorrow.

Speaking of dinner . . . It'd been slim pickings in the fresh produce aisle, so my and Cherry's tea was going to be quiche garnished with the few limp lettuce leaves I'd managed to forage for in the supermarket. I could rustle up a pretty good selection of pickles, but it still wasn't anything I was particularly proud of as a spread.

I could make a pasta salad. Yeah, that'd pad things out a bit. Make it look like I'd made a bit of an effort. I nodded to myself and put the water on to boil.

Twenty-five minutes later, I had a reasonably decent meal put together. And I still hadn't invited the bloody guest of honour. This was getting ridiculous. Time to stop faffing about. I'd put Phil off and everything; there was no point putting *this* off any longer. I dialled up Cherry's number and hit Call.

It went straight to voice mail. Sod it.

I hesitated, then did a quick internet search for the number of Ver Chambers, which was where Cherry hung out during work hours when she wasn't busy *m'ludd*ing in court. This time, I got an answer on the first ring, and recognised Jeanette-the-receptionist's chirpy tones immediately.

"'Ullo, love. It's Tom Paretski. Is my sister in today?"

"Ooh, hello, Tom, are you keeping well? Sorry, I think you've just missed her. She said she'd be going home early today."

I tried to keep the swearing under my breath. Why the bloody hell hadn't I pulled my sodding finger out and called her half an hour ago?

"Oh, hang on, no, she's on her way out now. Shall I get her for you?"

"Yes. Please," I said firmly.

I drummed my fingers on the kitchen counter to the sound of muffled conversations on the other end of the line. Then Cherry's voice came in loud and clear. "Tom?"

"Hi, Sis. Have you got to dash off somewhere?"

"No," she said in the sort of tone that suggested she really wanted to add a legal disclaimer.

"Fancy coming round to mine? I've got salad and stuff in for tea," I added, because if I knew my sister, the last thing she wanted to do was have to cook a meal when she got home.

"Tonight? You only saw me a couple of weeks ago." That had been at the bash for her fortieth birthday, which had been such a carbon copy of her and Greg's engagement do, I'd been honestly surprised they hadn't laid on a poisoning as entertainment. Still, having seen my sister almost fall victim to a murderer once, I was in no hurry to see anything like that ever again. "Don't tell me you're missing me already." It was more jokey than suspicious. She was wavering. Never let it be said that members of the legal profession aren't open to a bit of judicious bribery.

"I made that pasta salad you like," I said to sweeten the deal. "You know, the one with the goat's cheese."

"Oh?" Now she was more suspicious than jokey. "Anyone would think you were trying to butter me up for something."

Oops. Apparently I'd laid it on a bit too thick. "Well . . . there might have been something I sort of wanted to have a word about."

"Ah."

Funny how much you can learn from one short *Ah*. "Bloody hell, you knew, didn't you?"

"Knew what?"

"Don't play games with me, all right? You knew what I was going to find at the Morangie house, didn't you?" Which had basically been a load of old letters that told me the bloke I'd always called Dad wasn't, in fact, my father. Call me unreasonable, but I'd have thought my sis could have, I dunno, maybe *warned* me I was about to find out I was a bastard.

There was a pause. "I didn't *know*. But I could guess. All right, I've just got to phone Gregory. I'll see you in twenty minutes."

It was a tense twenty minutes, waiting for her. Actually, it was nearer a tense half an hour, but who was counting?

Oh, that's right. Me.

By the look of Cherry when I opened the door to her, she'd been a bit white-knuckled on the short drive over from Ver Chambers herself.

I sighed. "God, you've been waiting for this, haven't you? Ever since I went to that bloody house. Come in, sit down. Cup of tea?"

"I'm not sure. Am I going to need something stronger?" Cherry bustled in, dumped her handbag on the floor by the sofa, and then stood there, looking at me expectantly.

"Oi, I'm not letting you drunk-drive your way home. Greg would have my nuts. Probably stuff 'em and hang them from his rearview mirror." Gregory Titmus, canon of St. Leonards cathedral, was Cherry's fiancé. And a keen taxidermist.

"Do you have to be so vulgar? And of course I wouldn't drink and drive. You still have a spare room, don't you?"

"Yeah, but haven't you got work tomorrow?"

"Actually, no. I booked the day off."

"What, this soon after a bank holiday? Clients all off sunning themselves on the Costa del Crime, are they? All right for some, innit? Some of us have to work for a living."

Cherry *tsk*ed. "You know I do a lot of my paperwork at home. And the day off is so Gregory and I can get on with the wedding preparations. You wouldn't believe how much there is to do."

"Yeah, right. I'm Gary's best man, remember? And their wedding's in four weeks, not, what, eight months?" Cherry and Greg had the cathedral booked for next February. God knows why they'd gone for a winter wedding. Maybe Greg was too busy in the summer with other people getting hitched? Or maybe he fancied wearing his Doctor Who hat and scarf for the ceremony. I amused myself for a mo picturing my sis dressed up as one of the Doctor's companions—miniskirted Jo, maybe, or Leila in her jungle gear—but had to stop when Cherry started giving me funny looks.

"Some people spend *years* planning their weddings. I hardly think nine months"—trust Cherry to point out I'd got my maths wrong—"is too soon to get things sorted. Anyway, for God's sake, get me *something*. Preferably cold. I'm gasping. You know they say the heat wave is going to continue? It'll be hosepipe bans before we know it."

Like I hadn't had *that* conversation a dozen times already this week. I trooped dutifully into the kitchen. Ever hopeful, the cats trailed me like a couple of furry bridesmaids. "Lemonade all right?" I called with my head still in the fridge, enjoying the chill.

Cherry said something indistinct which I took as a yes, so I poured a couple of glasses and took them back into the living room. "I can bung a bit of vodka in if you want," I said, handing Cherry's to her.

She looked torn. "Probably better not. We're tasting cakes tomorrow."

"Yeah, well—anytime you change your mind . . . And are you hungry now, or do you want to wait a bit? It won't take long to get stuff ready."

I swear Cherry's ears pricked up like a dog's when I mentioned food. "Actually I'm ravenous. It was way too hot to eat much at lunchtime. I swear, there are days when I would *kill* to work in an air-conditioned office."

"Yeah, I know the feeling. I spent half my afternoon up in this woman's attic sorting out her water tank. Felt like diving in myself by the time I was finished. I seriously thought I was going to come down mummified." I left her to her lemonade and went back in the kitchen.

Judging by the way Cherry's eyes lit up when I brought the plates back, I needn't have worried about the food not being up to scratch.

"There you go. There's more pasta salad if you want it—actually, there's more everything, except the green stuff. Apparently nobody else in Fleetville can face the thought of hot food either. It must be killing trade for the local takeaways." I joined her on the sofa.

"I'm fine. This is lovely," Cherry said, already on her second mouthful by the time my bum hit the seat.

We chatted about this and that while we ate—Gary's forthcoming wedding, Cherry and Greg getting Wimbledon tickets, the arguments for and against nontraditional wedding cakes. Apparently Greg had a yen for a French-style croquembouche (which I had to get her to spell for me). Who'd have thought it?

Eventually, though, plates were put aside on the coffee table, we leaned back in our seats and an awkward silence fell with a plop like a brick in a cesspit. Cherry took a gulp of lemonade and swallowed it audibly.

Right. Time to talk about stuff. I half wished I'd gone for the vodka after all. "So. Down to business. You knew about the letter?"

"You mean Mum's letters? Or, well, that man's?"

"'That man' being my real dad? Yeah." Actually, I'd meant Auntie Lol's letter explaining stuff, but, well, if Cherry knew about the love letters, she didn't need the explanation, did she?

"Yes, I knew. But it's not like it really matters after all this time, though." Cherry's tone was even more dismissive than her words.

I stared at her. "You think it doesn't bloody *matter*? For Christ's sake, I found out Dad's not my dad, and you knew all along and didn't tell me! And you think it doesn't *matter*?"

"But it was all so long ago. Dad's perfectly fine about you now. It was just one of those things."

"Just one of those . . ." I couldn't seem to stop repeating what she said. "Sis, this is my bloody life we're talking about. I can't even . . . How long have you known?"

"Oh, years. You were about four when it all came out." She glared at me. "*You* won't remember, but it was horrible for the rest of us. Richard was in the middle of exams. It's amazing he didn't fail the lot of them."

"Well, excuse the *fuck* out of me for being born!" Jesus. And this was the woman I'd gone to the bother of making pasta salad for. Next time, she could have supermarket value-brand coleslaw and like it.

"There's no need to be bitchy about it." Cherry was tight-lipped. I couldn't believe she was blaming *me* for this. Then again, I was still, even after several months, struggling to believe it was even true. Mum? Having affairs? She'd always seemed so, well, *old* when I was a kid.

Not that I'm ageist, or anything. Obviously. Just, you sort of expect your mum and dad to have got that sort of thing out of their system by the time you're old enough to remember them. Which I supposed Mum had—at least, I *hoped* she hadn't had any more affairs while I was growing up. But, well, infidelity's like skinny jeans and designer stubble: looks better on the young.

"What happened?" I asked weakly.

"*You* did, obviously. Poking around in Mum and Dad's bedroom, finding things that should have stayed hidden." She was breathing hard, and I didn't think the pink in her cheeks was all down to the heat. "It'd all been over for years, and then you had to go and rake things up. I mean, I'm sure Dad must have at least *suspected*, but to have it all thrown in his face like that . . . You've no idea how hard it was on him."

She was right, I realised. I'd had no idea. Not once, not one time in all of my twenty-nine years, had he ever even hinted I might not be his. Not when I announced at seventeen I wasn't going to bother with school any longer. Not when I told him I was gay.

Not even when I'd brought Gary home for Christmas dinner.

Had he been more distant to me than to Richard and Cherry? I wasn't sure. He'd been, well, *older* when I was a kid. Not really up to football in the park, even if he'd wanted to. Or had that just been an excuse?

God, this was doing my head in.

Cherry leaned over and gave my knee a pat that looked as awkward as it felt. It didn't help that I was wearing shorts and her hand was hot and clammy. But it's the thought that counts. "You're still my brother, you know," she said. "And Richard feels the same."

"So basically, the whole sodding family knew about it except me?"

"Only the four of us. But yes. And it *didn't matter*."

"Bollocks."

"Language. Well, obviously it did at first. But you get used to these things. And I really don't see why Laura Morangie had to go and rake it all up again after her death."

"God, you make it sound like she's one of the undead. Rising from her grave to plague the living."

"I don't think it's very respectful to talk like that."

"What, and it's *respectful* to criticise her dying wish that I find out the truth?"

Cherry gave me a sharp look. "Tell me honestly—are you happier now you know?"

"Well, no, not exactly, but . . ."

"There you are, then." She gave a satisfied smile.

I got up and wandered around the coffee table for a bit. Merlin thought this was a great game and joined in, then tried to change the rules into *he who trips, wins*. I sat down again quick before he could make me fall down. "So is there anything else you can tell me? About my real dad? I mean, did Mum say anything about him?"

Cherry stopped smiling. "Well, no. I don't know what you're expecting here. I suppose she must have said something to Dad, but for God's sake, I was fourteen. She was hardly likely to tell *me* all the gory details. Most of the time, actually, I ended up having to look after you while they shut themselves up in the dining room and had all these discussions that always ended up with Mum in tears." Her mouth twisted. "One time Dad cried. It was horrible."

"Shit." Which was a pretty good description of how I felt. Dad had cried? *My* dad? Well, the bloke I'd always known as Dad.

And it had been because of me. I sat there in silence for a long moment, staring at the bubbles rising in my glass of lemonade. Cherry didn't say anything more either. She didn't really have to.

In the end, she shook herself like a damp dog, picked up her glass, took a final sip, put it back down on the coffee table, and stood up.

"Anyway, I've said all I had to say. You know how I feel about raking things up. I'll let myself out."

I stood up anyway. "Look, about Mum and Dad . . . I didn't realise, okay?" I managed a wonky smile. "Never really think about Dad having, well, feelings."

She nodded. "It's his generation. Which I suppose is why it was all so upsetting at the time. For us, I mean, but I suppose for him too. Look, why don't you come for lunch at Gregory's Sunday week? We're already booked this coming Sunday, but we've got nothing on the one after. You and Phil. Gregory was only saying the other night we should have you over again soon."

"Thanks, but seriously, roast dinners, this weather?" Greg had turned out to be a dab hand at stuffing a chicken, to nobody's surprise.

"Oh, the heat wave's bound to have broken by then. And anyway, did I mention a roast? We'll probably have cold meat and salad or something." Cherry gave me a sly look. "And it's usually nice and cool at the Old Deanery. Those old stone walls and high ceilings aren't so bad in summer."

I had a sneaking feeling Greg probably wanted the opportunity to collar me for some sort of wedding preparation duties, but I supposed I wasn't likely to escape them forever. "Yeah, okay, then. Twelve o'clock as usual?" It was earlier than I usually liked to eat lunch at the weekend, but Greg's Sundays were pretty much regulated by the services at the cathedral.

Cherry's look got even slyer. "You *could* always come for the service. Gregory's preaching that week."

"Er, thanks, Sis, but I think we'll let him give us the edited highlights over lunch."

"Worried you'd be struck by lightning if you stepped over the threshold?" Cherry *tutt*ed. "You know, most people in the Church of England are perfectly accepting of homosexuality. There's a very good theological case for it. Half the phrases in the Bible that people always quote as condemning it are simply mistranslated, misinterpreted, or both."

"Oi. I've been to your Greg's cathedral before. Didn't have the world's greatest experience, did I? Nah, I don't think Phil'd be up for it. He's a bit funny about religion."

More to the point, I thought he'd have a few choice words to say about being dragged out of bed on a Sunday morning just so he could hear Greg drone on from a pulpit.

"But lunch'll be great," I went on before she could muster another argument. "We'll see you at twelve, all right?"

After she'd gone, I couldn't seem to stop staring at the few photos I had of my real dad. He was dark, like me, and also like me not the tallest bloke in the world, unless Mum had been standing on a box for the photos. Having checked my face in the mirror, I knew Phil wasn't making it up when he said there was a resemblance between us, although we didn't look like twins or anything.

Of course, the pictures were taken thirty years ago. He probably looked a lot different these days. Although chances were that, unlike Dad and Richard, he still had a full head of hair.

It was well weird seeing Mum standing next to him, his arm around her waist, both of them smiling at the camera. I'd often wondered who'd taken the pics—some mate of one of theirs who was in the know? Or did they grab some passing stranger and ask them to do the honours? It was hard to tell from the backgrounds just where the photos had been taken. They were standing outside, around bushes or trees, and could have been in a park somewhere, or just as easily in someone's back garden. Mum looked happy but tense—unless I was reading too much into a faded smile. The time of year was hard to judge too. They weren't dressed for winter, and the trees were green, but it could have been spring, summer, or early autumn. Had she known she was pregnant already? Had he?

Had the bloke ever even found out I existed? Had he cared?

Sod it. I grabbed my phone from where it was charging on the kitchen counter and called Phil. "Wanna come over?"

"Thought you were seeing your sister tonight?"

"I did."

Phil huffed a laugh, presumably at my tone. "Went that well, did it? All right, I'll see you in ten."

Luckily we lived close enough to each other that I didn't have to feel too guilty about dragging him over for a couple of hours after having told him not to come round tonight. Plus I knew from experience that if it was hot in my house, it'd be like a tandoori oven in his attic flat, so he was probably only too glad to come over to mine. What with the weather and all, I'd half expected him to start dropping hints about moving in with me.

He hadn't. Not a dicky bird. Still, it was early days yet. We'd been together less than a year—more like eight months, give or take. Then again, how long does it take to get to know a bloke when you spend most of your leisure hours together?

I mean, obviously sometimes Phil had to work nights, and I had to work Saturdays, but we met up lunchtimes occasionally, which sort of made up for that. At any rate, it seemed pretty clear we were both serious about each other. And Phil hadn't batted an eyelid when I'd asked him round for what amounted to emotional support. It'd been a while since I'd been that comfortable with anyone I was seeing. A long while. Actually, I wasn't sure I'd *ever* been this comfortable with anyone before. It was, well, it was nice. And maybe just a little bit terrifying.

It'd been eight o'clock, near enough, when I'd rung him, and true to his word, Phil was round at mine before the clock had ticked round to quarter past. He let himself in.

"So what happened?" he asked, coming into the living room. "She threaten to get Greg to excommunicate you if you said anything about this Mike bloke to your mum?"

"Worse," I said, smiling up at him from my slump on the sofa. "Warned me Dad might start having feelings all over the shop." Making a slightly embarrassing contrast with my slobbing-around-the-house-in-a-heat-wave gear of shorts and a crumpled T-shirt, Phil was freshly shaved and wearing a crisply ironed short-sleeved shirt loose over a pair of chinos. The outfit did a very nice job of showing off his broad chest and shoulders and trim hips. You'd think a big bloke like him would feel the heat more—would show it, even, him being a blond and all—but he always managed to look cool whatever the weather. Maybe he kept ice cubes in his undies.

Nah, I'd have noticed. I mean, I don't like to brag, but I reckon I was pretty well acquainted with the contents of Phil's undies.

"God, I need a drink," I said.

Phil disappeared into the kitchen. Merlin jumped on my lap, and I stroked his furry little head, being all manly and stoic about the claws stuck painfully in my legs. I've had a lot of practice.

When Phil came back, he was holding a couple of glasses with generous measures of what had to be whiskey. Presumably from the bottle given to me last Christmas by the old bloke formerly known as Dad. "I meant a beer," I protested, taking a glass from his outstretched hand.

"Nah. If this doesn't call for the hard stuff, I don't know what does."

I took a sip, enjoying the smooth taste but glad he'd added ice. Condensation was forming on the outside of the glass, so I wiped my hand on my bare leg after I'd put my drink down on the coffee table. At least it cooled me off a bit. "I haven't even told you about it yet."

"Don't have to, do you? Not with that face on you." He sat down next to me, his muscular thigh a solid bulk next to mine.

I leaned into him, wishing the day would hurry up and cool down, at least to the point where we could snuggle without risking heat exhaustion. "I thought you liked my face?"

Phil grinned. "Nah, it's your arse I'm interested in."

"Yeah? That's the last blowjob you're getting, then."

"Like that's a threat you'd ever carry through on." He was right too, the smug git.

"So go on, then," he went on. "Tell me about it."

I scrubbed at my eyes with the heels of my hands. "I'm not asking Mum about this Mike bloke. Can't."

Phil *humph*ed. "Laid the guilt trip on you, did she? Your sister?"

"She said Dad *cried* when he found out."

"Fuck."

"Yeah, just a bit." I'd known that would get to him. Not the most comfortable of men around displays of masculine weakness, my Phil.

Was crying really weak, though? Or did it just mean you actually gave a shit? All I knew was that I'd rather drown myself in a bloody septic tank than be the cause of Dad doing it again.

"It's not your fault. None of it," Phil said, slipping an arm around my shoulders.

I managed a weak smile. "You reading my mind?"

"Yeah. It's on the advanced PI classes."

"Oh? They teach you that before or after the stuff about distance lip-reading and using sex as an interrogation method?"

"After. Course, I didn't do so well on the last one. Might have to get a bit of practice in at home."

"Are you trying to distract me with sex?"

"Might be."

"Try *harder*." I leered at him.

Phil raised an eyebrow. "Is that an innuendo in your pocket, or are you just pleased to see me?"

I flashed him my sultriest smile. "Why don't you, you know, *investigate*?"

All in all, it probably wasn't surprising we didn't get a lot more talking done that evening. Or that Phil's posh shirt had more wrinkles in it than my T-shirt by the time we'd finished.

CHAPTER FOUR

It was a couple of days later when we got on the subject of my dad again. Well, sort of. I'd been trying not to push Phil about researching stuff, seeing as he still had actual paid work he needed to be doing on a suspected infidelity case. Not to mention Marianne's little problem. I wasn't totally sure if he'd be getting paid for that one or not, seeing as no one had discussed money in my hearing. Still, last time Harry asked me to take a look at her plumbing (literally, not figuratively, I'd like to emphasize), she'd insisted on paying the going rate, no matter how often I'd told her a pint would cover it. So, yeah, my little problem was probably so far on the back burner it was starting to ice up.

We were in the kitchen at the time, Phil watching as I faffed around with packets of cat food and tried not to get mauled to death by the overeager recipients. He clearly thought I didn't have enough to do already, because he weighed in after a moment with, "You've got this ability, gift, whatever you want to call it. Why don't you try and do something with it?"

"What, like make a career out of it? Go on *Britain's Got Talent*? I've already got a job, thanks, and I don't need Simon bloody Cowell making me look like a right tit on the telly." I straightened up from the cats' bowls and bunged the empty sachets in the bin. Then I washed my hands, because in this heat, a little bit of cat food smell went a long way.

Merlin and Arthur didn't seem to have a problem with it—they were heads down and tails up, well on their way to polishing off their dinner already.

"No, you can manage that by yourself." Phil's smirk turned into a frown as he shoved his hands in his pockets. "But I don't get why you don't try and develop it. See how far you can go with it."

"How far . . .? I've found dead bodies, for fuck's sake. I found *you* before you turned into one, remember? How much more do you want me to do?"

"You say you can only find hidden stuff, right?"

"And water." I folded my arms.

Phil nodded a bit dismissively, like he didn't reckon that last bit was all that important. It just went to prove *he'd* never been stranded in the Sahara without a satnav and no idea which way to stagger to the nearest oasis. Which, fair enough, neither had I, but if it ever happened, I bet he'd be glad of my company. "Have you ever tried finding stuff that's only lost?"

"Course I've bloody tried! It doesn't work. End of."

"What have you tried it on?"

Stubborn git. "I don't know . . . Keys. Stuff in the van. It never works, I'm telling you."

"That's all stuff *you've* lost. Have you ever tried looking for things other people have lost?"

"No, because it doesn't work."

"Yeah, but have you tried?" My face probably told him what I thought of that. Phil stepped up to me and put his arms around my waist. "And what about expanding the way you look for the hidden stuff?"

"Like how?" One of Phil's hands had crept down to grope my arse. It made it a bit hard to keep my end up—of the argument, that was—which was probably his intention. Sneaky git.

"Well . . . you always reckon you need to be near where the thing is. What about using a map?"

"Using one how?"

"You've got this water-divining connection, haven't you? Why don't you try some of their tricks?"

"What, get myself a forked stick and wait for it to twitch?"

"If that's what works for you, yeah. Or there's wire rods, or pendulums."

"You've been reading bloody Wikipedia, haven't you?" Either that or he'd got hold of a copy of *Dowsing for Dummies*, but I'd checked online a while back and they still hadn't written one yet.

Phil's gaze went over my left shoulder. "Maybe. Look, I'm just saying, it's worth a try." He paused. "You want to find this Mike bloke, don't you? Maybe you could give it a go for that."

"Think Mum went all black widow on him and stashed the body somewhere, do you?" Ye gods. Talking about my mum like she was some kind of *femme* literally *fatale* was giving me the shivers.

"Don't be a prick. Look, would it kill you to give it a try?"

Would it kill him to stop bloody harassing me about it?

Oh, right. This was Phil. It probably would kill him. Plus, he now had his hand down the back of my kecks and was running a finger along my crack. All my blood had shot south, leaving me more than a bit light-headed. I caved. "Fine. I'll try it, all right?"

Phil smiled and stepped away from me, the smug bastard. "Good. I'll get the map."

"Oi, I didn't mean right now! Bloody prick-tease," I muttered to his departing back and went to grab the letters and stuff.

I felt like a right muppet, sitting on the sofa staring at my mum's old love letters and photos and then trying to pick up nonexistent vibes from last year's edition of the AA road map, spread out on the coffee table. Phil had me trying all sorts of stuff—hovering my hand over Britain's clearest mapping of the M25 (with added speed cameras); getting all touchy-feely with the pages; and, in a last act of desperation, swinging a pendulum we'd improvised from a bath plug.

The tight knot in my stomach that had formed at the thought of maybe actually finding something melted into disappointment—all right, maybe disappointment mingled with a tiny bit of relief.

"Shouldn't this be some mystic crystal or something?" I complained after five minutes of the plug hanging limply from my hand rather than mysteriously circling some spot on the map like Phil reckoned it was supposed to. "This plug's not even real rubber, just some cheap plastic. And the chrome plating on the chain's all worn off."

Phil huffed. "Why'd you buy it, then?"

"Didn't, did I? It's just something I had hanging around in the van after I replaced the fittings for a customer."

"Well, next time we'll go for the solid-gold stuff, all right, princess?"

"Nah, you've got to be careful with the gold stuff, or it looks tacky. Speaking of which, you know there's this place in Hong Kong that has a solid-gold toilet? I was reading about it online."

"Jesus wept."

"Too bloody right. Bet they skimped inside the cistern, though. Bet you anything when you open it up it's just your bog-standard bog fittings from Wickes. Well, the Chinese equivalent of Wickes, anyhow."

Phil rolled his eyes and sent a significant look map-wards. "Getting a bit off track here, aren't we?"

"Nope. To be getting off track, we'd have had to be *on* track in the first place. Which, in case you hadn't noticed, we weren't. I'm not even convinced there *is* a bloody track." I closed up the map and sat back on the sofa. "Face it: the map thing's a bust."

"Not necessarily." Phil looked thoughtful. "After all, your old man's probably not hiding—if he's even still around—so it was a long shot anyway. We need to give it a proper trial. Get someone to bury something somewhere, and see if you can find that."

I stood up, narked. "This was never about my sodding dad, was it? You knew I wouldn't find anything. You just wanted to get me trying stuff."

Phil stood up too and put his arms around me. "Maybe, but I still thought it was worth a shot. Look, I told you, I'm going to work on finding your dad. I'm going down to London tomorrow anyway. I can stop off in Edgware on the way back and kill two birds with one stone."

"Want me to come with?" I wouldn't be popular with the customers I had booked in, but none of them were emergencies. They'd survive.

"Best not. I'm going for the *old friend wanting to get back in touch* angle, so if you show up looking like, well, the long-lost illegitimate son, people might decide to clam up. Might think they're doing this Mike bloke a favour."

"What, like I'm going to go after him for thirty years' back pocket money?"

"Or just out to cause trouble generally. Your mum's still married to the same person as she was when they had the affair, isn't she? So maybe he is too."

I'd have been lying if I'd said it hadn't occurred to me he might have been married too, might have a wife and kids he'd stepped out on just like Mum had, but for some reason I couldn't see it. It didn't seem to fit, although I couldn't have explained why. "I don't know—can you see Mike with the stereotypical wife, mortgage and two point four kids?"

Phil grinned. "With you being the point four?"

I stepped back out of his arms, all the better to glare at him. "Bloody hell, don't you start with the height jokes and all."

Phil put on a face I reckoned was supposed to look innocent. It came over more like smug. "Did I say anything about your height? I might have been referring to the degree of estrangement."

"'Degree of estrangement,' my arse. Which, by the way, you're going to be feeling a degree of estrangement from if you keep up the gags at my expense."

"Touchy sod." Phil smiled as he pulled me back against him with two hands on the body part in question.

All right, he didn't have to pull that hard. "Yep, and don't you forget it. Hey, how far have you got on Marianne's case?"

"Not very. It's only been a couple of days, and I'm still working on the cheating-wife case."

"So is she?"

"What, cheating on him?" Phil huffed. "Nothing conclusive yet, but I'll tell you what, if I was married to that miserable git, I'd be bloody well tempted to cheat."

I pushed away from him. "All right, who are you and what have you done with Phil Morrison? I thought you were all about the sanctity of marriage vows?"

He smirked. "Said I'd be tempted. Didn't say I'd do it."

"God, the gleam from your bloody halo could put someone's eye out. So, what about Carey? Have you had a good look at him? Followed him around? Actually, hang about, shouldn't you be following him now?"

"I'm supposed to be digging into his background, not catching him with his trousers down."

"Right. So how come you're not down in Docklands? Digging."

"I just said I'm going to London tomorrow, didn't I? I had to spend today following Mrs. C. around. Which turned out to be a total waste of time and petrol, seeing as she only went to the supermarket, the gym, and her hairdresser's."

"So you haven't found anything out about Carey?"

"I wouldn't say that. Had a lot of downtime, didn't I, waiting for Mrs. C. to get her highlights done and fill up the supermarket trolley. See, there's this thing called the internet. Turns out it's pretty good for finding out stuff without having to get on a train—"

"All right, all right. Git."

"Plus, the bloke I want to talk to most is banged up in Nether Mallet."

"Sounds painful."

Phil gave me an exasperated look and a one-finger salute. "It's a category-C prison in Essex. And you can't just turn up, knock on the door, and ask if one of their inmates can come out to play. It could take weeks to arrange a visit—and that's *if* he agrees to see me."

"Yeah, but that's not likely to be a problem, is it? You're after the bastard who got him sent down. This Mortimer bloke ought to be biting your hand off."

"Maybe. Or maybe Carey's got him running scared, ever think of that? Mortimer's got family—wife and a couple of kids. He might want to keep his head down."

"Bloody hell. Who is this Carey bloke—second cousin to the Godfather?"

"Nope. Just a nasty little shit who's going to get his comeuppance. But it's going to take a bit of work."

"You'd better have a word with that wife, then. Tell her to hurry up and make a booty call so you can wrap up the case and concentrate on Carey."

"Yeah, I'll do that. I'm sure she'll be only too happy to oblige."

"What's she like, this Mrs. C.? Is she a looker?"

"Why? Are you thinking of helping me out by having a go at her yourself?" Phil sent me a sardonic look. "I'm supposed to be finding evidence of an affair, not manufacturing it."

I frowned. "You know, I hadn't thought of that."

"You weren't supposed to take it seriously."

"No, you prick. I mean, you could do that, couldn't you? Frame her so you get a payoff from the husband. I mean, not that you *would*, obviously, but some blokes might."

"They'd be daft. This isn't some no-win-no-fee thing. There'd be more money in stringing him along, conveniently *not* finding anything for weeks. Which I reckon he's going to accuse me of soon if I don't come up with anything."

"So what happens if you never do find anything? Some point, you've got to call it a day."

Phil nodded. "Yeah. All that happens is, I write up a report saying nothing doing, and send him a bill. Which he'll moan about but will pay in the end because he's worried if he doesn't, I'll squeal to the missus."

"Doesn't sound like a healthy relationship to me." I made a face. "What with Marianne and that git Carey, it makes you wonder how many are."

"What, healthy? Getting cynical in your old age, aren't you?"

"'Old age'? Hey, I'm the one who's still in his twenties, here." Just. "You're the one who's halfway to the carpet slippers and the pension book, not me." Phil had turned thirty just before we'd met—again—last year.

Course, I already had the walking stick—had done since I was seventeen—but it wasn't like I ever used it. My hip hardly even ached, in the summer.

Much.

"Yeah, well. Come next month, we'll see who's making the age jokes." Phil folded his arms, which was something he didn't do often enough. It made the muscles in his arms stand out very nicely indeed. "I'm still waiting for you to tell me what you want to do for your birthday."

I glared at him, not too happy to be jolted out of my warm, fuzzy feelings. Specially as they'd been turning a bit hotter and a lot less fuzzy. "That's not how I remember it. What I remember is me saying I didn't want to make a fuss about it. It's just another birthday. I'll go to work, get home, have a takeaway and a beer in front of the telly. That'll do me fine."

"Bloody hell, anyone'd think you were turning fifty, not thirty. Live a little."

"I don't get why you're making such a big deal about it. It's not like it's any kind of landmark or anything. What can you do at thirty that you can't do at twenty-one? Eighteen, even, now they've dropped the truck-driving age limit?"

He just sat there, looking at me, his arms still folded, the big, muscle-bound git.

"What?" I snapped.

Phil sent me a mocking look. "Just think you're a bit young for a midlife crisis, that's all."

"Oi! I am *not* having a bloody midlife crisis." I wasn't, all right? Thirty wasn't old or anything.

He laughed, the bastard. "Better be careful how much you protest there, princess."

I glared at him. "Less of the *princess*, all right? Or you'll be getting a tiara shoved where the sun doesn't shine. And anyway, I thought we were talking about Carey? You got some dirt on the bloke?"

Phil nodded, serious now. "I put out some feelers. He's been clever, has Carey—the Met's had their eye on him a couple of times, but there's never been enough evidence to prosecute."

"Bit like Mrs. C., then. Oi, don't suppose the *C* stands for—"

"Nope. It doesn't. And what Carey's been up to—allegedly—is a bit more serious than stepping out on the other half. Put it this way— if he *did* frame this Mortimer bloke for the drugs offence, he didn't exactly have to go out of his way to find the merchandise. Allegedly."

"Not just the knockoff iPads he's importing, then?"

"Apparently not. My mate Steve at the Met reckoned if I manage to find any dirt that'll stick, him and his whole department will be queuing up to buy me a drink."

That didn't exactly sound encouraging—after all, if the Metropolitan Police with all their resources couldn't pin anything on the bloke, what chance did Phil have? "Great. Hope Harry isn't holding her breath."

Phil shrugged. "The Mortimer angle might be a good one to follow. Steve reckoned he's as dodgy as Carey, so no one took him seriously when he cried foul."

"Huh. So to put Carey in jail, we've got to spring this bloke who probably deserves to stay in there with him."

"If that's what it takes, yeah. It's swings and roundabouts. At least Marianne and Harry'll be safe from Mortimer."

"S'pose." It still didn't seem right, us working to get a criminal out of jail. Still, if he hadn't actually done the crime he was in for, that was, as Phil would say, a boner fidey miscarriage of justice, wasn't it?

God, this was doing my head in.

What with Phil being out all day Friday, and me having a bath Saturday morning that seriously overran—that's installing it, not wallowing in it—it was Saturday night before I saw Phil again. Course, we'd texted in the meantime.

Well, all right, we'd sexted. So by the time I rolled up at Phil's on my way back from grabbing a burger for my tea, I was fairly gagging for a case update. Amongst other things.

When I let myself in, though, he had another man in there with him.

CHAPTER FIVE

Well, I say he had another man with him, but in fact Phil himself was nowhere in sight. If it hadn't been for the skylights, which would have been a neat trick anywhere but the attic, I'd have thought I'd got the wrong floor and walked into some other bloke's flat.

Said bloke was short, dark, and dressed in an expensive-looking suit, with an open-collared shirt and no tie. He was relaxing on the sofa with his arms flung over the back and one ankle crossed over the opposite knee, looking more at home in Phil's place than I'd ever felt around there, the bastard. Which was taking liberties and then some, seeing as it was Grant Carey, who, to the best of my knowledge, had never been round here before. And what the bloody hell was he doing here now? Had Phil got bored of trying to dig up the dirt on the bloke and decided to invite him round and ask?

Carey was better looking in the flesh than in his photos, and the hair didn't seem to be receding as much as I'd thought. He flashed me a cheery smile and a wave. "Hello, hello. Do come in. The more the merrier, I always say. Grant Carey—and you are . . .?"

"Tom Paretski." I didn't offer him a handshake. Or a business card.

He kept on smiling anyway. "Are you professionally involved with Philip, here?"

Was this bloke real? Also, what the bloody hell was he doing here? Which, yeah, I know I said before, but seriously, what the fuck?

"No," I said shortly, just as Phil grunted out his own negative, having stomped in from the kitchen while I was busy staring at Carey. Phil looked well ticked off, which I chose to interpret as being down to his other presumably uninvited guest, not me.

Carey's eyes went comically wide. "Oh. *Oh*. Do forgive me. The last thing I'd want to do is step on any toes, here. Philip and I were just having a friendly chat, weren't we? I was admiring this cosy little flat. Very compact. Of course, all this wood is something of a fire risk," he added, waving at the fixtures and fittings in a way that made my skin crawl. "But I'm sure you wouldn't take any unnecessary chances, would you, Philip?" He pursed his lips and sucked in a breath. "I imagine it would be rather unpleasant being here while everything went up in smoke. *Poof!*" Carey honest-to-God giggled at the end, like his idea of a fun Saturday night would be watching the building go up in flames with my Phil inside it. And while that little *poof* at the end might have simply been a bit of extra enthusiasm, my money was on it being a not-so-subtle dig at mine and Phil's sexuality.

Which was ironic, really, seeing as this bloke was camper than a Glastonbury field at festival time. He had one of those accents which was hard to place, like maybe he'd put it together from odds and ends he'd found lying around somewhere. Sort of posh, but with a hint that it wasn't quite how he'd grown up talking.

Course, Phil was all for social mobility. Which was neither here nor there, obviously. Speaking of which, Phil had buggered off back into the kitchen again.

"Popped round to sell Phil some fire extinguishers, did you?" I asked, sitting down opposite Carey and putting my feet up on the coffee table. Two could play at this comfier-than-thou bollocks.

"Oh no, you misunderstand me. No ulterior motives whatsoever." God, he was the picture of innocence, the git, with his wide brown eyes. "I just heard Philip here was interested in me, so I thought I'd save him a bit of trouble. Let him get it straight from the horse's mouth. So to speak."

"Your tea," Phil interrupted, thrusting a mug at him, stony-faced.

"So kind." Carey took the mug and put it down on the table so close to my ankle I had to shift an inch or get scalded. Apparently Carey took his tea black, like his shrivelled little heart. Phil had even left the bag in, so obviously he'd decided that while you might catch more flies with honey, drowning them in vinegar was way more satisfying.

"Very public-spirited of you." I laid on the sarcasm thick enough to lag a pipe.

"Oh, absolutely. I do *hate* to see people I've grown attached to take unnecessary risks. Philip and I have taken quite a shine to each other, haven't we?" Carey smiled.

Phil grunted something unintelligible.

"But tell me about you, Tom." Those big brown eyes gazed at me like I was the most fascinating thing they'd ever seen, and he was itching for a microscope and a scalpel. "What is it you do for a living, if you're not in the detective trade?"

I opened my mouth to give him a one-word answer, but Phil beat me to it. "Nothing you need to know about."

Carey shrugged. "Oh, well. Perhaps I'll have a look on the internet when I get home. Amazing, the things you can find out about people these days, all with the click of a mouse. Paretski . . . No, there can't be too many of those around here, can there?"

Shit. My blood ran cold as I realized Cherry's name would come up in any internet search. And Richard, and Mum and Dad . . . But he wouldn't really do anything to them, would he . . .?

His smile was getting more sharklike the longer I looked at it. Christ, I was beginning to see why Harry had such a low opinion of this bastard. And why she'd needed some help dealing with the little toad.

"Planning on staying much longer?" Phil asked so abruptly I jumped.

Carey didn't even blink, just uncrossed his legs and got up from the sofa with a sort of slinky, slimy grace, like a sharp-suited tapeworm. Not liking him looking down on me, I got up too.

Hah. I had at least an inch on him. Lucky I was still in my thick-soled work boots. Course, the steel toe caps might come in handy too. If, say, I wanted to give something a good kicking.

"Oh, I wouldn't want to impose on you any longer," Carey was saying. "I'm sure you and Tom have lots to talk about. I'll see myself out, don't worry."

Phil followed him to the door anyway. I didn't blame him—I was half tempted to trail along too, just to make sure the git had really gone. Instead, I walked over to the window and stared out until I could see him on the pavement below.

Carey turned, looked up, and waved at me, the bastard.

"Jesus, talk about your fucking awful timing," Phil muttered in my ear. When I turned, he was scrubbing his face with both hands. "Wish I'd never given you that bloody key."

"'Scuse me for existing," I snapped back, narked. "What, ruin your cosy little chat, did I?"

"Sod the bloody chat. You really think it's a good idea him knowing about us? And did you *have* to give him your full name just because he asked?"

"Well, someone had to make conversation, didn't they? You weren't exactly Mr. Effing Chatty, were you?"

"That's because you don't say anything more than you have to around a bloke like that. Ever heard the phrase 'anything you say can and will be used against you'? I've met blokes like him before—they're like bloody squirrels, ferreting away anything that gives 'em an edge."

I had to smile. "Make your mind up—is he a squirrel or a ferret?"

"Neither. He's a cockroach. And that's defamation of cockroaches."

I hesitated. "You don't think he'd actually, you know, do anything, do you?"

"Dunno. Why don't you ask Alan Mortimer? You know, the one he sent on holiday at Her Majesty's expense?"

Bloody hell, this was all getting a bit serious. "Oi, you don't reckon he's planted anything on you, do you?" I blurted out as the thought punched me in the gut. "Shit, why'd you leave him alone in here, anyway? You didn't have to offer him a cuppa." I glanced at Carey's untouched mug of tea, which was turning brackish. "It's not like he even drank any."

"He asked for it."

"That bastard was asking for a lot of things," I muttered. "And oi—what was that you just said about not giving him stuff just because he asked?"

Phil huffed. "Bloke like that asks for a piece of rope, you give it to him and hope he hangs himself. Don't reckon he had time to plant anything, though—not with you turning up like that. Still, wouldn't hurt for you to do your party piece and confirm it for us, would it, now?"

"Right." I stepped away from him a bit, not that I actually needed to, wiped my palms on my jeans, and listened.

Show me a house that hasn't got any hidden stuff, and I'll show you someone who's just a bit more cautious than the average homeowner and is keeping all their dirty little secrets well away from their own backyard. Phil's flat was no exception—there was the usual low-grade niggly stuff, the equivalent of sweeping the dirt under the carpet. Nothing big, at least not in this room. I frowned. "Did he stay in the living room all the time he was here?"

Phil thought about it. "Probably. Almost certainly."

"But he could have nipped into the bedroom, say, after you went to put the kettle on and before I turned up?" I folded my arms. "*Now* who wasn't being careful?"

"It was a calculated risk," Phil said steadily. Then the stone façade crumbled into a rueful smile. "All right, so he had me rattled, turning up like that. Needed a moment to get my brain in gear, didn't I?"

"Watch it," I said with a grin. "I might start thinking you're human. Right, so a full sweep's needed."

"You been watching spy films again? Go on, then, do your stuff."

I checked out the bedroom—nothing in there I wasn't already aware of, thanks—the bathroom (ditto), and then, for completeness, the kitchen.

Phil frowned at me. "He definitely didn't come in here."

"Yeah, so, I'm being thorough, all right? Maybe he snuck in without you noticing, with his evil cockroach powers." I was frowning too. There was something in here, all right. It was brighter than I'd have expected, though, for something Carey might have stashed. If *I'd* planted something incriminating on someone, I'd expect it to have a guilty, greasy feel to it. Although . . . a bloke like Carey—he might just have thought it was a bit of fun, mightn't he? I mean, looking at all the evidence with an impartial eye, he was a bit of a nutjob. "Top of that cupboard. There's something in there. Oi, you been taking lessons from my Auntie Lol, hiding stuff in the kitchen?"

Phil startled. "What? No," he said quickly. "That's not . . . I know what that is."

I blinked. "You sure?" It was, well, a bit too loud for anything I'd expect Phil to have hidden. "Better check, hadn't you? I mean, better safe than sorry."

"It's not . . . Fine," he huffed, and opened up the cupboard about six inches, stuck his head in for half a second if that, then closed it. "Told you. Nothing there that shouldn't be."

I folded my arms again and fixed him with a look.

"What?" he said.

"All I'm saying is, that had better be my birthday present you've got stashed in there."

He laughed. "Worried it's some bloke?"

"What, in your kitchen cupboard? Only if you're cheating on me with a midget."

"Could be one of Darren's mates." Phil smirked. "From what he tells me, the dwarf porn star community is very tight-knit."

"You know, I'm not sure I approve of you hanging around with him. He's a bad influence." I grinned and grabbed him around the waist. "I'm the only one who's allowed to be a bad influence on you."

"Is that so?" Phil melted into my touch. "Maybe it's time you got on with that, then."

It was a fair bit later by the time I remembered what I'd actually come round here for. Not that I was complaining about the way we'd spent our time, mind.

I heaved my head off the pillow before I went to sleep, and propped it up on my hand, leaning on an elbow. "Oi, are you ever going to tell me what you found out yesterday?"

Phil sighed and stretched. Jesus, he had big arms. Not that I was complaining about that either. "Bugger all about your dad. The only long-term resident I managed to talk to in your old street was eighty-four and senile. I spent most of my time trying to convince her I hadn't come to take her away to a home. When I finally got her onto the subject of your family, it got even worse."

"Yeah? Her and mum have a row over parking spaces or where she left her bins or something?"

"No. But apparently those Paretskis were a bad lot. She reckoned it came of being Polish." Phil laughed, no doubt at my expression. "Youngest son was the worst. Murdered a little girl in the local park when he was only a lad."

"Bloody hell! I hope you put her straight." God knows, this so-called gift of mine's brought me a fair bit of grief over the years, but I wasn't too chuffed at Mrs. Senile telling all and sundry I'd been a seven-year-old psycho.

"Did my best. Trouble was, *then* she gets it into her head I'm part of the Polish mafia, scouting out the territory, ready to murder her in her bed." He was laughing again, the sod.

"Argh!" I flopped back on the pillow and scrubbed both hands over my face. "If I ever meet my great-grandad in the afterlife, we're going to have serious words over this Polish bollocks." Great-grandad—or step-great-grandad, as I supposed I should probably call him these days—had toddled over from Germany to Britain sometime before 1914 and decided he liked it. When World War One broke out and being called Thomas Patschke started to seem like a bit of a bad idea—and not just because nobody could spell it, either—old great-gramps decided, like a whole load of other immigrants over the ages, to change his name.

*Un*like everybody else in the history of immigration, though, he didn't go for something British. Say, I don't know, Patterson or something. Maybe he still had a strong foreign accent and didn't reckon he could carry it off, who knows? And, let's face it, your average Brit in the early twentieth-century street was decades away from being able to tell one brand of "foreign" from another. But anyway, Thomas Patschke disappeared from public record, and up popped one Thomas Paretski. Just to be on the safe side, when his first son was born in 1917, six months after old Tom got married to a Derbyshire lass called Ethel, they named the lad George, after the one currently warming the throne.

Which was ironic, really, seeing as George V came from a long line of Germans, but there you go.

Phil prodded me in the stomach, and I jumped, batting his hand away and opening my eyes. "Oi, less of that."

"Thought you'd gone to sleep. Or started astrally projecting yourself onto the spirit plane to have a moan at your great-grandad."

"I was thinking. You should try it sometime. Oi, less of that and all." He'd given up on prodding and started tickling. It turned into a bit of a wrestling match, which, as usual, I was losing badly, until I got in a lucky grab to an area that would have had the Marquess of Queensberry screaming for the smelling salts. It could have developed into something he *really* wouldn't have been happy seeing in a boxing ring, but we both decided we were too hot and too bloody knackered, and flopped back down on the bed, chests heaving.

"God, that's me done for the day," I panted.

"Thank Christ for that." Phil grabbed a bottle of water from the floor on his side of the bed, took a swig, and passed it over.

"Cheers." I took a long swallow. "Hey, did you get down to Docklands? Any luck there?"

"Bit," Phil said. "Had some news from another quarter too." Then he fell silent, the git.

"Well?" I prompted.

"Get this—Mortimer's out on appeal. Seems his lawyer managed to dig up some new evidence. And guess what? They just happened to let him out of prison shortly before Carey turned up here." Phil gave a grim little laugh. "Puts a new perspective on Carey's undying love for Marianne, doesn't it?"

I thought about it. Then I thought about it some more. "You reckon Carey's running scared? Thinks his sins are about to catch him up, and wants to stop her telling anyone what she told us? Shit—you think he knows we know?" All the hairs on the back of my neck started to prickle. "Bloody hell. You don't think he's seriously dangerous, do you?"

Phil showed his teeth like a big, blond pit bull terrier about to savage someone. "You'd better be watching your step for the foreseeable."

"What about you?" I countered. "Don't get me wrong, I'm all in favour of digging up the dirt on the bastard, but you're the one doing the actual spadework. What if he tries to, well, take you out?" It might have been hotter than your average sauna in here, but all of a sudden, I felt cold.

"Doesn't need to, does he?"

"What?"

Now he was a world-weary pit bull exasperated with the naivety of younger dogs. "Think about it. The little prick's half my size. Physical intimidation isn't going to work. On the other hand, he knows my weak spot."

"Which is?"

"You, you moron."

"Oh." I lay back and stared through the skylight in the bedroom ceiling. The sky was an inky blue-black, a couple of faint stars twinkling away like there was no tomorrow. Not likely to be any rain tonight, then. Again.

"Yeah. Oh. So don't go taking any chances, all right? No running off to see what you can turn up on the bastard on your own or anything like that. Leave it to the professionals."

Not that I wasn't touched by his concern, but I was starting to get a bit narked by his attitude. "Right. Because those extra few inches you've got on me and him make all the difference, right? Does Darren know you're so bloody heightist?"

"It's got sod all to do with your sodding height, all right?"

"Yeah, right." Pull the other one; it's held together with metal pins and sticky tape.

I wished I'd said that last bit out loud when he fixed me with a patronizing look, the smug git. "It's about whether you're used to dealing with his sort. When it comes down to it, if I had to back either you or Darren against Carey, I know who my money'd be on."

Fucking marvellous. "Thanks so much for the vote of confidence."

He grinned and squeezed my arse. "You've got other qualities."

I rolled away from his grasp and got out of bed. "What am I, a sodding blow-up doll? Worried I'll get popped?" Jeans. Where were my jeans? Right. Living room.

"Where are you off to?"

"Home. Got to wrap myself in cotton wool and bung myself in a cupboard. Unless you think bubble wrap would be safer?" Underwear? That must be in here somewhere. Nah, sod it. Quicker to go commando.

"What the fuck are you on about?"

"What the . . .? You. I'm on about you, treating me like I'm made of sodding glass. Cheers, mate. Really good for the ego, that is."

"Oi. Tom. Come back here." He huffed a sigh. "Please? Stop being so bloody touchy, all right? So I worry about you getting hurt—it's not like it's never bloody happened before, is it? You think I want any more times on my conscience?"

Now *my* conscience was poking me. "You know I don't blame you for the hip," I muttered, parking my still-naked arse on the bed. Phil pulled me down to lie next to him, but didn't say anything, just ran his hands gently up and down my side.

After a moment, I realized he was stroking the scars left by the surgery to rebuild my hip when I was seventeen.

Shit. I twisted around in his arms. "I *don't*, all right? Wasn't your fault. It was an accident." Maybe I *had* been running away from Phil and his gang of bullies at the time, but hey, he couldn't have known I'd run straight into traffic.

I couldn't read his expression. "Yeah," he said. "You staying, then?"

"Yeah."

"Good. Go to sleep."

CHAPTER SIX

When I woke up at Phil's on Sunday morning, the sun was streaming through the thin curtains he had at the windows of his attic flat, giving me a whole new appreciation of the phrase *heat rises*. And not in a good way. I was sweating like I'd just got back from a five-mile run, and I hadn't even moved yet. My dick was all keen to get up close and personal with the six-foot hunk of lean muscle lying next to me, but the rest of me was saying no sodding way.

"Bloody hell," I grumbled, flinging an arm up over my eyes. That sun was vicious. "Too hot for sex. That's just sad. And, Christ, it's first thing in the morning. What's it going to be like at noon?"

Phil huffed. "Pretty similar to this, I'd say. It's ten to twelve, Sleeping Beauty."

"Oi, what is it with all these princess references? I'm telling you now, if you're hoping to get me into a poofy dress and a tiara, you're in for a big disappointment."

"Don't worry. I like you better in what you're wearing right now."

"Yeah, well, you can look, but don't touch."

That pretty much set the tone for the rest of the day, unfortunately. How is it a lie-in can make you feel even more tired than you were the night before? With hindsight, hanging around Phil's little oven of a flat all day probably wasn't the smartest idea we'd ever had. Trouble was, neither of us could face going out to frazzle even more in the direct sunlight. The news on the telly was full of dire warnings of what the heat wave was going to do to our reservoirs, our rivers, and our lily-white English skin, and the air quality was so bad it was off the scale. Oh, and my hip was playing up. Basically, there was zero incentive to move, especially as I'd already given Sharon at number twelve a bell and asked her to pop in and feed the cats.

But yeah, in retrospect, it would've been better to make the effort to get out of there. We were snippy with each other all day, and it came to a head just as we flopped into bed.

"Before I forget," Phil said as he turned out the light, "we're meeting up with Darren and Gary for lunch next Sunday. Soon as Gary's finished his church stuff."

I blinked into the darkness, not having got my night vision yet. "What? Next Sunday? Since when?" Next Sunday—that was ringing a bell, for some reason. And not the way Gary did.

"Since a couple of nights ago. I met up with Darren for a drink."

The little cogs whirred into place, and I remembered why Sunday was sounding iffy. "Shit. Sorry, but I sort of booked us up already. I told Cherry we'd go round to Greg's for Sunday lunch." I wiped my forehead with a hand, then dried my hand off on my hip. Then I wondered why I hadn't just used the sheet, seeing as I'd probably be sweating buckets into it tonight anyway. Jesus, it was hot. The air was so bloody still it was an effort to breathe.

Phil was frowning. "When was this?"

"Er... Monday? Tuesday? Yeah, Tuesday night, that was it. When she came over to talk about my dad. So, yeah, we can't really cancel."

He huffed. "And you were going to tell me about this *when*?"

"It slipped my mind, didn't it?"

"Bloody marvellous." He heaved himself out of bed and grabbed his phone from where it'd been charging. "Guess I'd better text Darren our excuses, then." He stood there, starkers, jabbing at the screen like a pissed-off Greek statue.

I sat up, narked he was making such a palaver about it. I mean, how much notice did he reckon Darren needed, for fuck's sake? "Oi, hang about. What you're basically saying is, you're pissed off with me for making arrangements without consulting you that bugger up the arrangements *you* made without consulting *me*." I folded my arms.

Phil threw his phone on the bed and folded *his* arms. Someone told me once—probably Phil, now I came to think of it—that mirroring posture's generally a good thing. I had a feeling this was one of the exceptions that proved the rule.

"No, what I'm basically saying is, I'd never have sodding well made those arrangements if you'd taken the time out of your busy schedule to let me know about yours."

"I just did, all right? Jesus, am I supposed to check with you before I do *anything*? Is that it? You're not my mum, for fuck's sake."

"No. I'm your partner. Last I heard, that was supposed to mean something."

"Yeah, it's supposed to mean you go along to family dinners without having a bloody hissy fit over it." I wasn't even going to get into what a seriously crap word *partner* was.

The Mysterious Mark had been his partner. Not me. They'd had it on a bloody certificate and everything.

"It's got nothing to do with your sodding family, all right? Just—Oh, for Christ's sake, forget it. I'm going to sleep." He dropped his bulk down on the bed, pulled up the sheet, and rolled over, leaving his back to me.

I got up.

I needed a glass of water, all right? I even managed to drink it, rather than throwing it all over the pigheaded git.

It was a bloody close one, mind.

That night, we had the thunderstorm from hell. And let me tell you, forked lightning takes on a whole new dimension when you're lying on the sofa looking up at it through a skylight. Yeah, the sofa. *Not* because me and Phil had had words before turning in—well, not entirely, at any rate. It was more that I couldn't sleep, and I didn't want to risk waking Phil with all my tossing and turning. We might have ended up having *more* words.

God, I wished I'd just gone back home for the night. I even considered making a late dash for it, but seeing as it was already 4 a.m. and the rain was coming down in sheets, it didn't seem entirely sensible. Also, it would have involved moving. I finally dozed off sometime after six, only to be woken at seven by my phone alarm, which I'd set deliberately early so I could sneak out before breakfast.

I staggered around Phil's flat, managed to find nearly all my clothes (who needs socks, anyhow?), and left him a note saying I had an early job.

Which was true, anyway. Just . . . not *that* early.

The sun was already scorching away all signs of last night's storm when I hit the pavement, and the air was getting heavy and muggy again, not fresh like you'd expect. Everywhere smelled damp and woodsy, mixed in with the fumes from the traffic that built up noticeably as I walked the half mile to my house.

By the time I got back to Fleetville, it was gone half seven and the local baker's was doing a brisk trade in bacon butties and cups of tea and coffee. I joined the queue, had a brief conversation about football with a bloke I'd seen down the Rats Castle a few times, then headed off home to munch on my sausage in a bun and try to wake myself up with my Americano. Oh, and put some Band-Aids on my blisters, because it turned out that socks were pretty essential after all when wearing heavy boots.

Work was going to be a bugger today.

What with one thing and another—all right, just one thing in particular, and that being a certain pigheaded git who was too stubborn to make a sodding phone call and apologise—I was pretty glad when Gary's Donna Summer ringtone blared out on Monday evening.

"Tom, darling, you *have* to come out with me tonight. I'm at a total loose end. Darren's abandoned me for the Cunning Linguists." This was Darren's GLBT Spanish conversation group. Which, by my book, meant that only around half of them were actual cunning linguists, but it seemed they were all pretty attached to the name. Apparently, your average language course didn't cover the sort of specialised vocab required by the modern queer abroad, although I'd always managed pretty well with a combination of English and hand gestures.

And stick-figure diagrams drawn on a beer mat on one occasion, as I vaguely recalled through a haze of time and alcohol. Fond memories.

"Haven't you got bell-ringing practice tonight?" I glanced at the calendar and, yep, it was still Monday. They'd used to meet on Wednesday but had to change to Mondays a couple of months ago on account of the new vicar in Brock's Hollow wanting the church for services or meetings or, I dunno, bingo or something. From what I'd heard, the replacement rev was a bit of a new broom and not everyone wanted to be swept, although Gary seemed to be pretty chummy with the new management.

"Cancelled," Gary said in the sort of tones usually used to announce someone's death. "Due to ill health."

All right, so he hadn't been so far off with the funereal tones. "Whose? Not yours, is it? 'Cos if it is, you probably shouldn't be drinking."

"*Moi*? I'm in the rudest of health, darling. Which can*not* be said for Treble, Four, and Seven, who have *all* been laid low with food poisoning."

"Yeah?" I said it maybe a bit sharper than I should have, poison still being a bit of a touchy subject for me.

"Mmm. Everyone's *saying* it's just one of those things, but between you, me, and the *News of the World*, blame is being laid firmly at the feet of Mrs. Four. Homemade mayonnaise, need I say more? Left out in the sun a tad too long at yesterday's barbecue. So the rest of us are just *bereft*."

"Can't the rest of you practice without them? Or, you know, double up or something?"

Gary sniffed. "Clearly you have no understanding of the noble art of campanology."

"Yeah, well, you know me. You've always been way ahead of me at anything camp."

"For that, darling, the first round is on you. I'll see you at the Dyke. Eight o'clock. Do *not* be late."

"Would I?" I asked, but he'd already hung up.

I was well in demand that evening. Five minutes after I'd got off the phone with Gary, Dave Southgate, our friendly neighbourhood detective inspector, rang and asked if I fancied a pint down the White Hart.

Dave's so straight you could use him as a spirit level and definitely not the sort to *pansy around* (his words) calling a spade an earth-moving implement, but he's an all right bloke really. Been a good mate of mine for a few years now, so I was sorry to have to let him down.

"Sorry, mate. I'm meeting Gary up at the Dyke. Still, more the merrier—want to join us?" I wasn't holding my breath. Dave and Gary had met before on a few occasions, and they hadn't exactly got on like bosom buddies. The phrase "handbags at dawn" had been uttered more than once.

"Do I sound like I've got a death wish? Persona non bleedin' grata around the Dyke these days, aren't I?"

"Why? What did you do? Make a pass at one of the barmaids?"

"Har bloody har. I had to send someone round to read 'em the riot act the other day. All thanks to a little slimeball who used to go out with one of the barmaids and is far too well acquainted with his bloody rights for my liking. If we go up there for a drink, the best I can hope for is Harry'll spit in my pint."

I winced. "Fair point. Another night, then, yeah? Oh, and how's the missus?"

"Jen?" Dave swore under his breath, but he sounded fond. "Swollen up like the bloody Michelin Man in this heat, and that's her words, not mine."

"What, already? I thought she was only four or five months gone?" It couldn't have been more than a couple of months ago Dave had dragged me out on the piss to celebrate the fact his gun still worked. Jen had been well impressed when I'd poured him out of the taxi and onto the doormat at 1 a.m. Not.

"Tell me about it. It's going to be a bloody long summer. *And* she's blaming me for it."

"I thought she was the one who wanted this kid?"

"Christ, I can tell you've never had a relationship with a woman. Everything's always my bleedin' fault, even if I had bugger all to do with it. You get used to it."

"I'll take your word for it. Better go, anyway—I'll see you around, yeah?"

Dave gave a melancholy grunt. I hung up and started getting ready for off, just in case Gary was fretting over some wedding thing.

Luckily, I'd already showered, and the T-shirt I'd put on after was one Gary had bought me as a saw-this-and-thought-of-you gift, so he couldn't possibly object to it. Unlike Phil, who'd taken one look at the slogan on the front (*Don't sleep with a drip—call a plumber!*) and made one of *those* faces, the poncey git. Maybe I should get him a sense of humour for his next birthday.

I hadn't even shown him the *Zombie plumbers want your drains* one yet.

Sod it. I squared my shoulders, grabbed my keys, and made a mental note not to even *think* of Phil all evening.

It's only a short drive up to the Dyke from Fleetville, and once you get out of the St. Albans sprawl and through Sandridge, it's all countryside. I cut through Nomansland Common, which was looking green and pleasant in the evening sun, if a bit parched around the edges. Apparently, last night's downpour had just been a drop in the dried-up ocean. Brock's Hollow's dog walkers were out in force, Frisbees were being thrown, and one optimistic sod was trying gamely to launch a kite for his kiddies while a teenage couple interrupted their snogging to stare in disbelief at his hopeless efforts.

The Dyke was tucked out of sight down some winding lanes through scrubby woodland—you'd never know it was there until you were pulling up in the car park. I parked the Fiesta next to a battered old Ford, then got out and wandered round the back to see if Gary was sitting outside.

He wasn't, and the cloud of midges that buzzed me made it easy to see why. Swatting the little sods away from my face, I made my way to the pub's back door. There was an abandoned cricket ball on the ground near one of the tables—must have been left over from some kids' game, though I dunno what their parents thought they were doing, letting the nippers play with a hard ball like that. I kicked it carefully to one side before anyone could tread on it and come a cropper, and pushed open the door into the public bar.

There's something about walking into your local that's like coming home after a hard day. Not that the Dyke was exactly *local*, for me at least—not compared to the Rats Castle, which is just round the corner from my house—but I went there enough that it counted. The Dyke's got this sort of cosy glow about it, what with the tobacco-coloured walls and the comfy, plush red seats, and unlike some St. Albans pubs I could mention, nobody ever gives Gary hassle there for being, well, Gary.

I spotted the man himself straight off. He was about as far from fretting as he could get, chatting merrily and with copious use of hand signals to a distracted-looking Marianne, while Julian rested his great doggy head on a barstool and soaked the seat with slobber. Gary was relatively soberly dressed in his *IT guys have bigger hard drives* T-shirt, which he'd got the same place he'd bought mine. I'd have worried it might make us look a bit coupley, but then again, his shirt was three sizes larger and bright pink.

I spotted the reason for Marianne's distraction too. Grant Carey was sitting at a table in the corner, arms spread on the back of the seat and one ankle crossed over the other leg, smiling away like he owned the bloody place.

CHAPTER SEVEN

Carey was with some blonde woman I'd never seen before, which was a bit of a surprise—not that I'd have put it past him to turn up with a new girlfriend to try to make Marianne jealous, but, to put it bluntly, if that was his aim, he'd gone for a strange sort of ammunition. Carey's smile got broader when he saw me—bit like a shark's does just before it bites your leg off—and he gave me a cheery wave I didn't return. The woman with him turned to see what all the fuss was about.

Now, I'd already noticed from the back view that, unlike Marianne, who was basically a stick figure with boobs, this woman was the comfortably well-padded sort. Seeing her face, I'd put her at around forty, which again didn't seem like Carey's usual type. But what really put the tin lid on it was the way she was dressed. Sensible skirt, grey cardi—and a dog collar.

And not the sort Julian was wearing either.

I frowned as I joined Gary at the bar. "What the hell's that all about?"

"What, darling?"

"Him and her in the corner." I smiled at Marianne. "Pint of Squirrel, love, when you're ready. And get one for yourself, all right?" From the wobbly smile she sent me in thanks, I reckoned she could probably do with a drink.

"*She* is our new vicar. Lillian." Gary gave me an appraising look. "*He* is just visiting. Although I must say he gave me pause when I walked in. I thought for a moment you must have a twin brother you've never told me about before. Which would be absolutely *criminal*, darling. You know I have a thing for twins."

"Oi, he doesn't look anything like me!" I frowned.

"Well, he does dress rather more smartly. But pop him in one of your lumberjack shirts, muss up the hair a little . . ." Gary trailed off, eyeing me with faint surprise. "Well. Who pooped in *your* potty?"

"That bloke," I said firmly, taking Gary by the elbow and leading him to a table as far away from Carey as we could get without actually going in the beer garden and getting eaten by midges, "is the bastard who's been hassling Marianne."

"Well, she never *said*." Gary pouted, looking hurt. "Neither did he, for that matter. He seemed quite sweet when I spoke to him earlier."

"Yeah, right. Sweet like . . ." I struggled to think. "Cyanide," I finished.

"I thought that was supposed to have a bitter taste? Like wedding favours after the divorce?"

"Look, that's not the point. Stay away from that bastard, all right? He's already threatened Harry, me, and Phil. And that was in the limited free time he gets from stalking Marianne and getting business rivals banged up in prison."

"Really?" Gary cast Carey a dubious look. Carey waved back at him happily.

"Yeah, really. So stop bloody looking at him, all right? I don't want you getting in his sights and all."

"Oh, I'm not worried. Julian will protect me, won't you, my precious boy?" Gary bent down to ruffle Julian's neck fur. "Yes, you *will*." It was a toss-up who was slobbering more right then.

"What was he talking to you about, anyway?"

"Oh, business matters, actually. He thought he might be in need of IT support in the near future. I gave him my card."

"Bloody marvellous." Now Carey knew where to find my best mate. I consoled myself with the thought it was actually pretty hard to lose Gary. "So what's he doing with the Rev?"

"Do I *look* like the sort of man who has his fingers in everybody else's pies?"

"You really want me to answer that?"

Gary sniffed. "Fine. Why don't you ask her yourself, then? I'll introduce you."

Carey had got up from the Rev's table and sauntered over to the bar, and was leaning on it smiling at a clearly uncomfortable Marianne.

I was torn—I felt like I ought to go and rescue her from him, but on the other hand it was a golden opportunity to find out what his game was with the Rev. And while I was at it, maybe warn her off the bastard.

After all, her immediate predecessor had come to a bit of a sticky end, hadn't he? It wouldn't look too good for the village church to have history start repeating itself.

"All right, then," I said, getting up. "Let's go for it."

We carried our drinks over to the corner table, Julian panting along in our wake.

"Lillian, darling, there's someone you simply must meet," Gary trilled out when we were in earshot. "If ever you need your pipes seen to, Lillian, Tom's your man."

She looked round, smiled, and actually stood up to greet me. This new Rev was a bit of a change from the old one. Poor old "Merry" Lewis had been tall, thin and nervous. Not to mention male. This one was about my height, not short of a bit of meat on her bones, and wore an open, friendly smile. She also had a firm handshake, I discovered. "Lillian James. I'm the new incumbent at St. Anthony's. Lovely to meet you."

"Tom Paretski. Plumber, in case you were wondering what Gary was on about."

"Yes, the T-shirt is a bit of a giveaway, there. And you don't look the sort for organ maintenance, which would be the other kind of pipes I have to deal with, of course."

Of course. And there was a *sort* for organ maintenance? Thin and skeletal, maybe, with a mask covering a terrible disfigurement and a nice line in evil laughter?

"Drinkies, Tom?" Gary put in, waving his empty martini glass under my nose. He'd put that one away quick.

"'S okay, I'll get them," I started, but he carried on getting up anyway, stepping carefully over Julian and sashaying around the old oak table.

"No, I insist. Lillian?"

"Not for me, thank you. I'll have to be going soon." She took a dainty sip from her small glass of white wine.

"Well, if you're sure . . ."

Gary wafted away, and I sat down next to the vicar and tried to remember how to make polite conversation. Well, I could hardly leap straight in with the interrogation. "You settling in all right at the vicarage?" Too late, I realised that might be a bit of an awkward question. I wondered if anyone had told her what had happened there last winter.

"Oh, absolutely. Well, I'm rattling around a bit, but one can never really have too much space, can one?"

"I know I can always do with a bit more." Chiefly when Phil was around at mine and spreading case files—or, as it might be, me—on the coffee table, but I didn't reckon she was after that kind of detail. "You're on your own, then?" I'd have pegged her for the married-with-kids sort, but I supposed it just went to show you couldn't judge the Good Book by its cover.

"At least until the end of the month. After that, I'm not sure—I've given up trying to predict what my children will get up to in their uni vacations." She smiled that sort of serene smile you often get on vicars. Maybe they teach it in theology college, along with the less advanced stuff like sermonising and baby-dunking. "I'm afraid I lost my husband a few years back, on a caravanning trip in Ireland."

I blinked and managed not to ask if they'd sent out a search party. "Sorry to hear that. Was he, um . . .?" About to say *in the God-bothering business too*, I realised in time that might not come across too well and gestured vaguely at her clergy get-up instead.

Luckily, she got what I was on about, rather than thinking I meant "on the cuddly side" or anything even more embarrassing. "Oh, no. Colin was a corporate lawyer." She dimpled. "He always used to say he only married me to have someone pray for his soul."

"Don't believe it for a second," I said with a smile, and she dimpled even more. "So did you have to move far for this job?"

"Just across from Norfolk. I was in a seaside parish, and I shan't miss the winters there, with the wind coming straight off the North Sea."

I nodded as my hip twinged in sympathy.

"And it's nice to be nearer to the children, of course," she went on, "with Emma in Oxford and Charlie at Imperial."

"Yeah? Sounds like you've got yourself a couple of highfliers there."

"Well, I do think I've been blessed. They work hard, which I always think is the most important thing." She picked up her glass of wine and drained it. "And now I need to follow their example, I'm afraid. It's been lovely to meet you, Tom." She stood up, just as I was about to ask her if she knew Cherry's Greg.

Bugger. Note to self: next time, less of the polite conversation, more of the third degree. "Yeah, you too. Er, I saw you talking to Grant Carey earlier...?" I left it hanging.

Lillian stalled in the act of leaving. "The young man at the bar? Yes, he came over and introduced himself. Is he a friend of yours?"

"Er... not exactly. What was he after? Um. If you don't mind me asking?"

She gave me a penetrating look. "That's rather a curious question. Still, I don't suppose he'd mind me telling you what we talked about. Marriage is, after all, a public declaration of commitment."

I stared. "He told you he was getting married?"

Lillian smiled. "Yes—to the young lady behind the bar. Now, I really must be going." She said it a bit more firmly this time.

I was still reeling from the nerve of that bastard. Unless Marianne really had agreed to marry him . . . No. He was just messing with us all. Wasn't he?

Shit. Maybe I should have a word with Marianne *toot*, as Darren would say, *sweet*. "Er, right. I'll say your farewells to Gary, then, shall I?"

"No need—I'll catch him on the way over."

Their paths crossed in the middle of the pub, just past the old blocked-up well which Flossie was currently guarding, i.e., sitting on top of the see-through cover. Lillian scratched the collie behind glossy black-and-white ears, submitted gracefully to a goodbye kiss from Gary in the region of *her* ear, then veered off to the bar for a word with Harry. If she was looking for new recruits to the God Squad, I reckoned she was well off track there, but you had to give her points for trying.

Gary set my pint down on the table and flopped back down on the seat with a world-weary air. "So did you manage to get all your pumping done with Lillian?"

"I hope you mean for information. Yeah, I heard enough. Cheers, mate." I took a sip of my pint. I'd have to leave talking to Marianne and/or Harry for a bit. Carey was still propping up the bar looking like butter wouldn't melt in his mouth.

Gary beamed. "Excellent. So what do you think of our new vicar? She's being an absolute *darling* about our blessing."

I blinked. "Your what?"

"Blessing, o ye of little faith. Lillian is going to bless Darren and my union in church, just as soon as we're back from our honeymoon."

"Isn't that a bit horse before cart? I mean, a blessing's like a church wedding, only not quite, is that right? Shouldn't you get the official stamp of approval before you go prancing off into the sunset?"

He pouted. "Next you'll be saying you'll expect me to be a virgin on my wedding day."

"Gary, you weren't a virgin on your *parents'* wedding day." Which was actually true, if you could believe Gary's story—although to be fair, they hadn't bothered to get hitched until he was fifteen, and only did it then because the travel company they were going to Goa with offered a free upgrade to honeymoon couples. God knew what the reps thought about teenage Gary tagging along. "Anyway, how come you're getting it done in Brock's Hollow? I'd have thought you'd be having the ceremony in St. Leonards cathedral, seeing as you and Greg are so chummy."

"Don't be ridiculous, darling. The cathedral? What do you think I am, some kind of diva?"

I raised both eyebrows. "Do I really have to answer that?"

"And anyway, the other bell ringers at St. Anthony's wanted to give us a peal. I could hardly say no to that, could I? Even if it does mean letting a novice ring my bell."

I grinned. "I'd have thought Darren would have something to say about you letting someone else ring your bell. I thought he was the only one who got to tug on your rope these days."

Gary gave an exaggerated roll of his eyes. "Really, Tom? I think *someone's* been a bad influence on you."

"You're probably right, there. And I'm looking straight at him."

"Hmm. I reserve judgement. So tell me, how goes it with the Neanderthal? I presume we're still expecting him as your plus-one for the wedding?" Gary sucked the olive off his cocktail stick with a thoughtful pop, chewed, and swallowed. "Of course, Darren seems to have taken quite a shine to him. He's such a sweetie."

"Who, Phil?" I said to wind him up.

Gary did a poor imitation of someone choking on his martini. "Please! I nearly snorted an ice cube. Darren, of course. Always ready to see the best in people. I've told him, 'You can't go looking at the world through rose-tinted spectacles all your life. Sooner or later grim, sordid reality will intrude.'"

My turn to splutter on my drink. "You what? He's an ex-porn star, for fuck's sake. I'm pretty sure your Darren knows all about the sordid side of life."

All I got for that was a dreamy smile. "And isn't it wonderful how he's kept his essential innocence?"

I drew in a breath, then changed my mind. Gary knew the score. If he wanted to pretend his fiancé was a cross between a fluffy kitten and Christopher Robin, who was I to burst his bubble? "Wonderful. Just wonderful," I said instead. "So how's all the wedding preparations going?"

That was Gary's cue to spend the next couple of hours bending my ear about wedding favours, florists, and the pianist they'd booked for the reception, who was apparently a *total* drama queen, fancied himself as Hertfordshire's answer to Sir Elton John, and had flounced off in a huff when asked to play a jazzed-up version of "Wind Beneath My Wings."

I kept half an eye on Carey, of course. He didn't collar anyone else for conversation after Lillian disappeared, just sat there doing genial everyone's-best-mate impersonations. You'd have thought he'd have got bored, but maybe stalking Marianne was entertainment enough. The only interesting thing that happened was when Flossie padded over to say hello. Living in a pub, Flossie's the friendliest dog you'll meet—with the possible exception of Julian, who's happy to slobber on anyone. But as soon as she got within three feet of Carey, the bloke tensed up like someone had set a Rottweiler on him. Obviously sensing the vibes, Flossie tensed up too, and it was an anxious moment all round until Harry snapped out, "Flossie!" in a low bark, and she scarpered back to her mistress at the bar.

Not long after that, Carey seemed to decide that, fun as this all was, he'd had enough. He got up from his seat like a snake uncurling from its nest, and slithered over to the bar. I couldn't hear what he said to Marianne, but it made her cringe away from him. Harry, hovering over her shoulder, looked like she'd cheerfully murder the bastard.

It wasn't right, this. I stared daggers as he sauntered out of the pub—then nearly choked on my Coke as he turned, smiled at me, and gave me a cheery wave.

Bastard.

Next time I went to get my round in, Harry sent Marianne down to the cellar to check on the beer stocks, then collared me. "How's your bloke getting on with the case?"

Great. Just when I was doing such a good job of *not* thinking about Phil. "Well, it's early days, innit? I'm sure he'll get in touch if he's got anything to tell you."

She gave me a sharp look at that—maybe my tone was a bit off or something. "Pity he's not here tonight. Would've given him a chance to get a good look at the little shit."

"Don't worry, he's had that already. We both did. Carey turned up at his flat the other day. Total nutjob. I'll tell you what, anyone who puts him out of commission is doing the whole bloody world a favour."

Harry scowled. "Did he threaten you?"

"Well . . . Yeah, I s'pose. Only not so's you could have the police on him or anything. But yeah." The little knot of anxiety in my gut I'd been managing to ignore up until now tightened.

She muttered something profane under her breath. "I'm sorry you got dragged into this. You take care, all right?"

"Nah, don't worry. I can look after myself. Look, are you sure there's nothing you can do? Legally, I mean. I thought we had laws against stalking in this country."

"Marianne won't make a complaint. Says she's worried what he'll do if she does. That turd's too bloody sharp to do anything definite, anyway." Harry looked away as she poured my Diet Coke. "We've had some other bloke hanging around and all. Don't tell Marianne. Big guy, shaved head. Could be Carey's hired himself some muscle. Or just someone to keep an eye on her while he's not around."

Bloody marvellous. "When you say 'hanging around'..."

"He hasn't been in. Just checking the place out."

"Hope you've got a good burglar alarm."

Harry gave a grim smile. "Anyone breaks in here, he won't know what's hit him. Being on the premises when we're open for business is one thing. But if he trespasses on my property after hours, all bets are off."

"Good. Better make sure Marianne's keeping her bedroom door locked at night, though. Just to be on the safe side."

"Don't worry. There's only two ways into her room—through my room or up the fireplace stairs. And they're bolted from the inside."

For some reason, back in the dark ages when the Dyke had been built, someone had thought it'd be dead handy to have a secret passageway leading from the upstairs rooms down to the walk-in fireplace in the lounge bar. Well, that was what I'd been told, at any rate. I'd never been up it, and neither had anyone I knew. Gary reckoned he'd nearly wet himself one day when Harry appeared from nowhere and caught him fiddling with the fire irons.

From the look on Harry's face, she'd love it if Carey tried going through her room to get to Marianne. I made a mental note to ask Cherry for the exact legal definition of reasonable force as applied to blokes breaking into a lady's boudoir.

That was when Marianne herself popped back up behind the bar, to report they had two barrels of the Squirrel and none of the other beers were in any danger of running out either, which I was pretty sure wasn't news to Harry.

"How are you doing, love?" I asked her.

Marianne smiled brightly, but it was brittle at the edges, and there were big orange streaks under her eyes where she'd covered up the dark circles with too much makeup. "I'm fine, Tom, how's you?"

"I'm good, cheers."

"Not with your Phil tonight?"

Christ, was there a bloody conspiracy to mention Phil every five minutes? "Not tonight. Hashing out wedding stuff with Gary." I waved in the direction of the bloke himself. Gary ostentatiously looked at his watch and mimed dying of thirst, holding both hands to his throat like he was choking and half sliding under the table.

"Um. Speaking of which, I take it there's no truth in the rumours about you and Carey getting hitched?"

She cringed. "What rumours? Who's been saying stuff about me and him?"

"He has, or at least, that's what the new vicar said he'd told her. And well, if you can't trust a woman of the cloth . . ."

"I'll kill 'im." Marianne glared so fiercely at the bar I was surprised the varnish didn't blister.

"Yeah, well, thought I ought to let you know what he'd been saying." I glanced over at Gary, who right now could've given Marianne a run for her money in a glare-off. "Looks like I'd better get back to Gary before he spontaneously combusts."

Marianne's smile made a brave effort to come back. "Bless 'im. You take care, now."

"You too, love." She'd need to, I thought as I took the drinks back to our table. What with all these blokes hanging around.

Maybe I'd better stop by a little more often. Just in case.

We stayed late enough that the bell for last orders was a distant memory. Harry had already packed Marianne off to bed by the time Gary drained his last martini and stood up, claiming Julian needed his beauty sleep. I'd been on soft drinks for the last couple of rounds, so I was fine to drive really, but after I'd waved them off on their walk back into the village, it still seemed like a good idea to get a bit of fresh air before I got into the car.

It was a warm night, so you might have expected people to linger in the beer garden but it was as deserted as it'd been when I got there. There weren't even any little pockets of smokers hanging around reminiscing about the good old days when they could light up in the main bar instead of getting kicked out along with other social undesirables like dogs and kiddies. Although come to think of it, dogs had always been allowed in the Dyke. I stood outside the door for a moment, enjoying the cooler air and the faint scent wafting over from the lilacs, although there wasn't much of a breeze. It was dead quiet—the Dyke's far enough from main roads that hardly any traffic noise carries. The only sounds I could hear now were the sort that make you feel more alone: a soft hoot that was probably an owl, followed by a furtive rustling sound that was probably the owl's supper.

I paced around the beer garden and looked up at what I was pretty sure was Marianne's window. Unless, of course, she'd nipped into the next room to warm Harry's bed for her. It didn't look all that secure. What with the low roof and the sturdy, old-fashioned windowsills, I reckoned I could probably climb up there easy without a ladder. And if I could do it, Carey probably could. Or this "muscle" of his. Shit.

About to go back inside and say something, I hesitated. Would Harry thank me for pointing out any security shortcomings? She was probably streets ahead of me on all this anyway. Plus, was sneaking in windows really Carey's style? It seemed a bit too overtly criminal for him. And probably less fun, to his twisted little mind, than simply knocking on the front door and using his slimy brand of coercion to get in.

Something tickled the back of my neck, and I slapped at it. Great. I was going to end up being eaten to death by those bloody midges for my trouble. I turned to head off to the Fiesta, which was sitting all on its little lonesome in the car park, the Billy-no-mates of the auto world—

—and that's all I remembered when I woke up with a dry mouth, a splitting headache, and a fuzzy-edged Phil looking down at me.

He looked well pissed off.

CHAPTER EIGHT

Good to see you too was what I meant to say, but what with my tongue sticking to the roof of my mouth at the end of the first word, I sort of gave up after that.

Phil looked even more pissed off and held a cup of water to my lips. It tasted bloody marvellous, and it's possible I might have whined a bit and tried to grab his arm when he took it away again. "Oi. Take it easy," he grunted, but he brought the cup back. "Drink it slow, if you want to keep it down."

Now he came to mention it, the contents of my stomach *did* feel like they might be getting ready to jump ship at the first opportunity. I sipped cautiously.

"Don't s'pose there's any chance of an aspirin?" I asked without a lot of hope once I'd glugged my fill. Heh. My Phil. I gave a weak chuckle, which got me a worried look from Phil.

"I could ask," he said in don't-bet-on-it tones.

I'd taken a look around by now, and what with the plain white blankets on the metal-framed bed I was lying in, and the NHS green paint on the walls, I reckoned it was a pretty safe guess I wasn't in Kansas anymore. "What happened?"

Phil huffed. "You're supposed to be telling me that. Back properly this time, are you?"

What? The last bit didn't make sense, so I ignored it. I tried to think back, but apparently some git had dug my brain out of my skull with a spoon while I wasn't looking and replaced it with soggy cotton wool. And then stomped on it. Seeing as how the effort of trying to remember made the room spin and upped the pain levels from *ow* to *bloody hell make it stop*, I gave up pretty quickly. "I went to the pub?" I hazarded.

"Yeah, and from what Harry told me, you had a couple of pints and about a gallon of Diet Coke, then walked out looking perfectly fine ten minutes before she came out to check for glasses and found you doing corpse impersonations in the beer garden." Phil glared at me like I'd done it for a laugh or something.

"Yeah . . . I remember going out there . . . So what happened?" I asked again. "Did I fall on my arse in the dark?"

"On your head, more like. Don't know what happened. Harry just said you'd knocked yourself out." Phil sighed heavily. "Christ, are you trying to give me a heart attack?"

I wasn't sure what to say to that. 'Specially as I'd just remembered we weren't on the best of terms right now. Although maybe getting hospitalised trumped all that. "What time is it?"

"Around two. In the morning. You were out for a couple of hours. If you include the bits where you were just pretending to be with it."

"What?"

"We've had this conversation before."

"Huh." We had? Sounded like I'd missed all the fun stuff, like getting loaded into the ambulance—at least, I assumed there'd been an ambulance? Maybe Harry or Phil or someone had bunged me in a car and driven me to hospital—and screeching up to A&E. Well, been there, done that. "So what's the verdict—am I going to live?"

For a split second, I seriously thought he was going to hit me. Phil looked fucking *furious*. "Don't you *ever* fucking joke about that," he snarled at me. Then he backed off a step and scrubbed his face with both hands. "Shit, I didn't mean . . . Jesus wept, I'm tired. Harry called the ambulance first off. I didn't get the call till gone midnight. Came straight here. They were doing all these tests and scans . . ." He took a deep breath and seemed to get a grip on himself. "Said you were lucky. Got a thick skull, so no surprise there. No bleeding on the brain, no major swelling. Yeah, you'll live."

And here I'd thought Phil was the boneheaded one in this relationship. "Are we all right, then?" I asked, feeling pretty tired myself.

Phil blinked at me. Then he nodded. "Yeah, we're all right."

After that, he insisted on calling a doctor in so she could have a good prod and a poke, and ask me what my name was, what year it was, and who the Prime Minister was. It all seemed a bit daft, and I thought about having a laugh with her, but I couldn't quite seem to work up the energy. In the end, the doc, who was a pretty young Pakistani woman who looked more tired than I felt, took a last eyeful of my eyeballs, pronounced me mildly concussed, and told me to get some rest. Phil gave me a kiss, squeezed my hand so hard it hurt, muttered something about how he wasn't supposed to be here anyway, and left me to it.

I'd been hoping they might let me go home the next morning—or, if you prefer, later the same morning—but no such luck. Then again, I wasn't feeling a lot like moving anyway, after a night in a hard bed where, every time I managed to drop off, I got prodded awake by nurses to check I hadn't tiptoed off this mortal coil while their backs were turned.

Gary popped along to see me during visiting hours. Well, he probably felt obliged to, after I'd staggered to the pay phone to let him know where I was, my mobile having disappeared along with my beloved. Gary was *gutted* he'd managed to toddle off home just five minutes before all the drama started.

"Darling, you could have *died*," he said, seizing me in a bear hug that cut off the oxygen to my brain and didn't do a right lot for the splitting headache. "Or been left a sad, shambling shell of a man." He backed off and squinted at me in concern. "Are you sure you really feel yourself?"

He didn't even go for the obvious innuendo. I was touched by how worried he clearly was. "I'm fine, honest. Just a bit of a bruise." All right, I felt pretty queasy too, but that was probably due to the hospital food I'd choked down for lunch.

"Just 'a bit of a bruise'? You were unconscious for *hours*. You do know who I am, don't you?"

With those big eyes looking soulfully at me, I reckoned I could have been forgiven for getting confused between him and his dog, but it was probably better not to mention that. "Gary, *I* rang *you*, remember? And it wasn't *hours*. Two at most. Less, if you don't count the bits where I was apparently babbling away but can't remember."

"Practically a coma." Gary shuddered. "All your muscles could have wasted away, leaving only a withered husk. There would have been *nothing left* of you. But stop distracting me. What I want to know is—"

I braced myself for a repetition of the whole *what-happened-I-dunno* conversation I'd had with Phil.

"—why am *I* here, and not your muscle-bound inamorato?"

What? I did a literal double take that left my head pounding so hard my eyes hurt. "Ow. You're a mate, aren't you? Why shouldn't you be here?" Then again, I *had* been wondering when Phil might show his face again. Not that he'd *said* he would, least as far as I remembered, but you sort of expect it, don't you?

"Because normally, Tommy dear," Gary was saying, "when one does fainting-damsel impersonations, it isn't for the benefit of one's *mates*. Mine is not the embrace into which you should be swooning." His hands now on his well-padded hips, Gary's eyes went flinty. "He'd better not be the one who put you here."

"You know, I'm starting to wonder which one of us got hit on the head here. Phil wasn't even there when it happened."

"When what happened?"

"Well . . . I dunno, do I? Can't remember."

"Aha!" Gary pointed a triumphant finger at me.

Shit. What was it Dave Southgate told me after Cherry got poisoned? Something about knocking down Phil's door if I ever came a cropper somehow? Apparently Dave and Gary had more in common than either of them would care to admit.

"No," I said shortly, wanting to nip this one firmly in the bud. "Not *aha*. Not any other eighties Europop band either. Me and Phil might have had a bit of a disagreement, but nobody's been bopping anyone else over the head about it."

"But there *was* a disagreement? What about?" Gary pouted. "And why am I only now hearing about it? I'm wounded. Pierced to the core. Impaled upon the rusty sword of your disregard. For goodness' sake, darling, I tell you *everything*."

"Gary, you tell everyone everything. And I didn't want to talk about it last night, all right? Wanted a break from it all."

"So go on, tell Uncle Gary all about it now." He perched on the edge of the bed, hands clasped around one knee, making his *I'm listening* face.

"It's nothing." I heaved a sigh. "Just, he goes on about me being touchy, and then he flies off the handle just because I forgot to tell him we're going over to Greg's for lunch next Sunday." I remembered who I was talking to and added quickly, "I mean, God knows I'd rather meet up with you and Darren, but it was all arranged with Cherry ages ago. I just forgot to mention it."

"Mm, you said that." Gary stared off into the distance, or at least as distant as you can get in an NHS room. Which was about three feet. "Darling, we've never really talked about this, but just how invested are you in this whole Phil thing?"

"He's not a bloody savings account. What do you mean, how invested am I?"

"Well. *You* know. Can you see you and Philip one day tiptoeing down the aisle together like my sweetie pie and me?"

I didn't know what to say. And not just because thinking of Darren as anyone's sweetie pie was giving me hives. "Well, nobody's got down on one knee yet," I said in the end.

"But is there," Gary paused significantly, "the potential?"

"I dunno, do I?" I hedged. "Potentially, yeah." It didn't feel right, somehow, talking about it with Gary before me and Phil had had the conversation. I mean, for all I knew, his short-lived civil partnership with the Mysterious Mark had put Phil off getting hitched for life.

And, well, it wasn't like he'd rushed round today to mop my fevered brow, was it?

Not that I was feeling neglected or anything.

Gary raised a pitying eyebrow. "Only the potential for potential? I'm sorry, darling, but that doesn't sound *très* romantic to me. Rather like, in fact, leaving you to languish upon your deathbed unvisited and unloved."

"Oi, this is *not* my deathbed. Unless you know something I don't—"

"Where to start, darling, where to start?" Gary murmured.

"—about my state of health, I was going to add. And Phil was here last night. This morning. Whatever. He's probably catching up on his sleep."

"At three in the afternoon? Still, I suppose it must be exhausting, carrying around that amount of muscle between the ears." Gary tittered.

"Oi, that's my inammo-whatsit you're talking about," I said, but I had a smile on my face. Then a thought struck. "Listen, before I forget, would you mind popping round to mine and feeding the cats? I can't keep asking Sharon to do it. Should've asked Phil to last night, but I wasn't exactly thinking straight. I mean, he might have done it anyway," I added loyally. "But I'd rather be sure."

"Mm. I've always suspected Arthur's only one meal away from turning man-eater. Will do, darling. I shall take Julian along to protect me from any attempts by the Beast of Fleetville to bite the hand that feeds."

"Cheers, Gary. You're a mate." I felt a rush of fondness for the big cuddly bastard.

"Anytime, darling." Gary patted my hand, and oh God, my eyes were welling up. If something didn't happen to distract me soon, this was about to get *seriously* embarrassing.

Thank God, there was a cough from the doorway. "Not interrupting anything, am I?"

I blinked a few times till my vision cleared, and pasted on a smile. "God, no. Dave, good to see you."

Dave stomped in. He'd put on weight now he was no longer on the healthy-sperm diet. If the beer gut got any bigger, you'd be hard pushed to tell if it was him or his missus who was expecting. "Right, then, Paretski. Who've you pissed off now?"

"You, by the looks of it."

"*I'll* say," Gary put in. "He didn't even bring flowers." Gary had turned up with flowers, a card, *and* a teddy bear dressed in dubious taste.

Dave grunted. "Christ, I could murder a cup of tea. S'pose it's all vending machine crap around here. God knows how they expect anyone to get well on that shite."

"There's a café down the hall," Gary told him with a helpful smile. "Serving teas, coffees, and hot and cold snacks." He sounded like one of those announcers you get on the trains when the buffet car's just opened.

I was suddenly gagging for a cuppa. "Gary, be a mate and scare us up a couple of teas, would you? Milk, no sugar for me."

Dave nodded. "Same for me, ta."

Gary rolled his eyes. "No need to ask what your last slave died of," he said, but headed off while Dave dropped his bulk into a chair, adjusted his crotch, and got out a notebook.

"I'm guessing this isn't a purely social call, then," I said.

Dave scowled. "*Someone's* got to get your statement about last night, haven't they?"

"You're taking witness statements now? Been demoted, have you?" Dave was a detective inspector, which I'd thought meant delegating all the grunt work.

"Witless statements, more bloody like. And no. Morrison filled me in, so I pulled up the file. Wasn't going to leave you to the tender mercies of some pimple-faced prat straight out of training, was I?"

"Phil called you?" I stared at him.

"Just said he did, didn't I?"

"When was that?"

"First thing this morning. So come on, what happened?" Dave prompted.

I frowned. "I was hoping someone was going to tell me."

Dave heaved a sigh. "Bloody marvellous. Right. You were at the Dyke, you went outside—did you see anyone? Anything?"

"Windows," I said. "I was looking at the windows. Marianne's window."

"Right, because what that kid really needs is another bloody stalker."

"I was . . ." Fuck, what *had* I been doing? "There was a reason. 'M sure there was."

"And then?"

"And then what?"

It was more a growl than a sigh this time. "That's the million-sodding-dollar question, innit? What happened?"

I was starting to get a bit narked. Here I was, still feeling like crap, getting the third bloody degree from my so-called mate, and *he* was the one getting pissed off. "Well, it's a bit of a stab in the dark, but I reckon I might have got a head injury somehow. What do you think?"

"Jesus, what does it take? Don't answer that. All right. Here's what we know: some nutter decided your head looked like a wicket and chucked a cricket ball at it. Who've you been pissing off in the village eleven?"

"I couldn't even pick the village eleven out of a police lineup." Well, maybe if they were wearing their whites. I paused. "Now you mention it, I did see a cricket ball lying around before I went in the pub. Shit. Are you sure it hit me? I didn't just manage a pratfall on the bloody thing and bash my head on the way down?"

"Positive. Unless you reckon it's someone else's blood and hair on the ball. Which might be what the lab'll tell us, *if* they ever get their bloody fingers out of their arses and run the tests, but I know what my money's on." He folded his arms. "You do realize people have died from that sort of thing?"

"What, you serious?" I reached for my glass of water, feeling a bit queasy. It was a toss-up as to whether it was down to the concussion or Dave's little revelation.

Dave nodded. "Yep."

"Shit. Don't tell Phil, will you?"

Dave looked around the room theatrically. "Not much danger of it right now, is there? So where is he, then? You two had a lovers' tiff? Find out he's been doing the nasty with your best mate?"

"Well, technically speaking, that's either Gary or you. Now I'm pretty sure Gary's devoted to his fiancé, so you tell me."

Dave shuddered. It made his gut wobble like a bouncy castle under a toddler onslaught. "Christ, give me nightmares, why don't you?"

"Oi, don't you come over all homophobic on me."

"I'm not homophobic, all right? We have sensitivity workshops and all that bollocks these days. Just saying, *if,* God forbid, I ever jumped into bed with a bloke, it wouldn't be with six feet of hulking great gamekeeper turned poacher."

I grinned. "You telling me you don't like 'em tall, well-built, and blond? No accounting for tastes. All right, then, seeing as we're talking hypotheticals, what would be your type?"

"Female."

"No, go on. If you had to shag a bloke—say all the women got killed in the zombie apocalypse or something—what'd he be like?"

"I dunno, do I?" He sighed. "Fine, then. Dark haired, I guess. I've always been into brunettes. Blonds might have more fun, but the blokes with 'em bloody well don't. *Not* built like a bloody brick shit-house. And he'd have to be shorter than me . . ."

Our gazes crossed, and like it was telepathy or something, we both realised at the exact same time just who around here was spot on with all Dave's requirements. At least, *I* did, and judging by the look of horror on Dave's face, which pretty much matched the way I felt, he'd got there too.

We each looked away in a hurry. Dave coughed.

"Right," I said, a bit too loud. "Bloody stupid idea, anyway. Seeing as you'd never . . . How's Jen today?"

"Good. Fine. Beautiful. Very . . ." Dave made vague but easily identifiable hand gestures in the region of his chest. "Blooming."

"How delightful." Gary was back with a couple of paper cups, each with a tea bag tag hanging over the side. "Your refreshments, gentlemen."

Dave took his drink and breathed in deeply, looking a lot happier. "Cheers. What do I owe you?"

Gary waved it away. "No, no, all part of the service. I'm honoured to support our heroic upholders of the law."

Ten to one Dave gave him a deeply suspicious look at that, but if he did, I missed it. I was too busy staring in dismay at the contents of my own cup. "What the bloody hell's this? It looks like dishwater. Christ, it smells like it and all."

"Camomile tea," Gary said primly. "I hardly think PG Tips would be a good idea on a dicky tummy."

"It's going to be a bloody sight more *dicky* if I drink this stuff. Where'd you even find it? The drains?"

"Most cafés have herbal teas these days." Gary sniffed. "I'll be getting along now, but don't hesitate to call should you need me for any further thankless menial drudgery." He flounced out.

I exchanged *oops* looks with Dave. We both grinned. Then he shocked the life out of me by passing me his tea. "Come on, hand over the herbal muck. I won't tell if you don't."

My eyebrows nearly hit the ceiling. "You're actually going to drink that?"

"Yeah, well. Jen's got in a cupboard full of the stuff—caffeine's bad for the baby and all that, and she reckons it's not fair if I drink stuff she can't in front of her. It's not so bad when you get used to it." He took a sip of the dishwater and didn't gag or anything.

"You're a braver man than I am." I took a sip of the actual, proper tea, and sighed. "Bloody hell, that hits the spot. What were we talking about again?"

"Your bloke." Dave frowned. "There'd better not be any suggestion *he's* the one who chucked that ball, or that lad's not going to know what's hit him."

"There isn't," I said firmly. Gary's suggestions didn't count. Seeing as they were bloody daft suggestions.

"Right. So we're looking at an opportunistic crime. Someone sees the ball lying around, and they see you, and they decide to put two and two together. So who'd want to knock some sense into your thick skull?"

"Buggered if I know." Christ. It was sinking in that someone had done this deliberately—had set out to hurt me. Maybe even to kill me.

I put my tea down on the bedside table, feeling sick. Maybe I should have stuck to the dishwater after all.

"Chatted up anyone who wasn't in the mood, lately?"

"Nope. I've got a bloke, remember?"

"Course you have." Dave scratched his armpit. "Thought your lot were a bit more free and easy about that sort of thing, though."

"Fuck off. You know I've never been into all that open-relationship stuff."

"Your Phil know that too, does he?"

"Yes, he sodding well does, all right?" Shit. "I think it might have been Grant Carey."

"What's he got against you? In fact, how come he even knows you exist?" Dave frowned. "You think he thought you were muscling in on his ex? Saw you peeping in her windows and jumped to conclusions?"

"Oi, there was no peeping. And no, not that. Not exactly."

"What, then? It's not like you know the bloke, is it?"

"Well . . . we've met."

"Bleedin' marvellous. What, up at the Dyke? Warn him off, did you?"

"Not as such." I took a sip of my cooling tea. It didn't do a lot to settle my stomach. "He was there that night. Well, earlier. He left a while before I did, I remember that. Didn't really notice the time. But that wasn't the first time we'd met. He pitched up at Phil's."

"Old drinking buddies, are they?"

"Yeah, right. No. He found out somehow that Phil was on his case." Shit. From the look on Dave's face, this was the first he'd heard about there even *being* a case.

Dave heaved a massive sigh. "Course your Phil's on his case. Course he is. Because otherwise, life just wouldn't have piled enough shit on my shoulders, now would it? Come on, then. Who hired him? Marianne Drinkwater, I presume?"

"Nah. Harry," I admitted with a twinge of guilt. "But it's pretty much the same thing, really, innit?"

"Christ. What a pretty little thing like that kid sees in Harry Shire, I'll never know. Carey, now, you can understand her getting sucked in by that slimy bastard. But Harry?" He shook his head. Dave Southgate: eternally baffled by the mysterious ways of the nonheterosexual. "I don't want to know what she hired him to do, do I?"

"Probably not. Um."

"What?"

I thought about not telling him, but I couldn't see how it could do any harm. Might even do some good—maybe get official wheels turning, that sort of thing. "Well, there was this thing about him framing a bloke. Least, that's what Marianne reckoned. Alan Mortimer, his name was. Is, even. Got done for possession of cocaine, but Marianne reckoned Carey planted the stuff. He's in Nether Mallet. Well, he was, until they let him out on appeal."

"And?"

"And, well, Phil thought it'd be a good line of enquiry. See if he could dig up any evidence to prove Carey framed this Mortimer bloke. You know, get him put away instead. Then he'd be off Marianne's back and out of Harry's hair." And well away from anyone else's body parts, at least around here.

Dave grunted. "Right. Because, of course, the local force who investigated at the time couldn't find their arses with both hands, not without Phil 'God's gift' Morrison helping them out."

"Come off it. Everyone makes mistakes. And maybe they didn't want to clear Mortimer, ever thought of that? Marianne seemed to think he was as dodgy as Carey."

"What, so you reckon the local bobbies thought if they couldn't get him for something he'd done, they'd have him for something he hadn't? I'm touched by the faith you've got in the integrity of me and my colleagues."

"Oi, I'm not saying they framed him. Just, it wouldn't be in their interests to waste their time trying to get the bloke off, that's all. Them being all short-staffed and overworked, as you keep telling me."

"Too bloody right." Dave heaved a sigh. "Right. So you reckon Carey got the wind up him about your bloke digging over the dirt. So how come it's you and not Morrison lying there with a bump on the head?"

"Well . . . Carey knows we're together."

"Christ, Tom, did you give him a copy of your CV and the key to your front door as well?"

I might have squirmed a bit. Not very comfortable, your average hospital bed. "He's good at worming stuff out of you. Making you say stuff without thinking about it first. Don't you bloody well get on at me about it."

Dave laughed. "Morrison have a few choice words to say to you, did he?"

"Might have," I muttered.

"Not a total waste of space, then. Right." He heroically downed the last of the camomile and heaved himself to his feet. "Some of us have jobs to do, you know. Can't waste all day lying about. When are they letting you out of here?"

"Tomorrow, I hope."

Dave nodded. "Make sure that bloke of yours takes care of you. I've had a concussion. It's a total bugger."

"Yeah? Get knocked on the head in the line of duty?"

"Manner of speaking." Dave's normally pretty ruddy face went a shade or two darker, but he was smiling, like it was a fond memory for some reason. "Me and Jen had this weekend away, didn't we? Second honeymoon, and all that bollocks. She insisted on a luxury hotel, four-poster bed, the works."

"And?"

"Well, that was the thing, wasn't it? We had a posh dinner, bottle of champagne, cocktails for pud. Enough to make anyone frisky, innit? Then we jump into bed together and there's these bloody posts where I'm not expecting 'em. Sodding hard and all."

I stared at him. "Seriously? You knocked yourself out shagging?"

"Well, technically we never actually got to the shagging bit. And I was only out for a couple of minutes. By which time, though, Jen's called an ambulance, and I wake up stark bollock naked to find the hotel manager—who, by the way, was camper than a bloody Butlin's with your mate Gary as chief redcoat—bending over me stroking my neck."

"Yeah, I think you probably hallucinated that bit." Dave's a good mate, but God's gift to queer men, he is not.

"Well, he claimed he was taking my pulse." Dave gave me a look. "I know what he was really after, though. Any excuse."

I laughed. "You wish. Must have been a bit of a downer, though—concussion on your second honeymoon."

"You'd think, wouldn't you? My Jen's got a great bedside manner, though. And the manager insisted on giving us another weekend break free of charge. Seems something Jen said made him think we were going to sue."

"Let me guess, she also let slip you were chummy with the legal profession?"

"Might've done. Might've done. You finished with that? I'll chuck it on the way out."

I nodded. "Cheers. You take care, all right?"

"Ever thought of taking your own advice? No, didn't think so." Dave plodded off, paper cups in hand, to go do whatever detective inspectors did when they weren't skiving off work to visit mates in hospital.

Funny how empty the room felt without him or Gary in it. I picked up the card Gary had left, and reread the dirty limerick he—or maybe Darren, now I came to think about it—had penned inside:

There was a young man from Nantucket
Who got hit on the head with a bucket
It started to throb

So he got out his knob
And got all the nurses to suck it.

I chuckled, then the hairs on the back of my neck started to prickle. I looked up to see Nurse Sarah (late twenties or early thirties, chirpy, on the cuddly side—she could have been Gary's twin sister) reading over my shoulder. "Sorry, love," she said. "This is the NHS. You'll have to go private if you want that kind of service."

"Nothing wrong with the service here," I said with a wink. "The food, now, that could definitely do with a bit of improvement."

"Ah, but if the food was good, people'd never want to leave. Got to free up these beds somehow, haven't we?" She gave me a roguish smile. "Though I doubt it'd be a problem with you. Bet you can't wait to get back home with your boyfriend. He's a love."

I blinked, and not just because she apparently thought Phil Morrison, my mean and moody significant other, was a *love*. "You met Phil? How long a shift do they have you working here?"

Nurse Sarah frowned. "I've been on since eight this morning—I'll be going home in an hour or so. But I thought his name was Gary?"

"Nah, he's just a mate. Phil's my bloke. He was here last night when they brought me in," I added quickly in case she was wondering where he was.

"I'm sure he'll come and visit you again soon," she said, and plumped up my pillows for me.

I thought, seeing as Phil hadn't come to visit in the afternoon, that he'd be here in the evening, but he was a no-show. I even dragged myself out to the public payphones next to the caff to give him a ring, just in case he'd, you know, forgotten I was here or something, but his phone went straight to voice mail.

The way back to my bed seemed a lot longer than it had this morning. My head was aching again, what with the clangs and the thuds, the constant bustle, and the occasional bursts of muffled laughter from the nurses. I suppose in their line of work, you have to take the lighter moments when you can.

I climbed back into bed, wondering how anyone ever got to sleep in hospital. Then I shut my eyes and went out like a light.

CHAPTER NINE

I was a bit hacked off, to be honest, when Wednesday morning rolled around and there was still no word from Phil. I'd tried ringing him again, but his phone was still going to voice mail.

It was a bit embarrassing, as the doctor said she wouldn't let me go if I didn't have someone with me. I ended up having to give Gary a ring to come and get me—Cherry, and pretty much everyone else for that matter, would be at work, and I really didn't fancy explaining everything to Mum and Dad. Gary works his IT wizardry from home, and he's always happy to take a break to help out a mate in need, bless him.

Course, as things were, he was a bit of a mixed blessing.

"You'll notice I'm not saying one word about the absence of a certain blond behemoth," he said as he breezed into my room. "Not one word. Not a syllable. My lips are sealed. Tighter than a gnat's derrière."

I sighed. "Can we get out of here?"

"Of course we can. Look, I've brought you your favourite T-shirt." It was the zombie one he'd bought me, which, given how much he'd gone on about me nearly dying, seemed a bit close to the bone. "And a decent pair of trousers, although, let me tell you, it took some searching in that offspring of an Oxfam shop you call your wardrobe."

He'd brought my pulling jeans, which were a total bastard to get on.

"Cheers," I said, because it's the thought that counts, and started to strip out of my hospital gown.

"Should I avert my gaze?" Gary asked, with a hint of an ogle in his eye.

I was feeling about as far from ogle-worthy as possible, but if that was what floated his boat, I wasn't going to deny it was giving my ego a much-needed boost. "Nah, knock yourself out," I said—and then we both burst out laughing. "Maybe not literally, though," I added. "It hurts like hell."

"Of course not, darling. I wouldn't want to steal your thunder." Gary frowned. "Do you need some help with those jeans? This sedentary lifestyle of yours may be beginning to take its toll."

"*One day* I've been laid up in bed. One day, all right? And no, they've always been this tight." I yanked the jeans up over my arse, the sudden motion making me feel a bit dizzy, not that I'd have admitted it to any passing medical staff in case they grounded me for a week. "There. They're on, see? And no, I'm not going to give you a twirl."

"Spoilsport. Now, have you got all your things?"

I stared at him. "This is a hospital, not the Waldorf bloody Astoria. I came here in an ambulance. I didn't stop to pack a suitcase."

"Where are the clothes you arrived in? Or did your evening get a *lot* more interesting after I left?" Gary's eyes lit up, presumably at the image of me prancing around starkers outside the Dyke before getting that bop on the head. At least, I hoped that look of relish didn't come from picturing whoever had laid me out nicking the shirt off my unconscious back as a souvenir. Not to mention the pants off my unconscious arse.

"Har bloody har. Phil took all my kit back with him when he visited, so what you see is what you get." I shoved my feet into my trainers, glad I didn't have to bend down to tie my laces up. I had a nasty feeling my breakfast might have made an appearance if I had.

Gary gave me a disapproving look. "I hope you're not planning to leave little Tommy to languish here."

"Uh..." I frowned at him. "Little Tommy's safe in my pants where he usually is, thanks."

"I wasn't talking about *that*, darling." Gary picked up the teddy he'd brought me. "See? He's even wearing a little lumberjack shirt, just like his daddy."

"Gary, I'm nobody's daddy. And no one notices the shirt when they look at that ted. They get too hung up on the leather posing pouch." The nurses had been having a right giggle over it.

"That wasn't *my* fault. It's sewn on."

"Sounds painful." Not to mention frustrating for poor little Tommy. "Where'd you get him, anyway? Bondage Toys'R'Us?"

"Darren found him for me. Isn't he adorable?" From the misty look in his eye, I was betting Gary was talking about his fiancé, not the cuddly toy. "He said if I'd given him another day, he could have found a little toy sink plunger for him to hold."

Well, there was a small mercy to be thankful for. "I'll be sure to buy him a drink next time I see him. Can we go now?"

"Of course, darling. *I'm* not the one who's holding us up."

Naturally, it wasn't as simple as just walking out of there. I mean, I'd got myself signed out and everything before Gary got there, but he insisted we said goodbye to the nurses, who all seemed to adore Gary. Some of 'em even remembered who I was too. By the time I'd finally managed to get out of that hospital and into the passenger seat of Gary's Toyota RAV4, I felt like my nonexistent suitcase. After it'd been treated to the tender mercies of Gatwick's baggage handlers.

"Go easy on the corners, yeah?" I said as I buckled my seat belt.

"Don't fret, Tommy dear. Your ride will be smoother than a freshly waxed chest."

"Cheers." I leaned my head back on the headrest, carefully avoiding the bruised bit, and closed my eyes.

Gary pulled out of the car park. "No need to thank me. I'm not being entirely altruistic. You've no *idea* how snippy some car valeting services get when asked to clean bodily fluids off leather seats."

"Yep, and I'm pretty happy keeping it that way," I muttered.

You've got to hand it to Gary: when he says he'll drive smoothly, he means it. I didn't look, but I could imagine we were leading a tailback of cars halfway to Hemel by the time he took the final corner and purred to a halt in front of my house. I opened my eyes. The parking space was empty, which reminded me the Fiesta must still be up at the Dyke. Great. Another thing to deal with.

Phil's Golf wasn't there either. Not that I'd been expecting it, or hoping it would be, or anything. Obviously.

"Somebody," Gary said as he unbuckled his seat belt, "is going to have to have words with that man of yours. Neglecting you in your hour of need. Do you think it bodes well for the future? Because I, darling, am having serious forebodings."

I was really not up for all this.

"Look, cheers for the lift. I'd ask you in, but I'd be pretty crap company right now. And I'm sure you've got work to do."

"Nice try, Tommy dear, but nobody's hit *me* on the head, and I distinctly remember you getting strict instructions from our Florence Nightingales *not* to be on your own for the next twenty-four hours. I've got my laptop in the back."

"I could give Phil another ring . . ." I said tiredly, and all right, not all that convincingly.

"No, you couldn't." He patted my knee and beamed at me. "Uncle Gary's going to take good care of you. Now, come on, let's get you in the house."

As we walked in my front door, I wondered if I should give Phil a bell anyway. Let him know I was out of hospital, at least. Even if he wasn't answering, I could leave him a voice mail. Or a text, maybe. Yeah, a text would be better.

I didn't want to seem, you know, desperate or anything. Plus, to be honest, I was starting to get a bit uneasy. This really wasn't like Phil. Even if he was pissed off with me. And let's face it, we already knew there was someone going around attacking people. What if Phil had fallen foul of him too? Only he hadn't been lucky enough to come a cropper somewhere public, like I had?

Jesus, my head was throbbing. I hobbled over to the sofa, where I managed a controlled collapse, the sort that wouldn't lead to either further agony in the head region or unpleasant reactions from the stomach area. For one thing, Arthur was milling around the coffee table, having jumped off the sofa like a lumberjack who'd seen which way the tree was falling, and if I chucked on him, he'd never speak to me again.

"Have the cats been fed this morning?" I asked, my eyes shut. God, I hoped the answer would be either *yes* or *I'll do it now*. The thought of moving from this sofa and opening up a can of cat food almost made my breakfast do a runner for the carpet. Maybe the cats would be satisfied if I gave them a couple of toes to chew on each.

"Do I look like the sort of man who neglects pussies?" Gary called back from the kitchen over the sounds of opening and closing cupboard doors.

"You really want me to answer that?" I managed weakly.

"I have the utmost affection for all our furry friends," Gary said reprovingly around the doorframe. "Except, perhaps, for the ones currently developing their own ecosystem in your bread bin. You really ought to pop your perishables in the fridge if you're going to be away for a day or two."

"Yeah, well, I'll try and remember that next time I go out to get my head bashed in."

Gary put on a sorrowful expression. "This head injury's making you a little tetchy, isn't it?"

I waved a couple of fingers in his general direction.

"Anyway, darling," Gary said brightly, "seeing as there's nothing in your kitchen that's fit to feed a rat, I'll just pop down the road and get some rolls or something. Maybe a muffin or two. Bye-ee!"

He disappeared, leaving a faint whiff of Givenchy Gentlemen Only and a sad little silence.

Sighing, I closed my eyes again and melted into the sofa cushions. Then Merlin jumped on my stomach, and I threw up on the floor. Gary was *not* impressed when he got back from the shops.

By midafternoon, I felt a whole lot better. Which was lucky, seeing as just as I was finishing up a very late lunch of chicken soup (Gary's Jewish great-grandmother apparently swore by it, and seeing as she made it to ninety-seven, I wasn't going to argue) there was a knock on the door. More to the point, it was the sort of knock they drum into the raw recruits at the police academy. Either that, or they pick it up from watching too many American cop shows.

It made my pulse jump for a moment, and I almost spilled my last spoonful of soup.

Gary came back from answering the door with a sour expression. "Your tea-addicted friend is here. I use *friend* in the loosest possible sense, of course. He still hasn't brought you any flowers."

I mustered up a smile with a lot less effort than I'd have thought possible a few hours ago. "Yeah, well, flowers for blokes aren't really Dave's thing. Go on, show him in."

If it was Dave, then odds-on it was either a social call or something about my little bop on the head. Nothing to do with Phil at all.

Except, if something *had* happened to him, wouldn't Dave stop by to tell me in person?

Shit.

"You're looking better," Dave said approvingly as he stomped into the living room. "Mind you, everyone looks like shite in hospital. It's the paint they put on the walls."

"Yeah, well, I'm feeling a lot better," I said, putting my bowl down and waving him to a seat.

Dave sat, and then he sniffed. "Someone chucked up in here?"

"It was one of the cats," I said truthfully if misleadingly.

Dave nodded. "You know, I could murder a—"

"The kettle," Gary interrupted pointedly, "is in the kitchen. Feel free to avail yourself of it." He flounced out of the room and up the stairs.

"Staying with you, is he?" Dave asked, with a jerk of his head in the direction Gary had disappeared to.

"Just for today. The hospital wouldn't let me go otherwise. And Gary does all his work out of his laptop and phone, so it's no skin off his nose." I waited for Dave to smirk and ask if Phil had done a runner, seeing as they weren't exactly bosom buddies, but it didn't come.

That prickle of unease I'd felt earlier came back with interest. I opened my mouth to ask Dave what he was here for, but he beat me to it. "Want a cup of anything?"

"Nah, I'm good, thanks."

Dave sat there for a moment. It looked like he was deciding whether a cup of tea would be worth the bother of getting up and making it. Inertia won.

"Dave? Not that I'm not touched by getting two visits in two days, but . . ."

"But you want to know what I'm here for, right?" Dave sighed. "I just got a call from the boys down in Docklands. Wanted to know what I could tell 'em about one Philip Morrison, currently gracing their cells."

"What? Why?" And, fucking hell, thank God.

He was all right.

"Seems he's been throwing his weight around. They got a call from a local businessman, and I bet you can't guess who that was. In fear of his life, apparently, due to a certain private investigator turning up at his place of work and making threats." Dave paused. "In front of witnesses, the fucking stupid sod."

"Oh Christ."

"Tell me about it. Actually, no, don't tell me about it, because I've had it up to here with your boyfriend for tonight. Just tell him, next time he wants someone to vouch for him with the local constabulary, he can drop someone else's name and leave me out of it. Got it?"

"Shit. I'm sorry, Dave."

"Yeah, yeah. Not your fault." At least Dave sounded a bit less pissed off now.

"Are they charging him?"

"Dunno. Up to them, innit?" He sighed heavily. "Did what I could. Harped on about the once-a-copper-always-a-copper bit. Told 'em Carey's a little shite, which, as it happened, wasn't news to 'em. Mentioned he's been causing trouble up here."

"Cheers, Dave. I owe you." I meant it too. Having to talk Phil up must have gone well against the grain for Dave—they always gave the impression of having a mutual agreement not to waste bodily fluids if one happened upon the other doing Guy Fawkes impersonations. I hoped he hadn't given himself an ulcer.

"No you fucking don't. It's your bloody boyfriend who owes me, and don't you let him forget it."

"Yeah, well. Drinks are on me next time. And cheers for letting me know about it, yeah? I was wondering where the hell he'd got to."

"Had a hot date, did you? Christ, I must be tired. Don't tell me. I do *not* want to know." Dave rubbed the back of his neck. "You all right, then? Your mate looking after you?"

"Yeah, Gary's been great." I smiled, but shit, I was coming over all emotional again. Bloody concussion.

"You and him ever . . . ?"

Okay, that startled me out of the emo overload pretty effectively. "What, Gary? No. Seriously, no. He's just a mate."

Dave frowned. "How's that work, then?"

I gave him a sidelong look. "It's like you and me, innit? We're mates."

"Yeah, but I'm not a poof."

"Yeah, and?"

Dave shifted in his seat. "Well . . . it's like, you and me, right, that's never going to happen. Right? 'Cos I'm straight."

"Yeah," I said cautiously.

"But you and him, now, that's different, innit? It's always there. In the background."

"What is?"

"Bloody hell, you know. *Sex.*"

I stared at him. "No, it's not."

"Come off it. You're queer, he's queer. Nothing stopping you, is there?"

"Apart from the fact we don't like each other that way? Seriously, Dave, just because we're both gay doesn't mean we want to shag each other. I mean, come on, you don't want to shag all the women you meet, do you?"

Dave looked uncomfortable. "Well, course not. Jen'd have my bollocks if she ever found out."

"Yeah, but say you and her had never got back together. You wouldn't want to jump into bed with every woman you met, would you? It's a, whatsit. Compatibility thing."

There were deep furrows ploughed into Dave's forehead. "Yeah, but you and that Gary get on all right, don't you? Are you seriously telling me that in all the years you've known him, you've never once thought about doing the nasty . . .? You know what? I have no idea why we're even talking about this."

"Oi, you started it."

"And I'm bloody well stopping it now." He stood up. "Right. Some of us have jobs to get back to. Try not to get yourself killed in the next week or so, will you? It's bollixing up my schedules something chronic. I'm supposed to be at a seminar right now. Sexual harassment in the sodding workplace. I ask you. Chance'd be a bloody fine thing."

I grinned. "I'll put a note in my diary. Stay alive until July. And cheers for helping Phil out, all right?"

"Don't mention it. And I mean that most sincerely."

The thing about being worried about people is, while you're still worried, you think everything'll be peachy if only they're okay. But once you know they're all right, you start thinking how bloody hacked off you are that they got into the situation in the first place.

I mean, seriously, what the bloody hell had got into Phil? Marching over to Carey's place and chucking his weight around? Like *that* was ever going to end well. Carey must have thought it was Christmas. He didn't even have to bother trying to stitch Phil up for something—the stupid sod had gone and done it all by himself.

By the time Phil finally rang, I was so far beyond tetchy that Gary was tiptoeing around me. Literally, which didn't help my mood any. I'd already gone through my diary rearranging this week's jobs and calling clients to apologise for no-shows, and was now sitting on the sofa going through VAT invoices, because apparently I wasn't hacked off enough already. I always hated percentages at school, so trying to grapple with them while concussed was probably not my smartest idea ever.

"Let you off with a caution, did they?" I said by way of hello.

Phil huffed down the phone, then was silent for a mo. "You've heard from Dave Southgate, then?"

"Just a bit. What the bloody hell were you thinking? You're supposed to be digging up stuff on Carey, not handing him your arse on a bloody platter."

"Christ, give me the benefit of the doubt, why don't you?"

"Yeah, well, feel free to fill me in on all this *doubt* that's going around." I stomped over to the window and opened it a bit wider. The early-evening air rolled in damply, like a heavy blanket just out of the tumble dryer. "All I heard was you went round to Carey's office and started acting like an East End heavy."

"Bollocks." He huffed again. "I'm on the train. I've had a fucking awful day, and all I want to do is have a shower and sleep. I'll see you at the weekend. If that's all right with you?"

You could cut the sarcasm with a knife, and now I felt like a bastard. "No," I found myself saying. "Come round, yeah? I mean, I'm still not supposed to be on my own." Which I wouldn't be, obviously, Gary having brought his doggy paw print jim-jams to stay over, but Phil didn't know that.

There was a long silence. "All right. I'll see you in half an hour."

We hung up, and I plodded to the stairs. "Gary?" I called. He was working in the spare bedroom again, claiming my bad mood was putting him off. "You're off duty. Phil's coming round."

Gary's heavy footsteps clomped down the stairs. "Are you sure about this? Given his wanton neglect of you all this time?"

"Yeah, well, he had an excuse."

"I hope it was a good one."

"Depends how you look at it. Nah, okay, it was a good excuse." I didn't reckon Phil would thank me for spreading it about, though.

Luckily, Gary didn't push. "So you won't be biting *his* head off? So to speak."

I grinned. "Wouldn't exactly be in my best interests, now would it?"

"Fine. I shall take my leave, then. He *will* turn up, won't he?" Gary's eyes narrowed. "If I find out later that he didn't, there will be *words* spoken."

"If he stands me up, I'll have a few things to say to him and all. Don't worry, mate. He'll be here."

"Promise to call if you need me?"

"Yeah. Cheers, Gary. You're a mate. I owe you one."

"Darling, I gave up keeping a tab years ago. Now, do you want me to linger until he arrives, or shall I begone?"

"I think I can survive the next twenty minutes till he gets here. I'll see you, all right?"

Gary fetched his laptop, made me promise—again—to call him if I needed anything, and left. That gave me plenty of time to shove the VAT invoices back in their file—I'd been losing the battle anyhow—and make sure there was plenty of beer in the fridge. Then I cracked one open for myself. It's thirsty work, tidying stuff.

Then I remembered I wasn't supposed to be drinking yet. Sod it.

Phil let himself in a few minutes later. Any smart comments I might have been about to make died at the sight of him. He had that worn and grimy look you only get after spending the day in the enforced company of our boys in blue. "You look like shit," I said, and handed him my beer.

"Cheers," he said, and I couldn't work out whether it was sarcastic or not. He took a long, long swallow and handed me the bottle back, empty. "You're looking good. Feeling all right, now?"

"Better." The headache was mostly gone, and the nausea. I wouldn't be running any marathons anytime soon, but from the look of him, neither would Phil. "Hungry?" I asked.

"Nope. But I could go for another beer."

I was halfway through fetching another bottle from the fridge when he grabbed me from behind. "Forget the beer. I need a shower. You up for joining me?"

"Want me to scrub your back?"

"I can think of better things you could be scrubbing."

We moved upstairs slowly, shedding items of sweaty clothing as we went and stepping over the cats, who didn't seem to see the point of moving just to accommodate two horny humans. Halfway there, I started making bets with myself on whether we'd make it to the shower.

I lost. Phil gently plastered me up against the wall on the upstairs landing and slid down to his knees.

"Oi," I said weakly. My back was sticking to the wallpaper, and the edge of a doorframe was digging into my shoulder. "I know blokes are supposed to come out of the nick desperate for a shag, but you were only in there one day."

He looked up at me, his eyes tired underneath sweat-dark hair. "Shut up," he said, one hand on my bollocks and his nose nudging my pubes. My cock was so hard it'd take an eye out if he wasn't careful.

I grinned down at him. "Don't talk with your mouth full."

Phil's always been good at taking a hint.

We had a long, leisurely shower after that, and then collapsed into bed. "Wanna talk about it?" I offered sleepily.

"Nope."

"Fair enough."

We were both snoring within seconds.

CHAPTER TEN

When I woke up next morning, my head felt clearer than it had in days. Well, since around midnight on Monday night, to be precise. The air coming in through the open window wasn't exactly cool, but at least it was (a) coming in and (b) didn't feel like it'd visited a sauna en route. Which was just as well, seeing as I had six foot two of solid muscle wrapped around me like a high-tog human duvet.

I thought about trying to wriggle out of his grasp without waking him, but seeing as a certain part of him was already bright-eyed, bushy-tailed, and poking me in the arse, I decided the rest of him wouldn't be too sorry to be dragged out of dreamland.

I wasn't wrong.

"You planning on working today?" Phil asked a fair bit later, with a hint of *you'd better not be if you know what's good for you* in his eyes.

Unless I was imagining it, obviously. "Nah. Thought I'd play safe and take it easy the next couple of days." I stretched, enjoying the way my body was aching in all the right places instead of the wrong ones.

Phil played idly with a nipple. Mine, not his. "Want to pay Alan Mortimer a visit with me?"

"Sure I won't get in the way of you two bonding over your Carey-induced jail experiences?"

"Not exactly an exclusive club, is it? People who've been done over by Grant Carey. I'm more interested in how Mortimer managed to get his conviction overturned."

"Hoping he'll end up doing your job for you?"

"Something like that. See if he wants any help. That bastard Carey needs neutering before he messes up anyone else's lives." Phil rolled out of bed, giving me a nice view of his perfectly sculpted arse. "I'll take first shower. You can make breakfast."

"Bloody hell, your concern for my health didn't last long, did it?"

Phil turned and gave me a look that was deadly serious. "I'm always concerned about your health, all right? Always. Don't you forget it."

Thank God I wasn't still going all weepy at stuff like that. It would've been well embarrassing. "Yeah, well, me too, right?"

I was halfway through cooking bacon and eggs before it occurred to me he might have had an ulterior motive for coming over all mushy.

Ah, well. I'd been gagging for a bit of home cooking too.

"So how come you called Dave to bail you out, anyway?" I asked when we were on the way to Mortimer's and, more importantly, Phil couldn't escape. "I thought you had your own mates in the Met?"

"*A* mate. Steve. Couldn't get hold of him, could I?" He huffed. "And the rest of 'em don't remember me quite so fondly."

"No? What did you used to do—hog all the choccy biccies at tea break time?"

"You know what it's like. Coppers take a dim view of anyone going private."

"I'd have thought they'd have a bit more loyalty, after all those years working together."

Phil grunted and stared at the road ahead, and we were silent for a moment.

"Anyway," I went on. "Are you going to tell me what happened to land you in the shit, or what?"

He muttered something that sounded a lot like *what.*

"Come on, spill." I didn't say anything about what a bloody idiot he'd been. I was a good boy, I was.

Phil was silent a moment longer, hands gripping the Golf's steering wheel like he was worried it might do a runner. "You were in hospital. You could have fucking *died.* That bastard was practically creaming himself over it all."

I gave him a sharp look. "He admitted it?"

"Course he bloody didn't. But come off it—who else could it have been?"

Funnily enough, I'd been doing a fair bit of thinking about that very subject. "Well . . . I'm not saying it was this, but everyone seems to reckon I look a bit like him. Carey. And let's face it, I was gawping up at Marianne's window at the time. In the dark. Oi, watch out!"

We'd actually swerved a bit, which is not generally recommended while zipping round the M25 at not-quite-legal speeds.

"You think it was Harry?" Phil asked, waving a hand at a driver who'd honked at us. She gave him a hard stare and changed lanes to one a bit farther away from us.

"No. I dunno, but . . . it's not her style, is it? If she was going to hit someone, she'd punch 'em in the face."

"So who, then?"

"Maybe it was just someone who thought he was doing her a favour. I mean, she's pretty popular, Harry is. Well, respected, anyway. And everyone likes Marianne—I mean, look at her. What's not to like?"

"Do I need to be worried?" Phil sounded amused.

"Well, I do have a bit of a thing for blonds," I said, giving the one in the driving seat an appreciative once-over. "Prefer 'em a bit more on the muscular side, though."

"Is that right? Got it. No worrying until Harry bleaches her hair or Marianne takes up body-building."

I laughed at the image that one presented. "She'd better not— Marianne, I mean. With arms that skinny, if she tried lifting weights, she'd snap."

Phil didn't answer, busy moving across lanes and towards the M40 exit. It wasn't long before we were out of the green belt and into the built-up areas that mark the start of the London sprawl, although we were still zipping through them at a fair old rate on the dual carriageway. Even when we turned off into the local shopping areas, the roads were still wide, fast, and busy, like it was a given people would be in a hurry to get out of there. You couldn't have paid me to live there.

I'd forgotten how tightly packed the houses are in London, even in the leafier part of Ealing, which was where Old Alan's gaff was, slap in the middle of a row of terraced houses. The place was nice enough, I supposed, but it had that London feel about it you don't get out in the sticks. I don't mean it was tatty or anything—God knows I'm not one to complain about that, seeing as how Fleetville's hardly the posh end of St. Albans. It wasn't the ethnic mix—where I live, there's more sari shops and halal butchers than there are pubs. And there are plenty of pubs. But it was, I dunno, less relaxed here or something. More businesslike, if by *businesslike* you mean *not having time for anything but making a profit.*

"It's smaller than I expected," I said, as we pulled up outside. There wasn't a space free to park along the kerb, so Phil blocked off Mortimer's driveway with the Golf.

Phil huffed. "Don't tell him that—we don't want to start by putting his back up. Had to downsize, didn't they? After he got banged up. Used to have a big place down in Rotherhithe."

"Must have been a bugger for the missus and the kiddies. All this going down in the world, I mean." The Mortimers had two, kiddies, that was. Mrs. M. was currently out on the school run, picking them up from the local primary school, and if she kept to the plan, taking them for a nice long play on the swings in the nearest park. You couldn't blame Mortimer for not wanting the nippers around while we chatted about his time inside, but I wasn't sure why he wanted their mum to be out as well. I mean, she must have *noticed* he'd gone to prison. "Still, kids that age are resilient. They probably coped a lot better than if they'd been in their teens already."

"Maybe," Phil said shortly, which was probably just his polite way of telling me I was talking through my arse.

We got out of the car, rang the bell, and waited. After the artificial chill in Phil's car, the air out here was thick and hot, smelling of exhaust fumes with a sickly overlay from the scrubby rose bushes in Mortimer's tiny front garden. Unlike neighbouring houses, though, there was no rubbish lurking in the flowerbeds, so clearly either Mr. or Mrs. M. still had some pride.

Phil had to lean on the doorbell a couple more times before it finally opened a grudging three inches. "Yes?"

"Phil Morrison. And this is Tom Paretski."

"Right." There was a pause, and then the door opened fully. "Come in."

It didn't sound all that welcoming. Not that it was all that unfriendly either, mind. Just . . . sort of flat. Not that interested in whether we came in or didn't. We trooped in, wiped our feet dutifully on the mat, and followed Mortimer into the small front room, where the grey light filtering through the net curtains gave me my first good look at him.

Mortimer was the thin, nervous sort, with greasy skin, damp palms, and a face like a pissed-off squirrel. I wondered who'd been messing with his nuts.

Then again, he *had* just been in prison. From what I hear, you have to expect that sort of thing in there.

He was wearing a suit and tie, which seemed a bit weird for a bloke in his own home with no job to go to. Still, he'd been expecting us. Maybe he thought we were worth dressing up for. I felt a bit bad about turning up in jeans, a T-shirt, and my work boots. Mind you, even Phil wasn't in a suit and tie today, and he actually had the sleeves of his designer shirt rolled up in deference to the heat, which was even worse here in the city than it had been in Hertfordshire.

Mortimer must have been melting—he was certainly sweating—but it didn't look like that jacket and tie were coming off while we were around.

"Tea?" he said abruptly.

"Not for me, ta," I said, just as Phil went, "Please."

I turned to give him a look as Mortimer scuttled off, presumably into the kitchen to bung the kettle on. "God, how can you drink hot tea in weather like this?"

"Not about the tea, is it?" Phil muttered. We sat down on the leather sofa, which was too big for the room. "It's about the ritual. The social aspect. Putting the bloke at his ease. You getting any vibes?"

"No, just whiplash from the sudden veer in subject." I listened for a moment. "Not sure. Might just be the usual background stuff. Bit quiet, actually." Maybe all Mortimer's secrets had got dragged out in the open, what with him going to prison.

Or maybe he'd kept the worst stuff in the office, and that had all gone down with the ship.

The bloke himself came back at that point, with three matching mugs from the posh china section in John Lewis—hey, I have to buy Christmas presents for people, all right? Not to mention find something to cross off Gary and Darren's wedding list, which, contrary to popular expectation, *hadn't* been lodged at the local fetish wear emporium. If there was such a thing, that was. Personally, I was quite happy not knowing.

"Milk, no sugar all right?" he asked, handing me one of them.

"That's great," I said with a cheery smile, despite the fact I'd asked for no milk, no sugar, and no tea either. "Ta." There weren't any coasters on the glass-topped coffee table, so I popped the mug down on a copy of last Sunday's *Observer Magazine.*

Phil took a sip from his tea before plonking the mug next to mine and looking up expectantly at Mortimer, who was still hovering, the final mug in his bony hand. Mortimer took the hint and sat down right on the edge of an armchair, as if actually relaxing might be the last mistake he'd ever make.

"Thanks for having us over," Phil started. "Can't have been an easy time for you, what with—"

Mortimer interrupted him. "I spoke to my solicitor after you telephoned. He's advised me not to say anything about the case to anyone." His pointy little chin came up. "How do I know you're not in league with—with someone?" he finished, and swallowed.

Phil leaned forward, his elbows on his knees, and gave Mortimer the benefit of his best trust-me-I'm-a-private-investigator face. "All we want is for the truth to come out. You just spent over a year in prison for something you didn't do. Don't you want the man who put you in there to get what he deserves?"

"We know he planted the stuff on you," I added, leaning forward as well. And carefully not mentioning Carey by name, since that seemed to be a thing we were doing. Not that I was sure why—was the bastard supposed to have spies everywhere?

From the sweat breaking out on Mortimer's forehead and the tense line of his shoulders, you'd have thought maybe Carey did have spies everywhere. "I can't speak to you. It's over now." He stood up abruptly. "For God's sake, why can't you let it be over?"

Phil stood up too. "Because Carey's going to carry on ruining people's lives until he's stopped." Huh. So we *were* mentioning his name, after all.

I felt a bit daft—not to mention, small—being the only one still on his bum, so I stood up as well. "Eye for an eye, innit? He put you in prison, so why not return the favour?"

Mortimer was clinging on to his mug of tea like it was the only thing stopping him from going completely to pieces. Maybe it was. I'd been wondering why he'd bothered offering us a cuppa if he was just going to chuck us straight out on our ears. "I can't help you," he said, his eyes fixed on a point over Phil's left shoulder and his voice higher in pitch than it had been a moment ago.

"Mr. Mortimer—" Phil started, but there was a sudden commotion out in the direction of the hallway. Mortimer jumped a mile, slopping tea everywhere, and we heard the front door open followed by high-pitched calls of "Daddy! Daddy!"

Two little kiddies in school uniform scrambled into the front room and clustered around Mortimer, ignoring me and Phil totally. "Daddy, Daddy, George hurt his knee and it bled and he cried." That was the biggest one, a gawky girl in bunches wearing big plasticky-looking glasses held on by a band around her head.

"No, I didn't! It really hurt, Daddy, and Mummy said it needs a plaster, and we had to come home and get one." The little lad, who was still chubby-cheeked from toddlerhood, gave a big sniff. To be fair, that *was* a nasty cut on his knee. The blood had trickled down all the way to one tumbled-down sock.

They were followed in by a pinched-looking woman with flat hair and no makeup to hide the deep, dark troughs under her eyes. "Julia, George, leave Daddy in peace. You'll give him one of his headaches. I'm sorry, Alan. I'll take them into the kitchen." She gave me and Phil a tired glance that held more than a hint of worry.

"I told you not to come back until five. I *told* you." The mug in Mortimer's hands was shaking. I hoped the carpet wasn't new. I also hoped this wasn't the way domestic life usually went in the Mortimer household, but the way Mrs. M. had blanched and the kiddies had gone quiet and slunk back around their mum's legs, like puppies in fear of a kick, didn't bode well.

I gave Mrs. M. a cheery smile. She looked like she could use one— in fact, she looked like she could use a nice long holiday, and not the sort her husband had just been on. "No harm done. Me and Phil were just on our way out anyway." I crouched down to turn the charm on Mortimer junior, and sucked in my lips. "Nasty graze you got there. Bet you were well brave about it though, yeah?"

George nodded, wide-eyed.

"He was standing on the swings, and he fell off," Julia chipped in, her eyes saucer-huge behind the thick glasses.

"Ah, well, a lad's gotta do what a lad's gotta do, right?"

I straightened and glanced over at Phil a bit guiltily, thinking I might have overstepped the mark with the *we're just going* bit, but he nodded. "Thanks for your time, Mr. Mortimer. If you change your mind, give me a call. Here's my card." He held one out, but Mortimer looked at it in horror as if it was about to slap the cuffs on him and drag him back to prison.

"I don't want it. You need to go. I can't help you." One of the kiddies made a noise, and Mortimer turned on Mrs. M., stepping forward with an ugly look on his face. "For God's sake, get them out of here!"

She went pink this time, and turned to us with a barely audible "I'm so sorry." George started to cry again as she grabbed the kiddies by an arm each and hurried them out of the room.

I frowned. "Oi, take it easy on the family, yeah?"

Phil grabbed *my* arm. "Leave it alone," he muttered. "You're not helping." He raised his voice as he turned back to Mortimer. "Sorry to have taken up your time." Then he frog-marched me out of there, slowing down to leave his card on the little table in the hall—lucky Mortimer didn't come to see us out, or I reckoned we'd be leaving in a shower of confetti—and then hustling me back to the car.

I pulled on the seat belt and rubbed my arm where he'd held it. "I can take a hint, you know. You didn't have to pull my arm out of the bloody socket."

"Stop whinging. I hardly touched you." Phil put the car in gear and whacked up the air-con to combat the greenhouse effect. "And nobody needed you going all vigilante back there."

"He'd better not be getting violent with her or the kiddies," I said grimly.

"They'll be fine. *We* were the problem there, not them. That poor bastard's on the knife edge of a nervous breakdown, not domestic violence."

"What, so suddenly you're the bloody expert?"

"Six years a copper, remember? I've seen my fair share of wife beaters." Phil stared straight ahead as he pulled out onto the main road, his jaw set. "The real sort, the ones you have to worry about, it's not about violence, not for its own sake. It's about control—where she goes, who she talks to, what she bloody wears, for Christ's sake. That poor bastard's barely in control of himself, let alone anyone else."

"Yeah, well, I bow to your superior experience and all that bollocks, but Mortimer looked pretty desperate to me. Desperate men do desperate stuff. Stuff they wouldn't normally."

"Trust me. He's not a danger to his family. He's more worried about everyone else being a danger to them."

I wasn't convinced, but I let it slide. "Yeah, well, anyway. We still wasted an afternoon there with nothing to show for it."

Phil shrugged. "Wouldn't be too sure about that."

"No? You got nothing, *I* got nothing, and we didn't even get to drink our tea. Don't mean to be a party pooper, but it strikes me we got bugger all out of that."

"Wait and see, wait and see."

Just as I was about to open my mouth and ask what the smug git thought he was waiting for, his phone rang. Phil drove one-handed and pulled it out of his pocket. "Phil Morrison."

Seeing as he probably didn't need anything else distracting him from the road right now, I restrained myself from pointing out it was illegal to drive and phone.

"Yes, that's right." Pause. "Uh, no. That's my partner. Tom Paretski." He handed me the phone. "Sarah Mortimer. She wants to talk to you."

Me? I gave him a startled look but took the phone. At least this way we were less likely to have an accident and/or get stopped by the police. "Hello?"

"Mr. Paretski?" Her voice was low and anxious.

"Call me Tom. What can I do for you, love?"

"I want to talk to you."

"Yeah? No problem."

"Can we meet?" She sounded breathy, like she was looking over her shoulder all the time. "Not . . . not now. Tomorrow. After school. I can tell Alan I'm taking the children to the swings again."

"Yeah, no problem. We'll be there." I'd actually been thinking about ringing a customer or two and saying I'd be able to do the work after all, but I reckoned she'd bolt if I didn't make it easy for her.

"Can it be just you?"

"Er . . . Phil's really the senior partner." I meant in the detective business. Obviously. And he'd better not get any funny ideas about it carrying over into our love life.

"Please?"

Shit. "Just a minute, love." I covered the bit you speak into and stage-whispered at Phil, "She wants to meet with just me."

He rolled his eyes. "So? Say yes, for God's sake."

I uncovered the phone. "Mrs. M.? Yeah, that's fine. No problem. So where are these swings, then?"

She gave me the where and when, and we hung up.

I looked up at Phil to find him grinning like the cat who'd just mounted a hostile takeover of United Dairies. And got them to throw in a catnip plantation for free. "What did I tell you?" he said, still smirking. "Still reckon we wasted our time?"

"Eff off," I said, glaring at him. "For all you know, she just fancies the pants off me. You'll be sorry when she uses her evil feminine wiles on my latent hetero tendencies and persuades me to run off with her and the kiddies."

"If I worried about that every time you worked your charm on a woman, I'd be a bloody nervous wreck. Besides, she's not your type."

I laughed, startled. "What, so I've got a *type* in women, have I? Go on, then. Let's hear it."

Phil tapped his nose. "That'd be telling. But she's not it."

I tried to get him to talk, but he wouldn't budge. In the end, I gave up—my head was a bit too fragile right now to go on banging it against the brick wall formerly known as Phil Morrison. "So how are we playing this tomorrow? You coming along too in case Mrs. M. changes her mind?"

"You mean, in case she wants to speak to the organ grinder, and not the monkey?"

"Oi, watch it or I'll be doing a bit of organ grinding myself."

"Promises, promises. No, you can go and hold Sarah Mortimer's hand on your own. You might want to wear something better, though. Make it look like you've made an effort."

"Want me to take her flowers and all? Seeing as this is apparently a date."

Phil gave me a look, but before I could work out what it meant, it was gone, and he was eyes front on the road ahead as we reached the junction for the M25.

When we got off the motorway and were back in St. Albans, I found myself looking at women on the street, trying to work out what Phil had meant by my *type*. Did he mean, like, a physical type? Or was it supposed to be a personality thing? And what had made him say that, anyway? Did he think I'd been getting too friendly with someone of the female persuasion lately? Who?

Then I reminded myself he'd been talking out of his arse, and went back to checking out the blokes like I usually did.

It's all right as long as you look and don't touch.

Funny how getting hit on the head can take it out of you. By the time we got back to my place, I was ready to drop. And not to give anybody twenty. "Coming in?" I said, admittedly a bit flatly, as I unbuckled my seat belt.

"Try not to kill me with all that enthusiasm." Phil leaned over and took hold of my chin. "You all right?"

"Yeah. Just tired. If you want dinner, you're cooking it."

"No worries. We'll get a takeaway. Pizza okay?"

Pizza sounded bloody marvellous. "Yeah."

"Come on. Let's get you inside."

I just about managed to keep my eyes open long enough to scarf down my half of an extra-large meat feast—Gary would have been all over the innuendo like lube on a condom—and slump on the sofa. Phil switched on the telly to watch the Grand Prix qualifying, and I snuggled in close.

Sometime later, I woke up to some bastard shaking my shoulder. "Buggroff," I muttered.

"Come on, Sleeping Beauty," Phil's voice rumbled in my ear. "You'll sleep better out of those jeans and in a proper bed."

"Any 'scuse . . ." I yawned and let him ease me upright. The room was oddly quiet, and I realised after a mo it was because the soothing *neeeow* sounds of souped-up cars going round in big circles had all stopped. "T'get m'pants off."

"Not that it's going to be worth my while tonight," Phil said in that warm tone he only uses when it's just me and him. "I'd get more action out of a week-old corpse."

"'S a word for that." I blinked at the oncoming doorway. Somehow Phil managed to manoeuvre us both through without taking the frame with us, and then we were on the stairs, his arm wrapped firmly around my waist as I dragged my leaden feet up each step. "Gonna read me a story?"

"Once upon a time, there was a handsome plumber," Phil started. "Mind your head on that doorway. Right. Where was I?"

I flopped down on the bed. I meant just to sit on the edge, but somehow I kept going until I was lying on the bed with my feet dangling off the end. I smiled up at Phil. "Handsome plumber," I told him. "Is he about to get a prick?"

"He wishes." Phil huffed a laugh and undid my jeans. "Shift your bum."

I shifted, and he pulled them off. "S'what happens?" I asked, and yawned again.

"He got into bed properly," Phil said and somehow managed to get me under the duvet and with my head on the pillow. "And went to sleep for eight hours solid."

"What, still no prick?"

"You've got pricks on the brain, you have." He bent over and kissed me softly.

I was about to say I could think of much better places to put pricks, but before I could get my mouth around the words—or anything else, for that matter—I fell asleep.

CHAPTER ELEVEN

I woke up feeling better than I had in weeks. Phil hadn't stayed—I suppose he'd thought I'd sleep better without him hogging the pillows and acting like an electric blanket. It was a bit of a shame, seeing as I was feeling so frisky. I had to content myself with an active imagination and an energetic shower.

I'd been advised by all and sundry to ease myself back to work after the head injury, so I only had a couple of jobs still booked in Friday morning—new tap down the road from me in Fleetville, and fixing a loo in Sandridge. The new tap was a bit of a faff—the old one was cemented in with a mountain of limescale I'd swear was older than the house itself—but I got the loo done in a jiffy. It felt good to be back into the swing of things, and I was whistling as I got back into the van.

Seeing as how Sandridge was only a couple of miles from Brock's Hollow, and I'd be spending the afternoon in Ealing with Mrs. M. anyway, I thought I might as well swing by the Dyke for a quick drink to wash down my cheese sarnie with. Reassure Harry I was still alive, that sort of thing.

And all right, maybe to see if Carey might turn up like the bad penny he was, and ask him what he'd been up to Monday evening when I was getting my head bashed in. Not that I reckoned I'd get a straight answer, but then again, his sort might not be able to resist the temptation to gloat. At any rate, if he was up there making a nuisance of himself, I could give Marianne and Harry a bit of moral support.

Turned out there was someone else giving Marianne grief when I walked into the pub. This bloke was a thug, no two ways about it. Belligerent snarl, shaven head, knuckles down by his knees, the works.

He was leaning on the bar, but not in a relaxed, God-I-need-a-pint sort of way. More in a looming-threateningly-over-the-barmaid sort of way.

Was this who Harry had been talking about Monday night, before my little trip to A&E? From what I could remember of her description of the man hanging around, this bloke fit the bill pretty well. The Devil's Dyke herself was eyeing him from the other end of the bar with not a lot of gruntlement in her gaze, but not interfering, which wasn't like her. Had Carey sent Rent-a-yob along to stir up trouble? I ambled over, figuring if he picked a fight with me instead of Harry, at least she wouldn't lose her licence over it. And I'd probably survive it.

Probably. I ignored the prickling on the back of my neck caused by wondering just where he'd been when I'd been getting my little object lesson in the finer arts of cricket.

"All right, Marianne?" I asked breezily, interrupting their conversation with nary a qualm of conscience. This bloke didn't seem to be the sort you'd waste manners on.

"All right, Tom," she said, trying to smile. "You all mended now?"

"Yeah, I'm fine. Well, it was my head I got bashed in, wasn't it? Not like I keep anything important up there."

Marianne laughed nervously, glancing up at the thug. Now I came to think of it, the bloke was giving me a very funny look. "This a mate of yours?" I asked her, making sure I kept one eye on him in case he didn't like her answer.

"It's just Kev. He's my brother, see? Kev, Tom's a friend. He's one of our regulars here."

Blimey. I stared at "Kev" and held out a hand before I could stop myself. It was hard to believe him and sweet little Marianne were the same species, let alone brother and sister. Kev was giving me the same sort of startled once-over I was giving him, though I wasn't sure what his excuse was. He didn't shake my hand, so at least I got out of that one with all fingers intact—good news for my income stream, seeing as it's a bit hard to do a manual job well when you're lacking one of the essentials. "Just over from Somerset, are you?"

He grunted, still eyeing me like I was the sort of bloke his mother had warned him a farm boy had to watch out for when he left the safety of the shires.

"Staying at the pub?" I went on.

Kev snorted, cast a glare in Harry's direction, and said something under his breath. It definitely had the word "dyke" in there somewhere, but whether he was referring to the pub or the landlady was anyone's guess.

"*Kev*," Marianne said urgently, managing to sound hurt, reproving, and a bit scared all in one syllable. Apparently she was better at speaking gorilla than I was.

He turned his back on me in favour of looming over her a bit more. "It's time you come 'ome," he said, a lot more clearly this time. "Dad's not 'appy, he ain't."

Marianne responded with a pointed phrase I was a bit taken aback to hear coming from her pastel-pink lips—especially about her old man. Kev wasn't looking any too *'appy* about it either. "You wash your mouth out. You don't talk about Dad like that, see?" If he loomed any farther, he was going to topple over the bar.

Or just topple the bar. One of the two.

Marianne stood her ground like a My Little Pony squaring up to the hordes of Genghis Khan. "After what he called me? I'll say what I like about 'im, and don't you go telling me I can't."

Unbelievably, the hordes backed off a bit. "You can't stay 'ere. It's not right."

"What, 'cos he's got to do his own cooking and cleaning now *that woman's* left?"

"You never used to mind doing your bit before Deborah come along. It's living in that there London. It's changed you, it has. And it ain't just about Dad needin' you. You gotta know what kind of place this is."

"It's a pub, Kev. And I ought to be working." She turned to me with a pointed air. "What're you having, Tom?"

"Just a Diet Coke, cheers, love, when you've got a mo."

She got out a glass and was about to start pouring my drink, when Kev leaned forward and grabbed her arm. "It's one of them there queer places," he growled.

"So what if it is?" she snapped back. "Maybe I'm queer, you ever thought of that?"

His grip tightened visibly. The dark looks he'd been sending me took on a new significance, although I was a bit surprised a bloke like this had any sort of functioning gaydar. Or brain, come to that. "You was normal before you left 'ome. 'Ad a bloke and everything. Is it her?" He jerked his head in Harry's direction. "She turned you queer?"

His tone implied that if he had his way, she'd shortly be regretting it. Marianne tried to twist out of his grasp. "You leave Harry out of this. Let go of me!"

"Oi," I butted in, just as Harry started to advance. "Hands off the young lady, all right? I don't care if she is your sister, there's no need to get physical."

He let go of Marianne all right, and turned to loom over me instead. "You can fuck off out of it."

"Right, that's it." Harry's voice cut through the atmosphere like a machete. "You? You're barred. I want you out that door now, or I'm calling the police, you got that?"

Kev's face turned even uglier as he glared at her. I was pleased to note the scrape of chairs as a couple of other patrons put down their drinks and stood up—at least, I assumed they were offering support, rather than preparing to leg it or looking forward to getting into a bar fight. "Think I want to hang around here with your sort? There ought to be a law against what you done."

Harry held up her phone. "You leaving, or am I dialling?"

Kev glowered at her, grunted something in the language of his people, and left.

"You all right, love?" I asked Marianne. She looked a bit pale and trembly now he'd gone.

Harry gave her a hug. "Go make yourself a cup of tea, and sit in the kitchen and drink it."

"No, I'm fine, really I am," Marianne protested, but she was already on her way out, Harry steering her firmly with a hefty arm around her bony little shoulders.

"What's the brother's story?" I asked Harry when she reappeared.

Harry *humph*ed. "Him? Don't reckon he's got the brains for a story. Lives on the dole, sponges off his dad, and spends half his life drinking the local Wetherspoons dry and the other half at the bookie's. Tried to make a go of it as a burglar, but ended up spending more time in the nick than in other people's houses. I told her not to tell 'em her address, but did she listen? Said she was worried something might happen to her dad, and she wouldn't know."

I winced at the venom in Harry's voice when she mentioned the pub chain. She wasn't exactly a fan of what she liked to call *money-grabbing bastards buying up our heritage*. Luckily for my eardrums, she was too worked up about Marianne's woes to spare a thought for the homogenisation of British watering holes right now.

"What's he doing around here, then? Long way to come just to give Marianne grief."

"Way I hear it, that's the main occupation of Drinkwater men—giving the women grief. They had Marianne's mum six feet under before she was fifty, and her dad's bit on the side moved in the day after the funeral." Harry snorted a laugh. "Sounds like she didn't last long. You heard what that waste of space said—they just want Marianne back so she can cook and clean for their lazy arses."

I frowned. "He mentioned Carey too—sort of. You don't reckon they're, well, chumming up together, do you? I mean, Kev seemed to like the idea of her having a bloke."

"Him and Carey? There's a match made in hell. Bastards like that think any man's better than two women together—unless it's in a bloody porno." Christ. Anyone who thought she was better off with Carey than with Harry needed a serious overhaul of their priorities. I hoped Harry had a decent first-aider on staff. If she clenched her fist any harder around that pint glass she was polishing, we'd be finding out pretty quick if there was any truth in the rumour she bled neat malt whiskey.

"Have you said anything about him to Phil?" I asked, thinking getting back on topic might be a good idea in more ways than one.

She frowned at me. "Thought you'd have done that."

"Got a bit distracted, didn't I?" I rubbed my head. Uncharacteristically, Harry ducked hers, like she was embarrassed or something. "I'll tell him tonight."

We hadn't *said* we'd be meeting up, but I reckoned he'd be pretty keen to find out what Mrs. M. had had to tell me. If anything. Speaking of which, I needed to get going, or I'd risk being late to meet her. Shame about the drink, but I couldn't count on the M25 not having a snarl-up right at the wrong moment. "Right, I'm going to have to love you and leave you. But listen, don't let that Kev give you any more grief, all right?"

Harry just nodded. And cracked her knuckles.

I nipped home to change before I headed off to Ealing. *Not* because of what Phil had said, all right? It was on the way, more or less, and steel toe caps are not exactly ideal summer footwear. While I was there, I put on a clean shirt as well, and some lightweight summer trousers Gary had persuaded me to buy last time I'd made the mistake of letting him drag me round the shops. I felt like some posh nob on his way to a Buckingham Palace garden party, but seeing as I also felt a lot cooler, I reckoned I could learn to live with it.

The traffic on the M25 wasn't too bad in the end. Apparently all sensible people were soaking up the sun in their back gardens rather than driving around London in a hot little metal box with no air-con. It was a relief to arrive in Ealing—at least the air outside the car ought to be marginally fresher.

The swings Mrs. M. had asked me to meet her at were in a small, closed-off area that was on the edge of a much larger, leafier park, bordered by areas of well-grown trees and bushes. I couldn't help thinking you'd be spoilt for choice for where to hide a body, and clamped down hard on my spidey-senses in case I found something I'd rather not. The kiddies' area, though, was bright and open—in fact it was a bit more exposed than I'd have expected Mrs. M. to go for, but then again, it was only a hop, skip, and a jump away from her kids' school.

And she'd have a better idea than I would as to whether him indoors was likely to come wandering along.

I parked the Fiesta under a chestnut tree down a side street and strolled over there. I was a bit early, so I sat down on one of the benches bordering the area and faffed about with my phone, trying not to look like some kind of pervert eyeing up the tots. There were only a handful of them, and soon after I'd got there, the last of them disappeared. Either they were being dragged off to pick up older brothers and sisters from school, or I looked more sinister than I thought.

One thing this playground could definitely have done with was a bit of shade. It was blistering hot out here in the sun, and the trees had been pruned back to well beyond the chain-link fence enclosing the play area. All they did was cut off entirely the feeble breeze that had cooled me down a fraction of a degree as I walked here.

I didn't have to be a deductive genius to work out when school ended. The noise levels coming from the primary school rose by a factor of about a thousand as the kiddies were let out of their stuffy classrooms and into the playground. It was around three minutes after that when the first of the mums trundled their buggies into the play area. They came in twos and threes, most of them, but Mrs. M. was on her own when she appeared. Well, apart from little George and Julia, of course, but they scarpered to the climbing frame the minute they got in the gate without even a backward glance for their poor old mum.

She gave a tight, relieved smile and a wave when she spotted me, and made her way over to my bench. "Thank you for coming. I don't know what I'd have . . . Anyway, thank you." Despite the obvious nerves, the whole impression she gave was fresher and prettier today, dressed in a floaty summer skirt and top that had to be in a whole different price range to the loose cropped trousers and vest tops sported by the other mums. It looked like she hadn't got around to downsizing her wardrobe yet. She'd done something with her hair too—it curved around her face instead of just hanging there.

"Good to see you. Kiddies all right on their own for a mo?"

"Oh, they'll be fine," she said. They ought to be—the playground was one of those with rubber flooring around the play equipment. God knew how George had managed to hurt his knee so badly yesterday. Maybe he'd hit the rubber bit and bounced onto the tarmac beyond.

I patted the bench next to me, and Mrs. M. sat down, smoothing her skirt so it wouldn't crease. Unless it was to draw my attention to the shape of her bum—but no, despite what I'd said to Phil, I couldn't really see her as being after a bit of the old extramaritals. She seemed the sort to stick with her man no matter how far he dragged her down.

I wasn't really sure why I felt so sorry for her, especially if old Alan had had his fingers in as many dodgy pies as Marianne reckoned. Yeah, the family had had a knock, but they weren't exactly living on the bread line. Mr. M. was even out of jail now. On paper, they should be celebrating. But I got the impression it was a long time since Mrs. M. had felt like cracking open a bottle of bubbly.

She'd fallen silent and was fiddling with the strap of her leather handbag. I drew in a breath to ask her what she wanted to talk to me about, but she beat me to it.

"Mr. Paretski, I—"

"Oi," I interrupted without thinking. "I told you to call me Tom, remember?"

That got me half a smile and an almost teasing suggestion of "I suppose Mr. Paretski's your father?"

Ouch. Mrs. M.'s face fell, and I guessed I must have winced visibly. "Er, yeah. Bit of a sore point that, these days."

Her hand flew to her mouth. "Oh God, I'm so sorry."

"Nah, nothing like that," I was quick to reassure her. "Fit as a fiddle, he is. Just, er . . ." I trailed off, realising we'd got seriously off track here, and gave her a wonky smile. "I'd tell you, but it's probably more information than you actually want. So what was it you wanted to—"

"I think my husband's being blackmailed," she blurted out. That handbag strap was going to be showing serious signs of wear and tear soon, the way she was twisting it in her fingers, decent bit of leather or no. "I think it's the man who framed him—he was innocent, you know that, don't you? He should never have gone to prison. Alan's never broken the law in his life."

That wasn't what I'd heard, but I let it slide. "This blackmailer—you know who he is?"

"Carey. Grant Carey. I never liked him." She stared out over the playground. Julia was on the climbing frame, but I couldn't see George at all. Still, at least he wasn't standing on the swings again.

"You met him, then?" I encouraged.

"Once or twice. Socially, you know. He had this girlfriend who was far too young for him—little blonde airhead, all legs and pumped-up breasts." Her lip curled in distaste.

I frowned. "Marianne?"

Mrs. M. nodded, still staring at the kiddies. "That was the name. A real *oo-arr* country-bumpkin type. From Somerset, I think."

All right, so I wasn't feeling quite so sorry for Mrs. M. right now. "Why do you think he's blackmailing your husband? Shouldn't it be the other way around? I mean, not that your husband would blackmail anyone," I added hastily as she gave me a sharp look. "I just mean, if he's managed to prove he didn't do the crime he went away for, maybe he's in a position to get Carey into trouble? Get him done for the frame-up?"

Mrs. M. bit her lip. "Alan won't tell me anything. But I think . . . I think Carey must have threatened to hurt me or the children." Her hands were clenched hard on her handbag strap, the knuckles white and trembling a bit. "I daren't let them out of my sight. If he comes *near* them . . ." She looked up, her eyes boring into me. "I'll kill him. I'll kill him for what he's done to us. Don't you understand? We were happy until this happened. Life was perfect. We had a lovely house, and holidays, and friends . . . I don't know anyone here. Everything's so different. Half the children in the school live in council houses, and they speak umpteen different languages. Punjabi, Somali, Polish . . ." She went a bit pink. "Not that I'm racist. Please don't think that. But it can't be good for their education."

I wasn't sure what to say to that. I mean, I could have reassured her I wasn't actually Polish, but that wasn't really the point. At least, not in my book, it wasn't. "Ah, kids manage better than you think. But what makes you think he's made these threats? Did you, I dunno, see them talking? Answer the phone to him?"

She nodded. "He came to our house soon after Alan was released. Brought me flowers—a housewarming gift, he said. And a bottle of champagne, to *celebrate*. We had to drink it with him." Her tone was bitter. Anyone listening in would probably wonder what she was complaining about, but having met the creep myself, I could sympathise. "Alan told me to put the children to bed early, and when I came downstairs again, that horrible man was gone, and Alan was sitting at the kitchen table with his head in his hands."

"Did you ask him about it?"

"I . . . I didn't like to. Alan's been so . . . You have to understand, prison was a terrible ordeal for him. People like us don't belong in there. He's found it so hard to get over it all. He still *is* finding it hard."

I ignored the *people like us* bit, and tried to put the next question delicately. "Did, um, anything really bad happen to him inside?"

"Well, of course, the whole experience was terrible for him," she said heatedly, like she thought I hadn't been listening properly.

Maybe I'd overdone the delicacy. "I meant, well, was he victimised in any way?"

Instead of answering, she stood up and called out to her daughter. "Julia! Let the other little girl have a turn on the swing. Come on. Now, or we're going home."

Julia got sulkily off the swing, and Mrs. M. sat down again. "I'm not sure how much more I can tell you," she said, her voice a bit shaky. "But you have to do something about Grant Carey. Alan said you wanted to get him put in prison—you do, don't you?"

I tried to look confident. "Yeah, that's right."

"Good. But you can't involve Alan." She reached out, took my hand between hers and gazed at me intently with eyes that seemed a lot bluer than they had yesterday. "You have to understand that. You can't involve him at all."

So that was a . . . Well, I wasn't sure what it was, to be honest. I racked my brains on the drive home, but I couldn't see how any of what Mrs. M. had said was going to help us. I mean, we already knew Carey was a dangerous little shit.

I got back to my house, kicked off my shoes in the hall, and wandered into the living room.

And got the fright of my life.

Carey was sitting on my sofa. Stroking my cat.

CHAPTER TWELVE

For one crazy moment, I thought he was going to open with "So, Mr. Paretski, we meet again. *Mwha-ha-ha-ha.*"

I stared at him for a long, long moment. "What the bloody hell—"

He smiled, a slightly rueful, lopsided effort that made his face look open and boyish, and I had to remind myself he was nothing of the sort. "Hope you don't mind. It was your neighbour who let me in—Sharon from number twelve. She saw I was waiting for you, and invited me in for a cup of tea, but then she had to go out. She *insisted* you wouldn't mind her using her spare key so I wouldn't have to wait around in the hot sun. Such a kind lady."

I was going to have to have words with Sharon. That key was supposed to be for emergencies, like feeding the cats when I was away or, as it might be, letting in the cavalry when I was being menaced by criminals who'd gone off their rocker. Not letting in said criminals and giving them the freedom of my bloody sofa.

"What do you want?" I snapped.

Arthur cracked open an eyelid and flicked his tail at me reproachfully from his position on Carey's lap.

"I think maybe we got off on the wrong foot?" Carey made a sort of oops-face. "I'm afraid I do have a tendency to get a teeny bit defensive around people like your boyfriend. Oh, don't get me wrong, I'm sure he's very good to you, but, well." He sighed. "I haven't had the best of experiences with people like that."

I wasn't sure what he was implying, but I was fairly certain I didn't like it. "People like what?"

"Oh, you know." Carey gave a sheepish little shrug. "Sometimes I think strength is all they understand, and, well, fake it until you make it, as they say. Still got the odd scar from bullies at school—psychologically, I mean. Well, most of them," he added, seeming embarrassed to admit it. Then he rolled his eyes. "I know what you're thinking, get *over* it already, but when you're faced with someone so much more physically intimidating, some habits are hard to break, aren't they?"

"Right," I said, thrown. He was being so . . . human, I s'pose. He even looked different today to my mental picture of evil-guy-in-a-suit—he was all casual in jeans and a T-shirt, his hair was rumpled like he'd just got out of bed, and he hadn't shaved. He was making me feel seriously overdressed. You'd be amazed how often that *doesn't* happen to me. Well. Maybe you wouldn't. "So what do you actually want?"

He ran a hand through his hair, ruffling it up even more. "God, it sounds so stupid. I just—I've been feeling really bad about some of the things I said. I babble on *insanely* when I'm nervous. I just wanted to say, well, I'm sorry. That's all." He made a face. "God, I'm sure you don't even *care*. I'm an idiot. I'll get out of your hair, now."

He stood up, even apologising to Arthur before gently encouraging him off his lap and onto the sofa.

"I just miss Marianne so much," he said, like he couldn't help it. "She was always . . ." He ducked his head and laughed under his breath, then glanced up again with a twisted smile. "*My moral compass* sounds so grandiose, doesn't it? But she was always so good at counteracting the cynic in me. Encouraging me to believe they're not all out to get me, and defence doesn't have to mean *off*ence. I miss that. I miss *her*. I know you're a friend of hers. She looks up to you." He held up a hand as I started to say *Oi, is this going where I think it is?* "I'm not asking you to help me get her back or anything like that. Just . . . It would be nice to think not *everyone* around her was an antagonist. You know?"

He flashed me another rueful, boyish smile and left. I stood there for a moment, then sank onto the sofa. It was still warm where he'd been sitting. Arthur gave me a snotty look, like I was a poor substitute for his new best friend, but grudgingly allowed me to stroke him.

That little visit had seriously done my head in. Carey had seemed so genuine. Was it possible we'd got him wrong?

No doubt about it, I knew where he was coming from. It's not always easy being a physically small bloke in a male-dominated line of business. Let alone a gay bloke—and yeah, Carey might not be gay, but you could bet your life a lot of blokes of the so-called macho variety would assume he *was*. He had that manner about him—something about the voice and his fussy little gestures.

I'd had to endure a fair few jokes at my expense when I'd started out in the plumbing trade—stuff like *Are you sure that wrench isn't too heavy for you?* and *You want to get a* man *to help you with that, love.* Even customers, sometimes, when I was wrestling with a total bastard of a tap that didn't want to break free from decades' worth of limescale, would stand there watching me for a while, then suggest helpfully that maybe I knew someone with a bit more muscle who might be able to get it done.

God knows what it's like for women. I've never actually met a female plumber, but ever since doing an internet search in an idle moment and finding there's a group of 'em called *Stopcocks*, I've decided it's probably safer that way.

So, yeah, I could get why he might think he had to come out with all guns blazing when someone like Phil seemed to threaten him. Because, yeah, it's okay for big blokes like Phil to make a whole song and dance about fighting fair, but if the other guy's a foot taller and a few stone heavier, what's fair about that? It's not just about thinking the other guy's going to deck you either. It's about respect. Because when the macho posturing starts in earnest, your average short bloke doesn't get a right lot of that.

Like we were all a bunch of bloody cavemen beating our chests and competing to drag off the best-looking lovers by the hair.

I still did a sweep of the house with my spidey-senses, mind. Not a thing.

Well, unless you counted the freshly dead mouse under the fridge that would've stunk the place out in a day or so. I gave Merlin a stern look as I carried the sad little corpse off for flushing. He tried to stare me out, but I had him bang to rights.

There had been some well guilty vibes coming off that mouse.

CHAPTER THIRTEEN

"**S**o basically it was an epic waste of time," I said, and took another swig of my beer. Phil was round at my house by then, and we were sitting at opposite ends of the sofa. I had a fat cat on my lap and my feet up on the coffee table.

I'd taken my shoes off, obviously. I'm not a slob. Actually, I'd got changed too. Didn't feel right, lounging round the house in a smart pair of trousers. I'd have been constantly worrying about spilling something down them. It was after dinner—ham salad, since you ask. I'd got some proper thick-sliced ham in from the organic butcher's in Brock's Hollow—cost me an arm and a leg, but seeing as the pig was a lot worse off, I couldn't grumble. Tasted bloody good with the Spiced Carrot and Pumpkin Chutney they'd flogged me on the side, although I'd had to bully Phil into trying it. And then wrestle the jar back from him before he scoffed the lot.

Fun times. Good thing we didn't have to worry about the food going cold.

"Worth a try." Phil smirked at me from the other end of the sofa. "Told you she fancied you, though."

I'd been giving him a rundown of my little tryst with Mrs. M. I hadn't mentioned Carey's visit yet, and wasn't exactly in a hurry to. Phil was only going to get all uptight about it and, well, it wasn't like he'd threatened me or anything. Total opposite, in fact.

I wasn't sure what it meant about who was responsible for my little tap on the head earlier in the week either. If you'd asked me before today, I'd have had Carey as odds-on favourite, but now I wasn't so sure. I mean, yeah, maybe he liked to mess with people's heads, but was he really the sort to bash them in with a cricket ball? Marianne's thug of a brother, on the other hand, I wouldn't trust any farther than I could throw him.

"Yeah, well, it isn't mutual." I frowned. "Still feel sorry for her, mind." Although less so, since talking to Carey. And her little dig about Marianne.

Phil gave me an assessing look. "When she met you in the park, how was she dressed? Put on a frock, did she? Bit of makeup?"

I frowned. "Skirt and top, actually, whatever the bloody hell *that's* got to do with anything."

He huffed a cynical laugh. "Thought so. Want to know what your type of woman is? *That's* your type. Pretty and girly and innocent, so you can put them up on a pedestal and come riding in to save them like Sir Prancelot on your bloody white charger."

I stared at him. "I'm gay, you twat! I'm not into"—*twat*, my mind supplied helpfully—"women like that."

"Never said you wanted to get them *off* the pedestal, did I?"

"Yeah, well, whatever. Met someone else today you might be interested in. Well, interested in avoiding at any rate. Marianne's big brother, Kev. He was making a nuisance of himself in the Dyke at lunchtime, trying to talk her into going back out west and leaving all the queers behind her."

Phil gave me a look. "Has he *seen* the number of gay bars in Bristol?"

"Yeah, well, I don't think logic is his strong point. Anyway, he definitely gave me the impression he'd be happy to see her back with a bloke—you know, in a *normal* relationship—so watch out for him and Carey chumming up."

Phil huffed dismissively. "If he's built like his sister, I don't think I'll need to worry too much."

"He's built like around ten of his sister. Arms like a gorilla and a brain to match, so watch out, yeah? About your height, shaved head—all the better to nut you with—and a snarl. You can't miss him. He's too bloody broad in the shoulder. Spent some time inside too. Housebreaking. Probably just head-butted his way in."

"I'll look out for him." Phil pursed his lips thoughtfully. "So you think he knows Carey?"

"Well . . . he never actually *said* so. Just that he was happier when she had a bloke. Then there was all this stuff about how their dad needed looking after, 'cos it wasn't right him having to do his own cooking, what with him being a bloke and all. Although if he's been trying to cook with his dick, I can sort of see why he's having trouble. Harry chucked him out," I added. "So I guess we'll find out if he's with Carey. You know, if that comes back to bite her on the bum."

"Thanks for the mental image," Phil said drily.

I grinned. "You're welcome." I hesitated, but I guessed I'd have to tell him about Carey's visit. I mean, I'd be pretty pissed off if I found out Phil was keeping secrets from me. "Um. Look, don't get all in a flap about it, but Carey was here earlier."

Phil's face went granite-hard. "Here. In your house."

"Yeah, he—"

"You let *Grant Carey* in your bloody house? Jesus, didn't you learn *anything* from having your sister's poisoner round here?"

"Oi! I didn't let him in, all right? Sharon at number twelve did. I was out."

"Christ, you want to tell me what's the sodding use of locking your door if you're going to give spare keys to the whole bloody neighbourhood?"

"It's not the whole bloody neighbourhood. It's just Sharon. And anyway, you had Carey round yours too," I reminded him pointedly.

Phil huffed a heavy sigh. "Please tell me you at least made a sweep afterwards for any little presents he might have left you."

"Course I did. I'm not daft. And nope, no nasty surprises there. Although I had to have a few words with the cats about the dead mouse under the fridge."

"Lovely. So what did Carey want, anyhow?" Phil's eyes went even sharper. "Did he threaten you?"

"No, nothing like that. Dunno what he came for, really. Just to give his side of the story, I s'pose."

Phil laughed. "What, that he's just misunderstood and 'stalking' is such a strong word? Manage to keep a straight face, did you?"

"Yeah, just about. He didn't stay long, anyway. You have any better luck with stuff today?" Which was my way of (a) changing the subject and (b) asking what he'd been up to while I'd been running all over the place working his case for him.

"Wrapped up the infidelity case."

"Yeah? Guilty or not guilty?"

"Not guilty, far as I could tell."

"Yeah? Satisfied client, then?"

Phil grunted. "He wasn't exactly cracking open the champagne. Didn't argue the bill, though, at any rate."

"You'd think he'd be happy the missus wasn't putting it about."

"Not always that simple, is it?" Phil took a long swig of beer. "When a marriage goes sour, sometimes it's easier if there's an excuse. If she'd been having an affair, he could have blamed her for it all. Now he's got to face facts. She hasn't fallen in love with someone else—just fallen out of love with him." He stared out of the window.

I wondered if we were still talking about Mr. and Mrs. C., or if a bit of Phil's short-lived civil partnership with the Mysterious Mark had crept in there when I wasn't looking.

"'Nother beer?" I asked, scooping armfuls of Arthur off my lap and pouring them onto the cushion next to me. I managed to escape major bloodshed in the process, so clearly he was feeling pretty lazy too. I stood up and stretched.

Phil snapped out of whatever bittersweet memories he'd got lost in, and turned back to me. "Wouldn't say no."

It wasn't the only thing he didn't say no to that evening either.

Sod's law, I had an early job next morning—Mrs. Z. just down the road from me who worked all week and wanted the new washer plumbed in before she had to take the twins to football—so I didn't get to reap the benefits of having Phil in my bed when I woke up. It's a bugger, this having-to-make-a-living lark. I left him with instructions to meet me up the Dyke for lunch. Well, all right, the Dyke had been his idea, seeing as he wanted to fill Harry in on developments anyway.

I'd have made a few innuendos about *filling people in* at that point, but it was too bloody early for sparkling repartee.

Mrs. Z. was petite and pretty in her colourful headscarf, her big brown eyes outlined with enough kohl to keep a power station burning for a week. She looked far too young to be the mother of two strapping ten-year-olds who were already as tall as she was. Let alone financial director of a local company.

She raised a perfectly shaped eyebrow when I told her that. "Am I paying extra for the flattery, or is it all part of the service?"

"'Flattery'?" I winked at her from under the kitchen worktop. "Don't know the meaning of the word. Just telling the truth as I see it, that's all."

"Sara warned me about you." She sounded amused. "Can I get you a cup of tea?"

Sara, I guessed, was her neighbour, Mrs. P., who I'd done some work for in the past. Nice to get a recommendation, 'specially when it's someone local. "Number seven? Lovely lady, she is. Tea'd be great, love. White, no sugar, ta."

"Sara also said could I ask you to pop next door when you've finished here, if you've got a moment. I think she wanted a quote for a new kitchen sink." Mrs. Z. gave me a knowing smile as she handed me a mug. The tea inside was just the right colour.

"Cheers, love." I took a sip. "Ah, that hits the spot. Right, how much of a hurry are you in? 'Cause your stand pipe's clogged up something chronic. No point me hooking up the new machine before it's cleaned out, or you're just going to end up with water all over the floor again."

Mrs. Z. muttered something I didn't catch, which was probably just as well. "That husband of mine! He *swore* it was the machine, not the pipe."

"Men, eh?" I said. "Can't live with 'em, can't flog 'em on eBay. Right, I'll be quick as I can."

It took a while, getting rid of the mess of soap scum, limescale, and fluff that had gummed up the stand pipe, and by the time I'd finished, the lads were bouncing off the walls while Mum hissed down her phone at their dad in angry Farsi.

"All done, love," I said, scribbling down an invoice. "Shouldn't be a problem now, but maybe run it empty on a hot wash every now and then, yeah? It'll help clear the pipes."

"Thank you. You're a lifesaver. Goodness knows what I'd have done with no washing machine, what with these two. And at least *you* don't cost me the earth." She said something vicious down the phone, then hung up and smiled at me again. "Don't forget to call on Sara."

I grinned. "Me, let a lady down? Never."

I had a couple of other jobs after that—well, another one was just doing a quote, but I still had to drive there, and it was right out in the old part of Hatfield—so I was a bit late getting to the Dyke for lunch. Phil had already got the first round in by the time I got there, and had bagged a shady table outside in the beer garden. I sat down and took a grateful swallow of cool beer. "Cheers, mate. Have you ordered the food yet?"

"Didn't know what you'd want."

"This weather? Salad. With a side order of salad. Well, maybe make it a ploughman's. Same for you?"

He nodded. "Ham, not cheese."

"Wouldn't want all those muscles to waste away from a lack of red meat. Right, I'll go and order. Have you spoken to Harry yet?"

"No. Marianne said she hasn't gone out, but unless she's down the bloody well, she's not in the bar."

"I'll see if I can scare her up for you." I ambled in the back door, intending to order the food and then ask about Harry, but Marianne was busy with some bloke who wanted to try every beer in the place before he took the dangerous step of committing himself to actually buying a pint. I thought I might as well try to find the boss myself while I was waiting. After I'd stuck my head in the lounge bar and found it deserted, no surprise there—it was a completely separate bar that was only ever used by families, and no parents were going to keep the kiddies cooped up indoors in weather like this—I unhitched the chain across the bottom of the stairs and wandered up, the wooden treads creaking under my feet.

"Harry?" I called out, mindful of what Harry had said earlier about uninvited guests. I'm very attached to my bollocks and I'd like to keep it that way. "You up there? It's Tom."

There was a pause, an odd noise, and then Harry appeared at the top of the staircase, looming over me like the angel of death.

She didn't look all that pleased to see me. "What is it?" she asked gruffly, pulling down her tank top over her belly, where it'd got rucked up a bit. She'd left the men's shirt off entirely today. Actually, when I looked closer, I saw her close-cropped hair was as messed up as it ever gets, so maybe she'd been having a nap. I felt a bit guilty for disturbing her—chances were she wasn't getting a lot of sleep at night right now.

"Sorry. Didn't mean to interrupt your break. It was just that Phil wanted a word."

"What about?"

"You know. The case." What did she think he'd want to talk to her about? The weather?

There was a noise from behind her. Harry looked round, then back at me. "I've got to go," she said curtly. "I'll be down in ten minutes."

"Right. Okay," I told her broad, retreating back, and ambled back down the stairs feeling a bit bemused.

Marianne had managed to sweet-talk the bloke with the beer into finally making a choice, so I was able to give her my food order. "How are you keeping, love?" I asked her when she'd written it down, all big curly letters and circles over the i's.

"I'm fine, thanks. How are you?" She didn't look fine. Her eyes had a pinched look about them, and even her hair wasn't as bouncy as usual.

"I'm good, cheers, love." I hesitated, but there wasn't any reason not to tell her. "Met up with Alan Mortimer's missus yesterday. That's one woman who's seriously delusional about her bloke—thinks he's pure as the driven snow, and I don't mean the sort they nicked him for selling either. She's pretty down on Carey and all."

Marianne gave me a wobbly smile. "She's nice, though, ain't she?"

Not to you, love, I could have said, but didn't. "Er, yeah."

"I met her a few times," Marianne said while I was still wondering whether to mention the other person I'd been chatting to. "We went out for dinner and that—me and Grant, and her and Alan. Dead posh places. The food was lush. She showed me pictures of her kiddies."

"Yeah, they're great kids, aren't they?" I said quickly, glad there was something I could be sincere about.

She nodded. "I thought, see, she'd be all stuck up, what with me being so much younger and her being all posh, but she weren't like that at all."

"Nobs oblige and all that," I said. "That brother of yours given you any more hassle?"

"Kev? No, ain't seen him again." She paused, her smile all gone. "We used to be that close when we was kids, me and him. He just got in with a bad lot when he was older. Well, and the drinking hasn't helped. But he's still my brother, see?"

I nodded. "Blood's thicker than a lot of stuff, innit?"

I wasn't sure I actually believed that anymore, but it seemed to be the thing to say.

Marianne brightened a bit, at any rate. "How's that sister of yours? We've not seen her in here for a long while."

"Cherry? Yeah, she's good. I'm seeing her tomorrow, matter of fact. Sunday lunch with her and the fiancé. Phil too."

"You have a lovely time," Marianne said, smiling properly now.

"We will," I said confidently. After all, it was just lunch with Cherry and Greg.

What could possibly go wrong?

CHAPTER FOURTEEN

Sunday dawned bright, warm, and sunny, with nary a cloud in the sky. All this good weather was well unsettling. I was lying in Phil's bed with him beside me, a couple of inches of space between us because while getting hot and sweaty together is fun up to a point, once that point's been reached, you start getting a bit desperate to cool off.

He'd been busy Saturday afternoon, but we'd met up in St. Albans in the evening to try out a new Indian place that'd opened up on Holywell Hill. The food had been good enough that we'd made right pigs of ourselves and couldn't be arsed to trek across town to mine, seeing as Phil's flat was only a hop, skip, and a jump away on London Road.

Or, as might be, an overfull stagger and a belch away. We hadn't even had the energy for a shag, which was why we'd been making up for it this morning.

I nudged Phil. "You know, I was reading somewhere that the earth flips poles sometimes. Do you reckon that's happened and no one noticed? And Hertfordshire's in Australia now? It'd explain why it's so bloody hot all of a sudden."

"I don't think that's how it works. It's just the magnetic poles that switch."

"What, so north is south and so on?" I frowned. "Won't all the homing pigeons get lost? They use all that magnetic stuff. I saw it on the telly. Bit sad, that—all these homeless pigeons. Someone ought to do something about that."

Phil laughed. "Christ, you're the living embodiment of 'a little learning is a dangerous thing.'"

"Who said that?"

"Pope."

"Since when are you a Catholic?"

"*Alexander* Pope. He was a poet."

"And since when are you into poetry?" I grinned at him. "Bit poofy, innit?"

"Up yours."

"You already have been."

"Could be again if you play your cards right."

"Promises, promises . . . Nah, sod it. No time. We've got lunch over at Greg's, remember? And I'll need to stop by mine first and feed the cats before they go feral and eat the neighbours."

"Thought lunch was only salad? It'll keep if we're a bit late."

I firmly disengaged his big, hot hands from certain parts of my anatomy. "My mum brought me up proper, all right? We'll get there on time." Or at least, not more than around twenty minutes late, which was good as, in my book, and seeing as that's what Cherry would expect, it'd be rude to turn up earlier, wouldn't it?

We drove over to St. Leonards in Phil's Golf, seeing as neither my van nor the Fiesta had air-conditioning. I was seriously considering making that a deal-breaker next time I replaced one of them, although sod's law, the minute I got sorted for hot weather, normal service would probably be resumed and we'd be back to brollies for the rest of the summer.

I should have twigged the moment I saw the Škoda parked on the gravel drive outside the Old Deanery. The fact that it was this year's model and I'd never seen it before was neither here nor there. I should've guessed, and then I could have faked an emergency call-out or a heart attack or a bloody zombie apocalypse or *something*, for God's sake. Instead, I blithely stepped up to the doorstep, rang Greg's bell (no sniggering in the cheap seats, please), and stood there like a muppet until he let us in and waved us into the front room for a predinner drink.

And brought us face-to-face with my mum and dad.

Look, I know what you're going to think. And yeah, maybe I wasn't exactly winning any awards for the world's best son, seeing as how I'd managed to avoid seeing them ever since I'd found out who my real dad was, back in January. But Christ, I'd known what it was going to be like. I stared at the round-shouldered, bald-headed old bloke who'd taught me how to drive, bought me my first bike, and sent me off to bed early when I was naughty—my *dad*, in other words— and all that went through my head was this bloody siren screaming *NOT DAD NOT DAD NOT DAD.*

I swallowed and turned to Phil for a bit of moral support, but he was busy doing rabbit impersonations, caught in the full-beam headlights of Mum's glare.

I'd always wondered what it'd take to rattle Phil's composure— apart from the sight of me in mortal peril, but call me vain, I liked to think that one went without saying. And now I knew: it was a tall, thin woman in her seventies without a scrap of makeup, her grey hair sculpted into rigid waves and her cardi buttoned up to the neck. Otherwise known as Mum.

Looked like it was up to me to break the silence and hopefully disrupt the waves of hostility rippling out from her towards my bloke.

"Um, 'lo, Mum. Dad. You all right?"

"I'm fine, thank you, Tom. But your father's knees have been giving him some trouble." There was the faintest tint of pink in her cheeks, and she stopped there, which wasn't like my mum at all.

Shit. She knew. She knew *I* knew.

"Ah," Greg said, and the embarrassed tone told me everything I needed to know about how close-lipped Cherry had been about the whole bastardy business, i.e. about as close-lipped as Gary with a juicy scandal. "Sherry, everyone?"

"Yeah, please," I said, wishing I could ask for something stronger but not daring with Mum here. There was a general chorus of agreement that alcoholic refreshment would be a bloody good idea. Even from Dad, who looked a bit startled when Mum then didn't chime in with an automatic *Not for you, Gerald, you're driving.*

Shit. Did *Dad* know I knew? Two thoughts zipped into my brain simultaneously. One: if he was the only one in the room who hadn't been told about the bloody great elephant prancing around in the corner and making dents in the floor, that was . . . That was beyond unfair. And two: no way on earth was I going to be the one to mention it to him.

"Excellent, excellent." Greg bustled around filling glasses and handing them out. "You know, I really can't think what's keeping Cherry."

Severe guilt pangs for setting me up like this, I hoped.

"Now," Greg went on, "I believe you already know Philip, Barbara?"

"We haven't seen him for a number of years," Mum said in a tone that managed to imply that the number hadn't been nearly big enough. She turned to me and tried to smile. "Cherry didn't mention you'd be here."

"Yeah, well, snap." I found myself biting a fingernail and quickly shoved my hand in my pocket before she could tell me off. "Um. Been up to much?"

"Oh, just the usual." We both drew in a breath and then changed our minds and didn't say anything.

Dad doddered over into the silence and gave Phil a watery stare. "You're a private investigator now, I hear?"

"Yeah. Yes," Phil said and cleared his throat.

"And before that, a policeman? Hmm. Interesting career progression." He wandered off to peer at Buster the stuffed border collie, who was today perched on a chair, looking out of the window.

Phil, who'd offered a handshake that Dad had either totally ignored or plain not noticed, looked wrong-footed and shoved *his* hand in his pocket.

Mum was glaring at him again. "How's your hip these days, Tom?" she asked pointedly.

"Good. It's fine. Hardly even notice it, weather like this."

Phil's lips had tightened. "I'll go and see if Cherry wants a hand." He tossed down his sherry and strode out of the room, presumably heading kitchenwards, although I wouldn't have blamed him if he'd done a runner all the way back to St. Albans.

"Mum . . . try and be nice, yeah? Please?" In the background, Greg was hand-wavingly explaining the finer points of taxidermy to Dad, whose expression was a cross between bemused and horrified.

Mum sipped her sherry and looked unhappy. I was going to *kill* Cherry for this. "I'm doing my best," she said in a firm, low voice. "But it's a little hard to be *nice* to the man responsible for crippling my youngest son."

I winced. On several levels. "Mum . . . I'm not a cripple, all right? And he never meant for anything like that to happen. You know that."

"I know nothing of the sort. It would never have happened if he and his friends hadn't terrorised you. For all we know, they stood there laughing while you lay in the road half-dead."

We were still speaking pretty quietly, but over in the corner, Greg's voice got noticeably louder and more manic.

"We were just kids then," I said, trying to keep it down a bit. "He's a different bloke now."

Her mouth turned down even further at the corners. "Even if he does regret it now, aren't you afraid . . ." She trailed off and turned away. It wasn't a good move, seeing as it had her staring directly at Mrs. Tiggywinkle the stuffed hedgehog. She seemed to have got a boyfriend from somewhere since I'd last visited—the hedgehog, that was, not Mum this time—and was getting a bit frisky with him on the mantelpiece.

"Afraid of what?" I prompted. "Look, I know he's big and all that, but he's not violent or anything. Phil'd never hurt me."

Mum's eyes opened wide. "That's not what I meant." Although it looked like she'd started to worry about that too, now.

"Then what?"

"How will you ever know if he's with you for the right reasons? And not, well, out of guilt, or because he feels sorry for you?" She looked down, her face pink and blotchy.

"He doesn't feel sorry for me, all right? There's nothing *to* feel sorry for. I told you, I'm fine." It came out a bit more heated than I'd meant it to.

"You used to love playing football," she said vaguely. Maybe she'd noticed I was feeling like someone had just booted one into my chest.

"That was when I was a kid. I'm a grown-up now, Mum. And I don't need his pity, or yours, or anyone else's. Right. I'm going to go and see how they're getting on." I looked at the sherry in my hand, but couldn't stomach it, so I left it for Mrs. Tiggywinkle and her bloke to fight over while I stomped off to the kitchen.

Not limping even a little bit.

As far as atmospheres went, the kitchen wasn't a lot better. Phil was leaning against a counter with his arms folded and his expression set in stone, while Cherry stirred furiously at a glass jug of what looked like homemade vinaigrette.

"You've got too much vinegar in that," I told her helpfully. "Bung a bit more oil in to balance it out."

I nearly dropped the jug when she thrust it into my unwary hands. "If you're such a bloody expert, you do it."

"Language, Sis. And oi, what's got you all in a lather?" I narrowed my eyes at her. "You're the one who's gone round springing Mum and Dad on the rest of us."

"Me!" Cherry squawked so loud they must have heard it in the front room, even over Greg's booming tones. "*That* was Gregory's idea. *And* he didn't see fit to inform me of it until five minutes before they arrived." Her hands twitched like they were regretting giving up the vinaigrette. Possibly because they wanted to throw it at her officiously reverend fiancé.

Which right then didn't sound like such a bad idea.

I put the jug down with a sigh. "S'pose he meant well."

Cherry just sniffed.

"Talk about your road to hell," Phil muttered from the sidelines. He heaved his bulk off the counter. "What else needs doing? For lunch, I mean," he added with a sharp look at me and Cherry.

"Nothing. It's all done, except the vinaigrette." Cherry glanced at me, but I was already there, chucking in a bit more of the extra virgin and giving it a whisk.

"Have you seasoned it already?"

Cherry gave me a blank look. "Are you supposed to? I thought it was just oil and vinegar."

At least she hadn't used malt vinegar, which in my book is lovely on chips and handy for getting rid of limescale, but shouldn't be allowed within ten feet of a lettuce leaf. "Got any honey? Mustard?" I asked as I ground in some salt and a little bit of pepper.

"This isn't bloody *MasterChef*," Phil huffed into my ear. "Just get it on the table. Sooner we eat, the sooner we're out of here."

"If we've got to sit through this lunch, we might as well have a decent bloody dressing on the salad." I was a bit narked at his implication he couldn't wait to get away from my family. Which, all right, was pretty much how I felt, but that was different. They were *my* family.

Lunch, when we finally got to sit down to eat, went pretty much as expected.

Unfortunately.

"Does your family still live on the council estate?" was Dad's opening conversational gambit to Phil.

"Yes," he said shortly.

"It's looking very run-down these days. Still, one would never think it to look at you," Dad finished on a cheery note.

Mum took the opportunity to give Phil a good once-over. "Of course, anyone can dress well these days, with so many designer outlets around. There's one in St. Albans now, although I can't see why anyone would want to shop there. It's just like a jumble sale, only more expensive."

Cherry and I shared an embarrassed look. "Phil's been trying to improve my wardrobe too," I offered, hoping to find them some common ground. Mum was always telling me off for being too scruffy. And the odd "You're going out in *that*?" comment from Phil counted, didn't it?

"Yeah, I'll have you doing the drains in Dolce & Gabbana in no time," Phil muttered with a face like he'd just found half a slug in his lettuce.

"I think people go too far with these things," Mum said as if she'd never heard of sarcasm.

Phil's jaw tensed, but he didn't say anything. I bit into my celery, and the crunch seemed to echo in the frigid silence.

"Would you pass the tomatoes, please, Gregory?" Dad chuckled. "I see you haven't stuffed these."

Nobody else laughed.

"Gregory's a very good cook, actually," Cherry ventured bravely.

"Oh, merely adequate," Greg protested. "And I must say you've outdone yourself with the salad dressing, my dear." He beamed.

Cherry's smile curdled. "Tom made it."

Dad lifted his gaze from his plate again to focus on me. "I suppose you and, er . . . Philip take turns, do you? Doing the cooking, of course," he explained quickly, which only drew our attention to all the other sorts of things we might have thought he was talking about.

Mum's eyes narrowed. "*Do* you cook, Philip?" she asked, menacing him with a slice of beetroot on the end of her fork.

"Not a lot," Phil answered shortly, which was utter bollocks. He might not enjoy cooking, like I did, but he could bloody well knock up a meal if he had to, and pretty often did.

Mum made a noise that sounded like *hmmf*. I imagined her adding it to the mental ten-things-I-hate-about-Phil list: *makes Tom do the cooking.*

"I like cooking," I said quickly. "'Sides, we don't always eat together. Phil's got his own place."

"Oh? Where's that?"

"London Road," Phil admitted.

"Really? Of course, it's such a mixture there. All those huge houses, mixed in with poky little flats. Do you have a house or a flat, Philip?"

"Flat," he ground out. "Could you pass the—"

"Bought or rented?" Christ, Mum was like a dog with a bone.

"Does it matter?" I interrupted. "What were you after, Phil? More ham?"

"Forget it. I changed my mind." He pushed his plate away, still half-full with food. Bloody hell, was he about to walk out?

"You know," Greg boomed out with desperate hand gestures. "I haven't told you about my sermon this morning. Quite a fascinating theme, all about the persecution of the early Christians—"

"I know how they felt," Phil muttered a bit too loudly for politeness.

"—and how their faith was strengthened as a result," Greg went on doggedly. His voice, never exactly quiet to begin with, reached ear-splitting levels by the end of the sentence.

"Cherry, is there any wine left?" Mum interrupted him.

We all looked down the end of the table at Cherry, who at that moment was emptying the last of the bottle of sauvignon plonk into her glass with a grim expression on her face. She turned pink. "I'll get another bottle."

"No more for your father, though. He's driving," Mum said, equilibrium apparently fully restored by that bit of Phil-baiting. "Did you bring the Fiesta, Tom?" she added in my direction.

"Nah, we came in Phil's car."

"He'd better not have any more either, then. We don't want any *more* accidents."

I swear I heard Phil's teeth grinding. I turned to Greg in desperation. "So, early church, yeah? Tell us all about it."

I'd planned to make our excuses as soon as politeness allowed, but Phil was making them for me before coffee was even served, pleading a "work commitment" I reckoned he'd made up on the spot. That dropped me right in it—either I got the family's backs up by nipping off early with him, or I pissed Phil off, stuck it out on my own, and had to hitch a lift back to St. Albans with Mum and Dad.

I nipped. I didn't have to bloody well like it, though. "Work commitment, my arse," I hissed at him as we crunched over the gravel drive to his Golf. "You could have waited half an hour, instead of making a run for it while Greg was still eating his pud. You ever hear of this thing called manners?"

"Come off it. Manners, *my* arse. Your mum made it plain she couldn't wait to see the back of me."

"She'd have warmed up to you in the end. *If* you'd put in a bit of effort. You didn't even bloody try!"

"So? Neither did she. In fact, scratch that. She went out of her way to make everything as fucking unpleasant for me as she could."

"Oi, don't you talk about my mum like that." I dropped into the passenger seat.

"Your dad wasn't any better." Phil slammed the driver's door shut behind him and buckled up with a vicious jab.

"You can leave him out of it and all. You're always telling me not to be so sodding touchy—why don't you take your own advice for once?" I was pissed off, I'll admit it. I'd spent *months* worrying what I was going to say to Mum about my real dad, and avoiding her until I could face it, and then when I finally got to see her, all we'd bloody well talked about had been Phil.

I was fed up with the whole bloody lot of them.

Phil wrenched the car around, managing to scatter even the densely packed gravel on the Old Deanery drive. "Had fun watching them put me in my place, did you?"

"Put you in your . . . For fuck's sake, Phil. All they did was ask about your family and stuff."

"Yeah, and make it crystal bloody clear they thought you were slumming it with me."

"Me, slumming it? You're the one in the sodding designer shirt!" And he had his posh loafers on again. *And* the fancy watch with two sets of hands. I was in jeans, trainers, and a shirt I got cheap down the market.

If I'd known Mum and Dad would be there, I might have dug out the garden-party gear again.

"For fuck's sake . . ." Phil screeched out of a junction, having glared the poor sod whose right of way it was into submission. "You're missing the point."

"Yeah, well, I'm sure you'll be only too happy to explain it to me."

"*Jesus.*" Phil zoomed up behind some old codger tootling along in a clapped-out Austin and thumped the dashboard. The old bloke turned off at the next junction. Probably because he wanted to live to tootle another day.

I stared out of the window as the streets of St. Leonards turned to open countryside. The fields were still brilliant green in the early summer sun, although they were definitely starting to go brown at the edges. All the people we passed were in shorts, sandals, and sunglasses, but the air-con in the car had me rolling my sleeves down against the chill. Or maybe it was just the frigid waves coming from Phil. Apparently determined to be a stubborn, pigheaded git, he drove in silence. Except when he was swearing under his breath at other road users.

I'd expected we'd be spending a fair proportion of the day over with Greg and Cherry, so we hadn't exactly made any plans for the evening. Which was good, because there was no way I was going to waste the rest of my Sunday listening to a muscle-bound poser with a chip on his shoulder the size of Epping Forest snipe at me and my family. As we neared my house in Fleetville, I opened my mouth.

"I need to sort out the van—"

Phil spoke at the same time. "Got some work I need to be doing—"

Huh. "Right, then," I said, chipper as I could. "Cheers for the lift, and I'll see you around."

There was a huff. "Tom . . ."

I pretended not to hear him. Amazing how distracted you can get, unbuckling your seat belt and opening the door. 'Specially if you don't bother waiting until the car's come to a full stop.

"See you, then," I said, and slammed the door behind me without waiting for an answer.

CHAPTER FIFTEEN

I got the van sorted out *and* got my bills and stuff up-to-date. Caught up with the laundry too—well, all the stuff that was mine, anyhow. Thought about shoving all Phil's designer socks and undies into a bin-bag and dropping them off at his place, but in the end I just left them at the bottom of the laundry basket. If he wanted them, he could sodding well come round and ask for them.

By evening, I was desperate to get out of the house. I thought about popping round the corner to get rat-faced in the Rats Castle—in fact, I'd pretty much decided that was what I was going to do—but somehow I found myself dialling up Gary instead.

"You busy tonight?" I asked after he'd given me his Leslie Phillips–style hel-*looo.*

"Mm. Funny you should ask. A hole does appear to have unexpectedly opened up in my schedule. I take it you'd be interested in filling said hole for me?"

"Yeah. Wanna meet up for a drink?"

"Do teddy bears like picnics? Ooh, that reminds me—how is little Tommy?"

"Little Tommy's fine. Sitting on my bed as we speak." At least, I assumed we were talking about the teddy bear. The way things were going, he might be the only one I'd be sharing it with for the foreseeable. "So are we having this drink or what?"

"Of course, darling. At the Dyke?"

"Uh, maybe not? Tell you what, why don't we try the Four Candles? Haven't been there in ages."

There was a silence.

"Gary?"

"Still here, darling. That was just me *not* commenting on the fact that you're clearly trying to avoid someone. Fine. We shall go find ourselves a cosy little table and gaze deeply into the river. In the philosophical sense, obviously, as the water's running rather low these days. It's the fish I feel sorry for, in all this global warming. They don't even *have* a carbon footprint."

"Yeah. Whatever. See you in twenty minutes?"

The Four Candles in Brock's Hollow is a nice enough pub, but a bit commercial, trading on its prime location in the middle of the village. It's the sort of place that, if you were driving through the village looking for a place to have lunch with the family, you'd go, *Oh, that looks nice*, and stop at. From the outside, it's your typical Olde English Pubbe, white-painted and framed with black timber, although it loses points for not having a thatched roof. There's a small beer garden, a play area for the kiddies that's knee-deep in bark chippings to fend off any potential lawsuits over grazed knees, and as Gary said, it's slap bang by the river, which is always good for a bit of duck spotting. You can get a decent enough meal there, but it's overpriced for what you get.

I managed to drive the short way down Four Candles Lane without meeting anyone coming the other way and having to have a staring match until one of us caved and backed out again—always a pain—and parked in the pub car park. Unlike a lot of pub car parks, it's large enough that there's never any trouble finding a space, which would be your first clue to how commercial the place is.

There were a few people having a quiet drink out the back, but no one I knew, which was how I liked it right now. I headed straight into the bar. They'd done the place up a bit since I'd last been in there—repapered the walls in deep crimson and taken down the nostalgic photos of Brock's Hollow in Ye Olde Tymes to put up a job lot of prints of farm animals. It might have made the place a bit more colourful, but to my mind it was now even more generic and soulless than it had been before. They'd also split off half of it into a proper restaurant bit, leaving the pub area a bit cramped and poky.

Of course, I probably wasn't in the right frame of mind to appreciate it properly.

Gary, bless him, had already got a round in. He was sitting at a table in the corner, Julian at his feet, next to a little square window that faced out onto the river. Just like he'd promised. I took a peek outside when I joined him and saw a couple of lads fishing from the bridge, plus one solitary moorhen on the water. The ducks must be on their break.

"You all right?" I asked as I dropped into my seat. "Cheers for the beer." I showed my appreciation by glugging down almost half of it.

Gary gave me a look over the rim of his martini glass. Either they'd put a cherry in it or that was some genetically modified breed of bright-red olive. "Bursting with health. Which is more than your liver will be if you keep that up. What's he done now, then? Come on, spill. Metaphorically, obviously. These trousers are dry-clean only, and Julian's just had his bath."

"Did I say Phil had done anything?"

"Did you need to?"

"Point." I took another swig from my pint, this one a bit smaller. Compared to the beer at the Dyke, it tasted over-fizzy and not fruity enough. Unsatisfying. "We had a row, all right?"

"About?"

"About him storming out of a family meal and basically calling my mum and dad a couple of snobs." Gary opened his mouth to speak, but I hadn't finished. "Like he's not desperate for the weather to turn cold so he can drag out the cashmere sweaters again."

I filled Gary in on the Sunday lunch from hell. "I'm not even sure who I'm more pissed off with," I said at the end, and took a long draught from my glass. I was on to my second pint already. At this rate, I wouldn't be fit to drive home. "Greg, for shoving his reverend bloody nose in and setting us up like that, or Phil, for being such a stubborn, pigheaded git, or . . ." I swallowed. "Or Mum." My insides knotted up just saying it. "I mean, I'm not saying what he said about her was right. Just, you know, *maybe* she could have made a bit more effort."

Gary *hmm*'ed. "You realise she was only using Phil as a distraction."

"What?"

"Your mother. She clearly didn't want the conversation turning to matters parental. 'The best defence is a good offence,'" he quoted sagely.

I had a flashback to Carey telling me how he felt like he had to pre-emptively throw his weight around to get anyone to take him seriously.

I dragged my mind back to the subject at hand. "What, like I was going to bring the subject up over Greg and Cherry's dinner table?"

Gary shrugged expansively, throwing his arms wide, and nearly knocked my pint over. Well, what was left of it. "Who's to say what a man might do, confronted with the knowledge that his whole life has been a lie?"

I picked up my glass quickly. "Okay, firstly, my dad is not my whole life. And secondly, I got confronted with it months ago, didn't I? I've had time to get used to it now."

"Have you?" He leaned forward to fix me with what was clearly supposed to be a significant look. On Gary, it was more like a leer. "Or have you simply been enjoying that North African river cruise?"

"You what?"

"In de-*Nile*?

"I haven't been denying stuff, all right? Just sort of . . . not dealing with it. I've been busy, haven't I? With stuff." Gary raised a doubting eyebrow. "Work and stuff. And," I added, wagging a finger at him as I got into the swing of it, "your wedding's taken up a fair bit of my time. Getting kitted out with the formal gear, writing my best man's speech . . ." Okay, so *technically* I hadn't actually started that one yet. But, you know, I'd been thinking about it.

Mostly I'd been thinking I didn't have the first bloody clue about making speeches.

"Ooh, I can't wait to hear it," Gary gushed. Then he frowned. "I hope you're not going to mention anything too indelicate. My mother will be there, you know."

"Gary, your mum already knows all your sordid little secrets. Because you tell her them."

"Mm, but she's getting very forgetful these days."

"Yeah, well, unless she's forgotten you completely, I don't reckon she'll be shocked by anything I come out with." I drained my glass. "Right, my round. Same again?"

"Please. And perhaps a glass of ice water as well. And perhaps a top-up for Julian's bowl."

"I'm surprised they even let you bring him in here," I said as I stood up.

"Oh, Madge at the bar is a total sweetie."

I raised an eyebrow. "Madge?"

"Madge," Gary confirmed, ruffling Julian's neck fur. "She knows how important it is for a big, handsome dog like you to stay hydrated, yes she *does*. Now tell me straight, darling," he added, looking back up at me. "Is this weather going to hold until the wedding day?"

"How the hell would I know?"

"Oh, you know. Your thingy. The watery bit."

"What's that got to do with it?"

"Rain is water, isn't it?"

"Yeah, but . . ." I shook my head. "I'm getting the drinks in, all right? You want a weather forecast, get on to the BBC."

I ended up getting a few rounds in that evening. Probably a few more than was really good for me, if I was honest, which I didn't feel much like being right then. Gary matched me drink for drink, but after a while, he gave up on the martinis and stuck to the ice water.

I thought about doing the same, but, well, beer's something like ninety percent water anyhow, right?

"I just dunno," I said glumly, toying with my pint glass. It was half-empty, which seemed deeply significant just then. "Me and Phil, I mean. What if it's, you know, run its course? What if, I dunno, he was only into me for the finding-things bollocks—"

"Or for your actual bollocks," Gary put in helpfully.

I ignored him. "And now the whatsit, novelty's worn off? I mean, look at him. Well, he's not here, so you can't, but imagine him. Remember him. Whatever. He's tall, he's good-looking, he's got more muscles than Popeye after a whole bloody field of spinach. He could have anyone he wants. Christ, I bet he's with some other bloke right now, shagging his brains out."

"Mm. Not quite, darling." Gary smirked.

I frowned, irrationally annoyed on Phil's behalf. "He could be if he wanted to."

"I don't mean to deny the physical attractions of your beloved, who I'm sure has the pulling power of a Sherman tank. *However*, in this particular instance, I'm quite certain his virtue has remained intact."

"Because he'd never cheat on me?" I blinked a bit of stray emotion out of my eye. Must be a leftover from the head injury.

"Because, darling, he's with Darren, who would never cheat on *me*." Gary beamed and poked a cocktail stick under my nose. "Want to pop my cherry?"

I stared at the lurid excuse for a fruit speared on the plastic stick. "Not hungry," I muttered. Then I thought, *Sod it*, and ate it anyway.

"There's a good boy," Gary said. "So you see, your Philip's virtue is quite safe, as he's currently moistening the shoulder of the truest man in Hertfordshire."

Gary dabbed delicately at his eyes, which had actually gone a bit misty—he wasn't just faking it. I tried to picture Phil crying on Darren's shoulder. Leaving aside the ridiculousness of the whole *Phil crying* bit, he'd have to bend down so far to reach it he'd probably topple over. I frowned. "What's he got to cry about, anyhow? He's the one who's being bloody unreasonable."

"Reasonable is as reasonable does," Gary said sagely. "More drinkies?"

I'd had so many drinkies I was weaving a bit when we finally stood up from the table at kicking-out time. "Don't think I'd better drive home," I muttered to the Gary on the left. The one on the right kept looking at me funny.

"Of course you shouldn't, darling." Left-hand Gary beamed. "You can sleep with me and Darren."

It was almost tempting. Then I remembered. "Phil," I said sadly as we walked to the door.

"I'm not sure we'll be able to squeeze him in as well. We've got a very large bed, but there are limits."

Something hot and heavy kept pressing against my legs, making it hard for them to go in the direction they wanted to. On the other hand, that *did* seem to mean I ended up going in a more or less straight line. I looked down to see Julian's enormous furry body flanking me. Maybe he had a bit of guide dog in him. Actually, come to think of it, he could probably fit in an entire guide dog and still have room for a rare steak and a couple of doggy treats. I sniggered a bit, picturing it.

"Good night, gentlemen. Safe journey home," someone—Madge?—called out, and I half turned in their direction and nearly tripped over the step down to the door.

"Oops-a-daisy," Gary said, catching me by the elbow and steadying me. "Time for Bedfordshire. Come on, let Uncle Gary take you home and tuck you up."

I fumbled for my phone. "Gonna call a taxi."

"Sure?"

I nodded. "Don't wanna . . ." I grimaced, and made a vague gesture. "Phil."

"Ah. Yes, I suppose there is a teensy possibility he might still be with Darren. We're continuing to avoid him, are we?"

I grunted something that could have been taken as a yes. It wasn't that I was avoiding him, exactly.

I just didn't want to see him, that was all.

Monday morning seemed to start around three hours too early for my liking, but the cobwebs had more or less cleared by lunchtime. Lucky I'd remembered to drink about a gallon of water before bed to stave off the hangover I probably deserved, or I might not have been so chirpy. Dehydration would have been a bugger in heat like this.

Normally, workdays, unless I'm meeting someone for lunch, I'll just have a sandwich in the van. Saves time, not to mention money. Today, though, I had a two-hour block between jobs—Mrs. H., in Hatfield, had asked me to come round an hour later than I'd booked her in to fit her new dishwasher, seeing as Mr. H. had taken the day off unexpectedly and was taking her out for a romantic birthday lunch. There had been the strong implication, when she'd called me, that he'd finally got her hint that gifts of domestic appliances weren't going to get him his conjugals in a hurry.

It was all right for some. The way things were going between me and Phil, I'd be lucky to get a cheap card for my upcoming birthday.

Anyway, I had time to kill. I could have gone home, but the cats would've given me funny looks and let's face it, I'd have the whole evening to spend sitting on that sofa on my own. Didn't really appeal.

So I decided to treat myself to a pub lunch. Again. At this rate, Harry was going to think I'd moved in and start charging me rent. Still, at least Marianne would have a smile for me—if I managed not to put my foot in it this time by bringing up the subject of her ex—and if Harry wanted to know how the case was going, I could take pleasure in directing her to bend the ear of one Phil sodding Morrison.

I got the local cab firm to give me a ride up to the Dyke, planning to walk down into the village and retrieve the Fiesta from the Four Candles car park after I'd eaten. It'd be a bit of a trek, but I was in the mood for some fresh air and exercise.

"Want to come in for a quick one?" I asked Al, the driver, when he dropped me off.

"Nah, cheers mate. Against my religion, innit?"

I stared at him. "Al, you don't have a religion. Unless private enterprise counts." As well as driving the cabs, Al also ran a thriving sari concern that Mrs. Al manned the till and did the books for, and the kiddies helped out in after school. They were all nominally Catholic, but I hadn't noticed any of 'em beating a path to St. Thomas's church on a Sunday.

"That's what I mean. Sitting around drinking when I could be making money? That's a cardinal sin, that is." He grinned and waved me off.

I ambled into the pub and made my way over to Marianne at the bar. She looked like she could do with a bit of cheering up, so I smiled at her. "All right, love?"

"Tom," she said, and stopped. She looked a bit distracted for a mo, then rallied just as I was starting to get worried. "What can I get you?"

"Anything good on the specials today?"

She cast a guilty glance at the blackboard, which was uncharacteristically bare. "Sorry. We're a bit . . . But the regular menu's on."

"No worries. I'll just have a pint of Squirrel and a cheese ploughman's."

Marianne nodded and scribbled in her notepad.

"At least that ex of yours is giving you a bit of space today," I said to make conversation.

Marianne seemed to shrink in on herself, and she looked around skittishly. "No, he's . . . he's not been in lately." She dropped the notepad and crouched down to pick it up. "I'll just take this through to the kitchen," she said and scurried off without looking at me.

Brilliant. I'd managed to catch her in the five minutes a day she *wasn't* worrying about Carey, and what did I do? I had to go and remind her about him. Well done, Paretski. Still, it had to be a good sign that he wasn't around. Maybe he'd realised he wasn't helping his case, hanging around all the time and making her nervous.

When I'd finally got my pint, I took it over to a table in the corner and scanned the place, trying to work out if there was anyone else around here who might have been giving her grief. It all seemed to be locals, though.

Maybe she was just a bit uncomfortable manning the place on her own, I decided. Because by the time I'd munched my way through my cheese, crusty bread, and pickled onions—let's face it, there was no one right now who'd give a monkey's about my breath stinking—the Devil's Dyke was still conspicuous by her absence.

"Boss not in today, love?" I wandered over to ask Marianne next time she had a free moment.

"She had to go see someone," Marianne said distractedly, tucking a stray curl behind her ear. It sprang back immediately, but she didn't seem to notice. Then she leaned over the bar with a brittle smile. "Um, Tom? Have you got a mo?"

Since I'd been spending my lunch hour with a leisurely pint, I couldn't exactly pretend I was rushed off my feet. "Course I have. Is it that tap in the ladies' loo playing up again?"

She shook her head, blonde curls bouncing. "No, the tap's fine. It's just, there's this funny smell in the cellar, see? And I think it's getting worse. Could you have a look and check it's not the drains?"

I frowned. "If your drains have burst, it's the water company you'll need to speak to. And shouldn't we wait to talk to Harry?" Harry wasn't the sort of person to put up with people—even mates—poking around her nether areas without permission.

"She won't be back for a couple of hours," she said. "And I'm worried it's going to start noticing out here, see? Someone might call environmental health, and we'd get into trouble." Marianne pulled out the big guns, opening her eyes wide and leaning over so far I was worried she'd topple right over the bar. Her being a bit top heavy and all. "Please?"

I didn't much feel like it—but on the other hand, it wasn't like I had anything to rush home for, was it? Not with me and Phil on the out-and-outs. I wondered what he'd been up to since I'd last seen him, and if he'd noticed a bloody great gaping hole in *his* life.

Then I told myself to stop being so bloody melodramatic. It was just a tiff, right? We'd get over it.

"All right," I said. "I'll give it a look-see."

There might have been a bit of self-interest in there too—call me squeamish, but if Harry had sewage from a burst drain seeping into her cellars, I'd just as soon know about it before I ordered another pint and a ploughman's.

Marianne smiled her relief. "Thanks, Tom. You're a treasure."

So I finished my pint and followed her down the steps to the cellars, half my mind on whether I'd still got the number for that bloke in pest control, in case it turned out to be a dead rat or something.

Which, funnily enough, wasn't too far from the mark.

Although believe me, I wasn't laughing.

CHAPTER SIXTEEN

ames Dean didn't have a bloody clue what he was on about. In my
experience, which isn't as limited as I'd like it to be, *nobody* has a
good-looking corpse.

Grant Carey certainly wasn't bucking the trend. He looked
smaller, dead. Insignificant. Like a kid who'd been playing the tough
guy, until some bigger kid came along and cut him brutally down to
size. And his face... I was going to see his face in my dreams. Bloated,
blackened—and Christ, the stench. Thinking of it only made it worse,
and I backed off, my hand over my mouth, trying not to breathe.

"What is it? Did you find something?" Marianne's voice was
shrill and nervous.

I grabbed her hand and carried on moving. I'd have had to draw
in a breath to say anything, and I just couldn't. Dragging Marianne
along with me, I went up those bloody stairs faster than Merlin when
he hears the can opener—*Jesus, God, don't think about eating*—
through the kitchen door and out into the sunshine. Then I leaned
against the wall, my head down and my hands on my knees, and
gasped in lungfuls of blessed fresh air while I waited for my stomach
to stop heaving.

"What did you find?" Marianne kept asking.

"Oi, what's going on here?" A bloke I knew by sight had come
through from the bar and followed us out—probably to find out
where the bloody hell his next pint was coming from—and was staring
at us. "Somefin' wrong?"

I gave him a twisted smile. "Just a bit, yeah. Christ. Call the police,
will you?"

"What, you had a break-in?" he said over Marianne's "The police?
Oh my God!"

"Yeah." I had to clear my throat. "Some bastard broke into the cellar and died there." Shit. Harry was going to kill me for dragging the name of her pub through the mud.

Marianne put a shaky hand on my arm. "Did . . . did you see who it was?" She went a bit pink. "I mean, was it anyone you seen before?" She went even pinker.

I frowned. Shit, was she going to have hysterics if I told her? I mean, the way she'd been talking about him all along, she might just be glad he was dead, but she'd been with him a long time. Maybe she still cared a bit? Like he'd still cared for her? "Er, yeah. Sorry, love. It's Carey."

"What, Grant Carey?" the bloke from the pub interrupted. "Short lad, up from London? Looks a bit like you?"

He fucking well didn't anymore. I swallowed. "Yeah. You know him?"

Pub-bloke shrugged. "He seemed like an all right sort. What'd he die of, then?" He laughed and nudged Marianne just below her left boob. "'Ere, I hope it wasn't the beer."

I stared blankly at him, while Marianne gave a loud sob and disappeared back inside. "Police?" I reminded him, giving a pointed look at the phone he was holding.

"Oh. Right. Yeah. Sorry, love," he yelled through the door and finally punched in the numbers.

By the time he'd finished giving all the details, with so much bloody backwardsing and forwardsing between me, him, and the operator, I was wishing I'd cut out the middle man and just rung Dave Southgate, Harry had got back from wherever she'd been.

She stomped up from the car park and gave me a look that didn't bode well for my future welcome at the Dyke. "What's going on?"

"You've got a problem," I said, managing to stand up straight. "Grant Carey's in your cellar. Dead. *Well* dead. Cops are on their way."

She didn't look surprised, but then I'd seen Harry open a gag gift of a live frog that hopped out of the box and onto her arm without turning a close-cropped hair. She folded her arms. "And we know this because?"

"'Cos Marianne was worried about the drains and sent me down there to have a butcher's, all right?"

There might have been a slight softening of the granite that made up her features. "Christ, that little turd. Even when he's dead, he's a pain in my arse. Drink? You look like you could use one."

"Yeah. Just a beer, okay?" I added in case she was planning to dose me up on the hard stuff, which really didn't feel like a good idea right now.

"Wait there."

Harry went back inside.

Pub-bloke cleared his throat. "Right. I'll be off, then," he said and scarpered.

I should probably have got his name and address, in case the police wanted to talk to him, but chances were Harry knew who he was. And anyway, all he'd done was make a phone call.

Harry was gone long enough I reckoned she must have gone down into the cellar to take a look for herself. Or maybe she was just checking on Marianne. At any rate, she came out a few minutes later with an opened bottle for me and one for herself. Not that *she* looked like she needed it. Feeling honestly a bit narked that she was taking this so much better than I was, I took the bottle with a nod of thanks and slid down the wall to sit on the ground with my back to it. I sipped the beer cautiously, not sure how my stomach was going to take it, but it went down beautifully, the familiar bitter taste washing away the cloying, fetid sweetness in the back of my throat.

"Cheers," I said, feeling a bit better.

Harry nodded, her face stony as she loomed over me. She was probably thinking about how bad this was going to be for business—after all, they closed places down if they found a dead rat, didn't they? God knows what they did for a dead man. Maybe Phil would know—God, Phil. I had to tell him about this. I might not be too happy with him at the mo, but I was pretty sure dead bodies trumped domestics. And he needed to know, what with the case and everything.

I was *not* just desperate for a bit of comforting from my bloke, all right?

I fumbled my phone out of my pocket and managed to hit his number on the second or third go.

"Tom?" Phil's voice, when he answered, was such a bloody relief I'd have been embarrassed to admit it. He sounded a bit wary, like he was worried what I was about to say.

Hah. Little did he know.

"Yeah. I'm up at the Dyke. With Harry." I pulled myself together. "You can stop worrying about how to nail something on Carey. Someone else has done the honours. He's here. Dead."

"Shit."

"Yeah."

"You called your mate Dave?"

"Someone called the police. Dunno who they'll send."

"You found him?"

"'S what I do, innit?" I tried to smile, but it felt so weird I decided it wasn't worth the bother. "He was in the cellar."

"How'd he die?"

"Dunno. Didn't exactly stick around to examine the body."

"Are you sure he's dead?"

"Trust me, I'm sure." My stomach gave a gentle heave at the memory. "Been dead a day at least, I'd reckon." Even in this heat, it'd have to take a while to get him looking—and smelling—that bad, wouldn't it? I thought about it.

Then I decided I really didn't want to think about it anymore.

"Shit."

That was when I heard the sirens. "I'm gonna have to go." I hesitated, then said it anyway. "See you tonight?" I hoped I didn't sound as pathetic as I felt.

All right, maybe I was just a *little* bit desperate for some comforting.

If Phil noticed anything, he was kind enough not to mention it. "I'll come round to yours. And Tom?"

"Yeah?"

"Take care, okay? I'll see you tonight."

Something ice-cold in the pit of my stomach thawed, just a bit, as I hung up.

Must be the beer. I took another swig.

Yeah, that was it. The beer.

I spent an exhausting couple of hours at Dave's police station, drinking crap vending machine coffee and cursing the dodgy air-conditioning along with everyone else. By the time they'd finished with me—and this being a suspicious death, it was all by the book, so I had to deal with junior officers who didn't know me from Adam and weren't particularly disposed to like me—I could have recited my story in my sleep. Which given that it was basically just "There was a nasty niff and I found a body," I could probably have managed without all the intensive rehearsal they seemed to think necessary down the nick.

Trouble was, they didn't just want to know about me finding him. They wanted to know everything I knew about the bloke, including our cosy little chat at Phil's place, *and* the fact that Harry had hired Phil to discredit him.

I didn't know what to say. I felt like I was dropping Phil *and* Harry in it by snitching about all this stuff, but what was I supposed to do? The coppers, in my experience, tend to get pissed off if they find out you haven't been telling them the whole truth, and it wasn't like I had a chance to talk things over with all interested parties first.

It was a bit of a bugger.

And was I supposed to say anything about Mortimer? Not to mention Mrs. M., and her throwaway comment about killing Carey, which had been weighing on my mind more than a little.

I decided to let that one slide. I mean, *I* knew she hadn't meant it, but the police tend to take death threats on the serious side. And Christ, hadn't her and the kiddies suffered enough?

Not as much as Carey, though, my mind chipped in with, helpfully.

The worst part, though, was when I finally got to talk to Dave. I was ushered into his office, where he was sitting glumly at his desk, fiddling with a half-dismantled fan. There were big sweat patches under his arms, and he looked as hot and bothered as I'd ever seen him. The afternoon sun was streaming in through his window, which probably had something to do with it.

"You ought to get 'em to fix that air-conditioning," I said, flopping into the visitor chair. I was feeling a bit hot and bothered myself.

Dave grunted and put the fan down. "They *have* fixed it. Or so they tell me. Apparently, I can't have it bearable in here without it being ten degrees below zero in reception. Which we can't have, obviously, because God forbid any members of the bloody public freeze their bollocks off when they come in to complain about us."

"Take it from me, Dave, no one's going to be complaining about the cold around here."

"You say that, but you don't have to deal with the support staff. You could take the whole bleedin' lot of 'em to the Sahara bloody Desert and they'd still complain about draughts. I had Lesley from filing in here today moaning about how she had to put on a cardi when she came to work and it wasn't bloody natural. *Natural*. I ask you. What's so bloody natural about having to work in a bloody sauna?" He sighed and fanned himself with a copy of *Billboard*, which seemed like a funny name for a police magazine until the penny dropped with a clunk. Christ, this heat was killing off my brain cells wholesale.

I wrestled the few survivors into submission and came up with an idea of why I might be still here. "Got a lead on who offed Carey?"

Dave sighed again, a bit more heavily this time. "We need to talk about your boyfriend."

"Thought that sort of stuff was all a bit too much information for you."

Dave didn't laugh. He didn't even smile. "How much time have you spent with him since last Thursday?"

I was still in question-answering mode, so I didn't think anything about it at first. "Thursday . . . That was the day we went into London. Yeah, that's right. He came over that evening and stayed over. And I met him for lunch the next day. But hang about, why d'you want to know?"

"And after that? Did he spend the weekend at yours?"

"Some of it. We had Sunday lunch over with Cherry and Greg." And Mum and Dad, not to mention the elephant in the room.

Dave nodded. "How's your sister doing these days?"

"She's fine. What do you want to know about me and Phil's movements for? Reckon we did it? Duffed Carey up between us and bunged him in Harry's cellar?"

"Tom, you're a mate. Of course I don't bloody think *you* did it."

He didn't meet my eye, and that emphasis on the *you* was all too significant.

"What, you're after Phil? Come off it. You can't seriously think he did it."

"No? That bump on the head affected your memory, has it? Because I've got a very clear recollection of him getting himself arrested for threatening Carey only last week."

I stared at him. "That was bollocks. You know it was. Carey made it all up and got the witness to go along with it." I felt a twist of guilt as I said it, though. *Don't speak ill of the dead* and all that. All I could think of was the way Carey had seemed when he'd come round to mine.

"Did he? He's not making this up, though, is he? Not unless he's got one bloody vivid imagination." Dave gave me a long, hard look. Then he sighed. "Look, here's what we know. What we *think* we know. Carey took one blow to the side of the head—probably from a fist—and went down, hard. Hit his head on something on the way down, and that's what finished him." I winced. There, but for the grace of God . . . Dave went on, and when I realised where he was going, there was an ice-cold prickle in my chest despite the heat. "I don't reckon Phil killed him deliberately. Unlucky punch, wasn't it?"

No. Sudden, furious anger fizzed in my veins. "It wasn't any bloody punch! It wasn't Phil, all right? What the fuck is this? You still pissed off with him about— Fuck, I don't even know why you're pissed off with him!" I was practically shouting in Dave's face at this point.

"Oi. Sit down. *Sit. Down.* Tom. I know you don't want to think about it, but you've gotta face facts. The bloke's got form."

I sat down. Before I fell down. "The . . . What?"

Christ. Now Dave's expression was pitying. "He did tell you why he left the force, right?"

"Well, yeah. He wanted to go it alone. Always did. He only joined your lot for the training."

Dave looked away, swearing. "Sorry, mate, but that's not what it says in his file."

"What do you mean, *his file*? Since when have you got a file on my bloke?"

"*I* haven't. His old force have. I got 'em to give me the edited highlights, after he enlisted my help with the Met the other day. Thought I'd better know exactly who I was vouching for. Turns out, there was an incident. Basically involved one Sergeant Morrison following a suspect home and beating the crap out of him."

"Phil?" My stomach was one big, swirling pit of nausea. I couldn't fucking believe it. Phil was chucked out of the force for police brutality? *My* Phil? "Did they send him down?"

Dave shook his head. "Never went to court. He got suspended, and everyone breathed a bloody great sigh of relief when he decided not to come back." He gave me a significant look. "Want to know what the bloke he beat up was in for questioning about?"

"No. Yeah. Maybe. Shit, just tell me, all right?"

"Domestic violence. So it wouldn't be too far out of the bounds of possibility to think maybe blokes beating on women is a bit of a red rag to him now, would it? Seeing as he never liked them in the first place, *and* one of 'em cost him his job."

"But he'd never . . . Phil'd never kill anyone." My mind was spinning. He wouldn't, would he? "And Carey never hit Marianne, all right? She said that." It struck me suddenly that pretty much all we knew about Carey, we'd got from Marianne.

But she wouldn't have lied. Not sweet little Marianne. She was just a kid.

"Tom . . . Look, I believe you, all right? But the bloke who did this, chances are he *didn't* mean it to go so far." Dave sighed. "Look, I know you like him, though God knows why from what you told me about you and him at school. But Morrison's bad news. His sort never change."

I felt hollow. Empty. "No. You're wrong about him. He's done good stuff. For fuck's sake, he's saved my life."

"Yeah, funny how every time you're in danger, he always seems to be involved, though, innit?" Dave held up his hands. "I'm not saying he doesn't care about you, all right? In his way. I'm just saying, when push comes to shove, you can't count on him not to shove just that little bit too hard."

I gave Dave a rundown of my and Phil's whereabouts for the past few days to the best of my knowledge and recollection. Including the damning fact that I hadn't seen a whisker of Phil since Sunday lunchtime, or for large chunks of Saturday, either. And then I walked out of there in a daze.

I couldn't believe it. I'd thought I knew Phil. Could trust him. Yeah, he'd been a bit of a bully at school. But that was half a lifetime ago. I'd thought he was past all that.

Here was Dave telling me Phil had cold-bloodedly assaulted someone. I wanted to think it wasn't true, but there was this little voice in my head reminding me of all the times I'd called him stubborn and pigheaded. Didn't seem too far a stretch from him being firmly convinced something had to be done, to actually doing it himself. Christ, no wonder he'd become a PI. Talk about taking the law into your own hands . . .

There was no way, though, he'd ever have gone so far as to kill someone. *No way.*

Then again, only this morning I'd have said he'd never beat someone up, and look how wrong I'd turned out to be on that. Maybe it was like Dave said, and he hadn't meant to kill him? God. My insides were tied up in bloody knots. Looking at it objectively, I realised I knew sod all about it.

The only thing I was certain of was that Phil had lied to me.

Given the mood I was in, it wasn't the best night for Phil to have let himself into my house to wait for me. He was sitting on the sofa with a beer when I got in, his feet up on the coffee table like he didn't have a care in the world—or a dark secret either.

I saw red. Christ, I saw fucking crimson. I stomped over to him, fighting the urge to dash the beer bottle from his hand.

"You fucking . . . What the *fuck* were you thinking? *Were* you thinking? At all? What about back then? Shit, I can't believe it." I felt sick.

Phil's face twisted as he put down his beer and stood up. "What's happened? Who's been saying stuff?"

"Dave. In the course of asking just where you were when Carey was getting himself killed. So there I was, all 'No, mate, you're barking up the wrong tree, my Phil wouldn't hurt a fly,' and then I've got Dave giving me pitying looks while he tells me you bloody nearly got done for GBH!" I was so furious I could barely see straight.

"Tom . . ." Phil put a hand on my arm. I shook it off. I didn't want him touching me right now.

"I felt like a right dick. And not a *private* one either. Spouting all that *crap* you told me about you leaving the force on purpose so you could set up on your own. You lied to me, you bastard."

Now Phil was frowning too. "Bollocks."

"Fuck that. You didn't jump, you were sodding well pushed."

"Look, just because I never told you something doesn't mean I lied about it."

"Christ, what is this? Bloody word games? You said you only joined the police to get their training."

"Yeah, and?" Phil folded his arms, the git.

"*And* it's fucking bollocks. To coin a phrase."

"That what your precious *mate* told you? He's a fucking liar. Or he doesn't have a fucking clue what he's talking about. Both, I'd guess. Jesus Christ, Tom. I can't believe you're taking that sad fat old tosser's word over mine."

"Oi. You don't bloody well talk about Dave like that. Where the bloody hell would you have been without him last week?" Fucking ungrateful bastard. I struggled to keep my voice—and my fists— down. "Come on, then—you reckon Dave's talking bollocks, you tell me how it really was."

We glared at each other. Phil's face was hard. "All right, then, I'll tell you how it was. This *cunt* puts his missus in the hospital and just laughs in our fucking faces because he's got her too scared to make a statement. I lost it, okay? I lost it, and I wiped that fucking smirk off his face with my fist. Happy now?"

Not much, no.

I couldn't tear my gaze from him. Christ, just when I thought I knew him . . . If I was honest, I'd always found it a bit of a turn-on, him being bigger than me. Stronger than me. Now, though . . . Now, I wasn't so sure.

A muscle twitched in his jaw. "I just lost it, okay?" he said, quieter this time.

"Oh." My voice sounded funny, which wasn't that surprising given how much my throat hurt. "So that's all right, then. 'Cos you just lost it. Still, at least I know what to watch out for now if you and me ever have a major bust-up."

Phil froze. I couldn't read his expression, but it didn't look good. Something hit my hip, and I realized I'd stepped back into the doorway. "You think I'd . . . Jesus *fuck*, Tom, you really think I'd ever . . ." He swallowed. Then he closed his eyes briefly. "I . . . Fuck this. Just fuck it."

Then he turned and walked out of the house.

CHAPTER SEVENTEEN

Christ, I needed to talk to someone. I also needed a drink, but that was more easily arranged. I grabbed a glass and the bottle of whiskey and slumped onto the sofa.

I didn't know who to call.

Gary would be sympathetic, but he wasn't exactly the most impartial observer where Phil was concerned, and I couldn't have stuck it if he'd let slip how pleased he was to be proved right. I couldn't face talking to Dave either, not with him being all *I-told-you-so* and shaking his head sadly.

Cherry? She'd be upset, and probably worried about both of us. It'd taken her a while to warm to Phil, but I reckoned she was fond of him in her way. But she had enough on her plate, what with the job and the wedding preparations and all. She didn't need to deal with my break-up on top. If that was what it was.

Was it?

I wasn't even sure what I wanted it to be, let alone what it actually was. It'd rocked me, no question, hearing him admit to beating this bloke up. I'd thought he'd changed. The crap he'd got up to at school—the insults, the pushing and shoving in the corridors, in PE lessons—I'd thought that was just him coming to terms with, well, fancying me. And the whole being-gay thing. But this . . . this had been *years* after school. When he was a copper, for God's sake. Sworn to uphold the law and all that.

My face burned as I remembered how I'd defended him to Dave. I'd been so bloody sure Phil was innocent. I felt stupid, now. Stupid and naive. Embarrassed too—Dave was a mate, for fuck's sake.

But Christ, the way Phil had looked at me . . . Like *I'd* hurt *him*. Shit, I shouldn't have said what I had. Just 'cos he lost it with some wife-beating wanker didn't mean he'd lose it with me, did it? From what Phil said, the bastard had deserved it, and then some.

From what Phil said.

I wasn't sure what it meant about Carey. I didn't want to think about that. I mean, if Carey really had done all the stuff Marianne said he had, would it really be so bad if Phil had just . . .? No. I didn't want to think about it.

I ended up calling Mum and letting her drone on about her garden and how the roses all had greenfly and she didn't reckon these European ladybirds were doing their job properly, these red-on-black ones, and they weren't as nice to look at either, which was adding insult to injury, and wasn't it terrible about all the bees? All I had to do was say "Yeah" and "Mm" every time she paused for breath, and just let her words wash over me. I was actually starting to feel a bit better, when her tone changed and I realized she'd asked me a question. "Sorry, Mum, didn't catch that."

"I said, 'How's Philip?'"

Cheers, Mum. Great timing on finally starting to care if he lived or died. I swallowed. "He's good," I lied.

"Oh, good," she said, sounding distracted. Or maybe just disappointed. "He seemed a bit out of sorts on Sunday, but I suppose you know him better than I do. There isn't anything wrong, is there?"

"No, course not," I lied through my teeth.

"Well, you don't usually ring up just for a chat, do you?" She sounded like she was teasing, but it still caused an uncomfortable twinge in the guilt muscles.

"Yeah, but that's 'cos when I do, I get the third degree," I said, trying to keep it light. "Um. I'd better go—stuff to do, you know. You look after yourself, yeah? Give my love to—to Dad." Shit, had she noticed the hesitation?

"He's only in the next room, you know. Did you want to speak to him?"

"Nah, that's okay. He's, well, he's keeping all right, isn't he?" Daft question. He'd been fine at Sunday lunch. Then again, things changed, didn't they?

"Oh, much as ever." She paused. "I think he'd be pleased to see you, if you could find the time to pop round."

There was a little wobble in her voice as she said it. I'd been right. She knew I'd found out the truth.

Oh God, I couldn't deal with this now. "Sorry, Mum, gotta run. I'll speak to you soon, yeah?"

I hung up, my heart thumping, and poured myself another whiskey. It could've done with some ice in it—the evening, instead of cooling off, had turned sticky and muggy, promising a night of tossing and turning and chucking off the duvet—but the fridge seemed like half a mile away. I could make do.

I switched on the telly, but nothing held my interest long enough to even begin distracting me. Even *Ramsay's Kitchen Nightmares* seemed stupid and pointless right now. Merlin stalked into the room and I patted the sofa cushion beside me. Having him on my lap would probably involve death by heat exhaustion, but the company would be nice.

Of course, this being my luck, Merlin looked at me, then spooked at nothing and scarpered up the stairs. Probably to join Arthur as a furry hot water bottle on my bed. If I was really lucky, one of them would have picked up fleas from somewhere and would be introducing them to the bedbugs right about now.

I picked up the paper. Threw it down again—nothing likely to cheer me up in those pages. Maybe I should start reading books or something. I wondered if they did self-help manuals for people whose significant others turned out to be murderers.

Oh God.

I'd have switched on my laptop, but there'd have been emails, and I couldn't face the thought of actually having to deal with stuff right now. Plus I might have been tempted to look up how long it took bodies to start to go off, and I had a strong suspicion my stomach wasn't up to what I might find. I got myself another drink instead.

Then I thought, *Sod it*, and called Cherry. So she had a lot on her plate; didn't we all? And for some of us, that plate was piled high with shit. In fact, the plate was more like a sodding toilet. *And* the seat was cracked.

She could suck it up and deal.

Cherry answered on the second or third ring. "Tom?"

"Hey, Sis." I paused.

"Tom?" she said again. "Are you all right?"

"Not exactly. Think I might have broke up with Phil."

There was a long pause on her end. "Oh, Tom. What happened?"

"Oh, nothing much. Just, Dave reckons he might be a murderer, only he didn't mean it, and he beat up this other bloke when he was a copper. And when I told him, he got pissed off. And, well, pissed off."

"You're not making sense."

"No. Prob'ly not. Shit, I think I'm just tired. Sorry. I'll speak to you later, all right?" Christ, it was muggy this evening. I trudged over to the window, but it was already open and not a breath of air was coming through.

"Tom! Don't put the phone down. Where are you?"

"Home. Alone." If any comedy burglars dropped by, they'd be welcome to whatever they could find. I couldn't be arsed to stop them.

"I'll come over."

"Nah, you don't wanna do that. It's getting late." Well, maybe not *that* late, but it'd take her a good twenty minutes to get to mine from Pluck's End, and she'd have to drive back too.

"Don't be ridiculous. I'll see you soon." She hung up.

Great. Now I'd have to tidy up.

Nah, sod it. It was only my sister. I slumped back on the sofa and switched the telly back on.

It was actually more than half an hour before Cherry got to my house, and I soon found out why. She'd brought Gary with her, the traitor. Her, not him, although to tell the truth, I was a bit hacked off with both of them, conspiring behind my back. When your best mate and your big sister get all chummy and gang up on you, it's just wrong.

Cherry was wearing a girly sundress and clumpy sandals that made her look younger than the big four-oh she'd reached earlier this year, and her nose was so shiny from the heat you could see your face in it.

Gary, looking cuddly in cargo shorts and his Pavlov's Bitch T-shirt, was all sorrowful eyes and pouting lips. "Tommy, darling, give your Uncle Gary a big hug." Seeing as he currently had both my arms pinned firmly to my sides in his python-like embrace, I wondered how he thought I was going to manage that. "Now, sit down and tell us *all* about it."

I wobbled a bit when he released me, trying to get the air back in my lungs. Gary had parked his bum on the sofa and was patting his knee expectantly.

"There is no way on earth I'm sitting on your lap," I told him firmly and dropped into one of the chairs at what was hopefully a safe distance. "Christ. You want a beer?"

"I'm making tea," Cherry yelled from the kitchen. "And I brought some cakes round."

Got it. No more alcohol for Tom tonight. Bloody marvellous.

"Ooh, are they those ones with the cherries on top?" Gary piped up. "I do love nibbling on a cherry."

Bloody hell. If that was Gary flirting with my sister, I was out of here.

"No, you ate all those," Cherry said, apparently oblivious to innuendo as she brought in an open biscuit tin full of cupcakes with butter icing and little ball bearings on top.

Since when did Gary and Cherry meet up for cupcakes? In fact, come to that . . . "Oi, since when do you bake cakes, Sis?"

"Don't be silly. *I* didn't bake them. Mrs. Ormerod baked these. Careful when you eat them. I lost a filling to one of those little silver balls the last batch she baked. And *Mr.* Ormerod didn't have a tooth left in his head when he passed away in February, bless him."

I groaned. "Great. So not only have I lost the love of my life, I'm about to lose a few teeth and all."

Not that Phil was, you know, actually the love of my life.

Probably.

Shit. How did my life get this fucked up?

"But look on the bright side, darling," Gary put in, leaning forward and unerringly grabbing the largest cake. "When it comes to blowjobs, the fewer teeth the better, I've always found."

"Don't be silly, Tom," Cherry said briskly, pretending she was far too well brought up to have heard what Gary had said. "I'm sure it's all just a misunderstanding." She bustled out and returned a moment later with three mugs of tea. "There you are, Gary. Tom. Now, what's all this nonsense about breaking up with Phil?"

I didn't want to tell them. I sat there with my hands wrapped around my mug—not that I needed any extra heat, but Cherry had put about half a pint of milk in so it was barely even warm—and struggled to think what to say.

"You said, well, you said he'd beaten someone up. When he was in the police force," Cherry prompted, leaning forward with an earnest look on her face to match the one Gary was wearing. With them lined up on the sofa opposite me, it felt like interrogation by committee. "Tom, he hasn't been, well, violent towards you, has he?"

"Course he hasn't!" I took a sip of tea, managed not to gag too visibly, and put my mug down on the coffee table. I ran a hand through my hair. It felt sweaty and horrible.

"So what's the problem?" Gary asked, beaming as he took another cupcake. How he could pack them away like that, I had no idea. I felt queasy just watching.

Well, maybe it was from the tea.

"It's, well . . . Fuck it. We had a bit of a row about it, all right? About him keeping secrets—"

"But, darling, everyone has secrets," Gary interrupted. "It's how we preserve our mystique."

Not helping, ta very much. And since when was Gary on Phil's side, anyhow? I was starting to think Darren was a bad influence in more ways than one.

"And he lied about why he left the force. Made it out to be some big career plan, when they actually gave him the heave-ho. *And* he called Dave Southgate a sad fat old tosser."

"Well, *that* wasn't very nice," Cherry said primly.

"Sticks and stones, darling, sticks and stones." Gary took a delicate slurp of his tea.

"And then, *then* he had the nerve to get the hump with *me* about it all."

Cherry nibbled thoughtfully on a cupcake. "Are you sure you didn't overreact?" Something in my face must have tipped her off to what I thought about that, as she went on in a hurry. "Not that I think you *would*. It's just, well, Phil always seems so civilised, these days. And I realise that doesn't mean anything in terms of domestic violence, but you just said there hadn't been any of that."

"Aren't you supposed to be on my side here? Strikes me this tea-and-sympathy party is a bit lacking in one of the essential ingredients." And that was being charitable about the so-called tea.

"Of *course* we're on your side, Tommy," Gary answered for her. "We just want you to be happy, don't we, Cherry Pop?"

Cherry Pop? This was getting worse and worse.

"Absolutely. And, well, Phil's been making you happy, hasn't he?" Cherry leaned forward to pat my knee. "And if he was disposed towards violence, I'm sure we'd have seen some sign of it by now. Not that I'm saying you get on people's nerves, obviously, but, well..." She trailed off.

"*Well*, what?" I demanded, narked.

"There's that thing you do with your hands when you're stressed."

"What thing?"

"Oh, you know. *You* know, don't you, Gary?"

Gary nodded sagely. "Look, he's doing it now."

"I'm not . . ." I stood up and shoved both hands in my jeans pockets.

"And there's the . . ." Gary made a vague hand-wavy gesture towards his right ear, for God's sake.

"Oh God, yes," Cherry said and laughed. "Every time . . . Tom? *Tom?* What's the matter? Oh, come on. It's not that bad. We're just saying maybe your friend Dave is being a little overprotective. I mean, it's understandable Phil wouldn't have wanted to tell you about leaving the police under a cloud. If it even happened."

"It happened. He admitted it."

"Even so. He'd be hardly likely to go out of his way to tell you things that don't reflect well on him." She frowned and put down her cupcake. "Tom, this isn't about Mum and Dad not liking him, is it?"

"It's . . ." I waved my hands expansively, then wondered if that was the *thing* she'd been on about and jammed them back in my pockets. "It's got nothing to do with Mum and Dad, all right?"

Gary stood up and threw his arms around me. It was like being hugged by Winnie the Pooh. Well, if old Winnie had grown to six foot and had developed a slight case of wandering paws. "So what is it about, Tommy dear? You haven't really said."

I hadn't? What the bloody hell had I been talking about all this time?

God, I was tired. I sagged against Gary's soft, warm chest. He probably *was* stuffed with fluff. Cherry patted my shoulder awkwardly—at least, I hope it was Cherry. Otherwise one of the hands on my arse would have had to belong to her. "Dave thinks Phil did it."

"Did what?" It came in stereo.

"The murder."

"Whose murder?" Cherry asked, her voice shrill. Gary stiffened. And not in any way Darren would be after my nadgers for.

I lifted my head to stare at them in turn. Where had they *been*? "Carey's murder."

"Grant Carey's been murdered?" Gary demanded, sounding shocked, at the same time as Cherry went, "Who's Carey?"

I pushed away from them both and headed for the whiskey. "Sod the tea and sympathy. I need a drink."

CHAPTER EIGHTEEN

I woke up with a headache next morning. Trust Cherry's god-awful tea to be the one thing that could give me a hangover.

I popped up to the Dyke midmorning. *Not* for a hair of the dog but to see how Harry and Marianne were doing. And, all right, maybe to reassure myself Marianne wasn't the sort to lie to anyone. I grabbed a bacon roll from the baker's in Brock's Hollow on the way, seeing as pub grub was likely to be off the menu for the foreseeable. I'd already heard a couple of off-colour jokes en route about what might have gone into the Devil's Dyke steak-and-ale pie.

I was expecting the pub to be closed, but I wasn't expecting the whole place to be shut up and silent as an all-too-appropriate proverbial. There wasn't any police sticky tape on the front door, so I banged on it, but got no answer. "Harry?" I called. "It's me. Tom."

Still no answer. Just as I was about to give it up for a bad job, Marianne's crumpled curls stuck out of an upstairs window. "Tom?"

"Yeah. Everything all right, love?"

She didn't answer, and the curls disappeared. I waited, and after half a minute or so, the door opened.

Marianne's face was red, blotchy, and bare of makeup. All her bubbles had gone flat. Seeing her like that, common sense chipped in and told me in no uncertain terms she was nothing more than the victim in all this. No question about it. She gave a loud sniff and looked at me like she couldn't trust herself to speak.

"How are you holding up, love?" I said and got an armful of barmaid for my trouble.

She felt very . . . soft. And fragile, like if I hugged her too hard she'd snap. The front of my T-shirt was rapidly getting wet. In between sobs, all I could make out were the words *Harry* and *my fault*.

"Hey," I said, patting her hair and getting a waft of strawberry shampoo. "Come on. Let's get you back inside, sit you down. Cup of tea, that'll do the trick."

"I'll put the kettle on," said a vaguely familiar voice, which nearly made me jump out of my skin.

I squinted into the relative darkness of the lounge bar, and was surprised to make out the motherly figure of the new vicar, dog collar and all. What was her name? Gillian? No—Lillian. "Oh—'ullo," I said awkwardly. "Didn't realise Marianne had company." I hoped she hadn't taken advantage of the situation to try to get Marianne to sign up for the God Squad. Seemed a bit calculating for a woman of the cloth.

Then I told myself to stop being such a suspicious git. Chances were she was just being supportive.

"I didn't think Marianne should be here on her own," Lillian said and bustled off kitchenwards while I wondered if I'd been too transparent with my suspicions, or if Him upstairs had given her a nod.

"All right, love?" I steered Marianne to a comfy chair and peeled her limp-spaghetti arms from my neck. "You sit yourself down. Got a tissue?"

Marianne gave a loud, hiccuppy sniff, which I took as a no. I scrabbled in my pockets and found a mostly clean handkerchief. "There you go. Have a good blow."

She took the hanky but didn't take my advice—just sat there holding it like a kiddie with a favourite bit of old blanket. Well, as long as it helped somehow.

Lillian was back with a trio of mugs a lot faster than I'd expected. She seemed to have found her way around the private areas here pretty quick. She popped a mug down on the table in front of Marianne, and then handed me one. "I hope white, two sugars is all right?"

I flashed her a smile. Can't stand sweet tea, but it's the thought that counts. "Lovely. Harry not here, then?" I was surprised she'd have left Marianne at a time like this.

The Rev's face was grim. "She's been taken in for questioning."

Marianne burst out sobbing again.

I stared at Lillian. "Sh—sugar, they can't think she did it. Seriously? *Harry*? She wouldn't hurt a . . ." *Fly-weight*, my brain helpfully provided, as I remembered her boxing past.

"I'm sure it's just routine," Lillian said, but she didn't look any more convinced than I felt.

I took a sip of tea, and another as well before the god-awful syrupy taste sank in.

"Was she actually arrested?"

"No, just asked politely to come and answer some questions down at the police station. But you know what that means." Lillian sipped her own tea.

"Sh—sugar," I said again, this time with feeling.

Lillian raised an eyebrow. "I do have a teenage son, you know. I think I can cope with the odd expletive."

"Er, yeah. Sorry," I said, then wondered why I was apologising for *not* swearing.

"Anyway," she went on. "You needn't worry about Marianne. I'll stay with her until Harry gets back."

"Don't you have"—I stopped myself just in time before I said *God-bothering*—"vicar stuff to do?"

Lillian smiled. "Nothing that won't keep. Our Lord told the parable of the lost sheep for a reason." Somehow it didn't sound as preachy as it would have if Greg, say, had said it.

"Right. Okay, then." I turned to Marianne, who was holding her tea like a liquid security blanket and sniffling. "You going to be all right?"

She nodded bravely.

"I'll just put my cup in the kitchen," I said, standing up. At least I'd be able to chuck the vile stuff down the sink.

As I passed the steps down to the cellars, I was hit with a memory of the smell last time I'd been down there. It was so vivid, I shuddered and almost gagged. The cellars weren't even taped off—apparently the police had decided they'd got all they could out of them. For a weird moment, I had a daft urge to go down the steps and take another look around, though what I'd have been looking for, I had no idea.

I wondered if the clean-up people had been round yet, and how Marianne could stand to stay there if they hadn't. God, maybe the smell hadn't been just a memory . . .

"Going to take the quick way out, all right?" I yelled back to the ladies, and legged it through the kitchen door that led straight outside.

I managed to make it out and into the fresh air in time to stave off a reappearance of my bacon butty.

After I'd left the Dyke, I marched round to the cop shop like a one-man protest rally, barely holding my anger in check. The bloke on reception knew me by sight, luckily, or I'd have had to march straight back home again. "DI Southgate?" he asked before I got a word out. "I'll see if he's free."

There was a short conversation on the internal phone, then I got ushered into Dave's office. "Mr. Paretski to see you, sir."

"Oi. I want a word with you." It was probably a bit of a rude greeting, but I was narked.

Dave sighed. "Course you bleedin' do. Cheers, Keith."

Reception-bloke—Keith, presumably; I filed the name away for later—nodded and left.

"Come on, then, I haven't got all day." Dave rolled his shoulders and winced as something cracked. "What's got your knickers in a twist? Let me guess—wouldn't be one Harry Shire, now would it?"

"You can't seriously think she did it. Harry?"

"Has she been charged? No, she has not. Which means we're keeping an open mind, all right? Something you might want to consider. Think about it, sunshine. She's a proud woman, Harry Shire. How'd you think she felt, a little turd like Carey having her over a barrel?"

"What, so you reckon she snapped, and shoved him *under* a barrel?"

"Would you blame her?"

"Maybe not, but your lot sodding well would. *And* I don't believe she'd do it. Not Harry."

"Someone bloody well did it, didn't they? And if it wasn't your Phil, who's the obvious suspect? I'm not saying she meant to kill him. Like I said before, could have been an accident—maybe she hit him just that little bit too hard. Once a boxer . . . And there's another thing." Dave leaned forward and looked me right in the eye. "You ever think maybe she might have been the one who put you in hospital?"

"What?" I stared back at him. "Jesus, what? I don't even know where to start with that. Why the bloody hell would she do anything to me?"

"Because, as has been pointed out to me, both you and Carey are dark-haired little squirts, and one shadowy figure looks a lot like another in the dark. You said yourself, you were staring up at Marianne's window like a bleedin' Peeping Tom. Why the bloody hell *wouldn't* Ms. Shire assume it was her girlfriend's stalker?" Dave gave me a sharp look. "Found you pretty soon after it happened, didn't she?"

"No. I mean, yeah, she did, but no, it couldn't have been her."

"No? We know she's got the strength to chuck a ball that hard. And Carey had been in that pub pissing her off all night. Everyone's got their limits. Could've been the last straw, seeing him—as she thought—gawping at her girlfriend while she got her kit off for bed."

Shit. What had Harry said about people on her premises after hours?

That they'd get what was coming to them, or words to that effect.

"No," I said, and even I could hear it didn't sound all that certain anymore. "Chucking a ball? That's not her style. Punch a bloke in the face, maybe. But not chuck a ball at the back of his head."

Dave sighed. "People do all kinds of bollocks. Especially for love. Maybe she had it in her hand—picked it up to put it away or something—and just gave in to the impulse. *Obviously* she regretted it when she realised it was you all along. *And* it would have made her even madder at Carey, so she'd be even more likely to snap next time he got in her face."

"No." I stood up. "It wasn't her, all right? Harry wouldn't do that."

But all I could think of was her face when she'd talked about him. And how some *idiot* had told her anyone wiping Carey off the face of the earth would be performing a public service.

"And all that business with Marianne getting you to check the cellar out? Fishier than a dolphin's arse, if you ask me." Dave clearly wasn't as finished here as I was. "Wouldn't surprise me if she had a pretty good idea already what you were going to find down there, her and Harry both."

"For fuck's sake, why would they hide a body in their own bloody cellar?"

"People do stupid stuff when they're panicked."

"Harry, panic? Seriously?"

Dave shrugged. "You ever seen her with a body to hide? People don't always react how you'd expect them to. Maybe she needed to get him out of sight sharpish, so she bunged him down there for temporary safekeeping and then never got the chance to move the bastard? You know what it's like up at the Dyke—always someone coming and going." He gave a grim smile. "Maybe she didn't reckon he'd go off so quick. Your average corpse doesn't come with a best-before date. So there she is, stuck with a body in the cellar that's starting to stink the place out. Not to mention, isn't quite as solid and easily portable as it used to be."

Cheers for the mental image, Dave.

"She's got to get rid of him somehow," he carried on, "if for no other reason than he's starting to put the punters off their pints. So what does she do? She knows nobody'd buy her getting a man to do her dirty work for her. So she buggers off for a bit and gets the girlfriend to call in our resident corpse-finder general, otherwise known as one Thomas Paretski. That way, Harry's one step removed from the whole bloody palaver, she's got a witness to her and Marianne not knowing what was down there—allegedly—*and* she gets someone else to cart away the late Grant Carey's mouldering mortal remains for her. Peachy."

"Peachy, my arse. So basically, what you're saying is, either my bloke's a murderer or Harry is. Hey, maybe they were in it together, ever think of that? Sure you don't want to check out my alibi and all? Maybe I wanted to get back at Carey for chucking that ball at me?"

Dave just looked at me.

"Shit. You *have* checked out my bloody alibi, haven't you?"

"Look, before you get on your high horse, just remember I'm accountable to the public here. I've got to follow procedure. Course I don't reckon you did anyone in. But if my boss hauls my bollocks over the coals, I can't just tell him 'No worries, Tom's a mate,' now can I? And that goes for the rest of 'em too." He paused, ran a finger around his collar and grimaced. "I'd get a bloody good arse-kicking if anyone knew I'd been telling you about the case, and all. Just be careful around Harry, that's all I'm saying. *And* that bloke of yours."

"Phil'd never hurt me," I said. Loyal to the last and all that bollocks.

"None of 'em ever would." Dave's tone was more sad than cynical. "Until they bloody well do."

I drove back to Fleetville on autopilot. It was all bollocks. I *knew* that. Harry'd never kill someone.

Except . . . My guts twisted as I thought of how Marianne had been when I'd found the body. Something hadn't rung true about her reaction. She'd been upset, of course she had.

But . . . she hadn't seemed all that shocked.

Almost as if she'd already known what I was going to find. And there was another thing—she'd just taken my word for it when I'd said what I'd found. If someone told you they'd found a dead body in your house, you'd want to have a look, wouldn't you? See for yourself they hadn't just panicked over a bundle of old rags or something. Unless, of course, you already knew full well there was a dead body there, because that was where you'd left it . . .

Or, say, where you'd seen someone else leave it. Let's face it, the thought of little stick-figure Marianne hitting a bloke so hard he'd died was laughable. So was the thought of her carting a dead body down into the cellar all by her little lonesome. If Marianne had done it, she'd had help—and who was the obvious suspect?

No. I couldn't believe it. Not Harry and Marianne. This was seriously doing my head in. I needed to talk it over with Phil.

Shame we weren't actually speaking to each other at the mo.

CHAPTER NINETEEN

I felt . . . I dunno. Lost, I suppose, which, given my well-known talent for finding things, should have been bloody hilarious.

I wasn't really appreciating the joke right now.

I called off the afternoon's job, then wished I hadn't. It left me wandering around the house feeling like I ought to have stuff to do, but I wasn't sure what it was. I mean, the cats had been fed probably a bit more than the vet would approve of and even Arthur was starting to get seriously hacked off with me stroking him all the time. Plus, I'd run out of laundry (don't think about Phil's stuff at the bottom of the basket, just don't) and cleaned out the fridge.

Yeah, there was plenty of paperwork to catch up on, but . . . I just couldn't. I switched on the telly, hoping to find some sport to pass the time, but all the BBC were showing was women's gymnastics, and I didn't think I was really their target audience.

The house felt empty. Too big and too small at the same time, somehow. I couldn't stay there.

It was like I didn't know who *anyone* was anymore. Including me. If Phil wasn't who I thought he was, if Harry wasn't . . .

I just wanted something I could be certain about.

Failing that, I went round to Mum and Dad's.

They still lived in the house I'd grown up in—well, since I was seven or eight, when we'd moved from London. Much to my then-teenage sister's disgust, as she'd had to leave behind all her mates and her boyfriend, who'd promptly sought consolation with her former best friend. Not that she was still bitter about it, or anything. Well, that was what she said, but then, why make a point of telling me a few months ago about how she'd blamed me at the time?

I mean, seriously, if she wanted to blame someone, why not blame the bastard who murdered a little girl and then hid her body in the park for yours truly to come wandering across? Or blame Mum for deciding the city wasn't a safe place to live anymore.

So anyway, we'd moved to St. Albans, which was far enough out of London to feel totally separate, but still near enough for Dad to get in to work on the trains for the last few years he had to go before retirement. I'd settled in all right, as far as I could remember—primary school age kids usually do, I suppose. It was Cherry and Richard who found it hard moving away from all their mates. If Mum and Dad had the same problem, I was too young to notice—and in any case, Mum chummed up pretty quick with Auntie Lol next door.

Funny that. If they'd never met—if we'd never moved, even— would I ever have found out the truth about myself? Or would I have died thinking Dad was, well, my dad?

I wasn't sure how I felt about that. It was hard not to be mad at Mum for keeping something so bloody important from me—but then again, if I'd never found out, would I be feeling so ... Shit. I wasn't sure *how* I felt.

Lost, I supposed.

Bugger it. I got out my key and opened the door.

After wandering into the living room and calling out "Anyone home?" umpteen times and getting no answer, I had a look round the house. Just in case Dad's hearing had finally gone completely and Mum was, I dunno, upstairs in the bedroom with the door shut. And *The Archers* on full blast.

There was no one around. It was like a dry-land version of the *Marie Celeste*. Only the dust bunnies in my old bedroom gave me a cheerful wave when I opened the door. It was always weird, seeing the room without all my stuff in it, even after all this time. Like it was a hotel room I'd stayed in once. Mum wasn't one for keeping shrines to departed children—every time one of us moved out, it was all hands on deck for a scurry of redecoration and pointed threats that if we didn't take our junk with us it was going in the skip.

Which I'd never fully understood, with them having all this space here they never actually used. They spent more time in the conservatory than they did upstairs, during the day at least ... It finally dawned on me. A hot summer's day like today? They wouldn't be in the house.

I ran downstairs again and headed into the garden, and there they were, installed comfortably on lawn chairs with faded flowery cushions, sunhats firmly wedged on heads. The glare from Dad's pale summer trousers nearly blinded me. Mum was shelling broad beans into a colander. It was like I'd walked into a time warp, or a museum exhibit of the 1950s suburban family. I half expected someone to start talking about the coronation, or how those new-fangled televisions would never catch on.

"Oh, hello, Tom," Mum said, looking up from her vegetables. Dad didn't react, and a closer look confirmed my suspicion he'd nodded off under his Panama. "We weren't expecting you today."

Cheers, Mum. Way to make me feel welcome. "Yeah, I just thought I'd pop round."

"Well, it's always nice to see you. Gerald," she said in a louder voice, "Tom's here. *Gerald.*"

As if in answer, Dad gave an exceptionally loud snore, and then he woke up with a start. "What? Speak up, dear. Oh, Tom. We weren't expecting you today."

"Yeah, I kind of got that. Thought I'd pop round. You all right?"

"Fine, fine. Did you hear about that business in Brock's Hollow? They found a body in the pub. Terrible. Still, I hear he wasn't a local."

I s'pose it was the same sort of thing as newsreaders making a point of telling us how many casualties in some far-flung disaster were British, like nobody gave a monkey's about the rest, but it still sounded a bit harsh.

"Yeah." I grabbed a spare folding chair from the conservatory, wrestled it open, and sat down. "Bad news for Harry—she's the landlady. Mate of mine. Not good for business, this."

And no, I wasn't planning on mentioning I'd found the body, and luckily it hadn't made the news reports either. Mum moved out here to get away from thoughts of me finding dead bodies. I didn't want to remind her about all that sort of stuff.

"Oh, I don't know," Mum said with a sniff. "She'll probably get all sorts up there now. Gothic punks and whatnot. People are terribly ghoulish these days."

Dad perked up. "There's a pub in St. Albans that does ghost tours. She could try that."

Cheers, Dad. It was bad enough having the memory of Grant Carey's mortal remains stuck in my head. The last thing I needed when I went up the Dyke for a relaxing pint was his unquiet bloody spirit haunting the pumps. "Aren't the ghosts in the White Hart centuries old? I don't reckon it's quite the same if they've only just died. Bit too close for comfort and all that."

"Would you like a cup of tea?" Mum offered, probably so she could get away from all this morbid stuff.

"I'll make it," I said, jumping up from my chair and almost knocking it over. "Dad? You on for a cup of tea?"

"Oh, yes. Lovely." He closed his eyes.

I legged it back to the kitchen and put the kettle on. They'd had new kitchen cupboards put in since I'd left home, but since they were identical to the old ones except for the door fronts, I had no problem finding stuff. Even managed to dig out a tin with a nice fresh batch of tea loaf. Whistling, I buttered a few slices and bunged them on a plate, then got a tray and loaded it up with mugs and plates.

Mum had finished shelling the beans by the time I got back out there with the provisions. Dad was asleep—at least, until Mum nudged him. "Gerald? Tea."

"What? Oh yes. Lovely." He took his mug, raised it as if he was about to make a toast, then bent down to put it carefully on the grass without tasting it. And closed his eyes again.

"Hope you weren't saving the cake for anything," I said, offering Mum a slice.

"Oh, I can always make another one," she said, leaving me not sure if I should be feeling guilty or not.

Still, I knew what would make me feel better. A nice slice of cake. I took the biggest piece and tucked in. It was pretty good. "You been busy?" I asked.

"Don't talk with your mouth full. No, not really. Well, there's always so much to do in the garden. It's been getting into a terrible state."

I gazed around me at the pristine flowerbeds and the roses in their regimented rows. "Looks all right to me."

"Everything's been growing like wildfire, the weather we've been having. The buddleia's getting *completely* out of hand."

"That's the one with the butterflies? Looks fine to me."

"It needs cutting back. And we've got honeysuckle down the back that's getting all over everything."

"Well, if you need a hand . . ."

Mum gave me a look. "You always seem so busy lately."

I sighed, thinking of just who I'd been busy with. Lately.

Should have remembered Mum was sharp as a pair of secateurs when it came to stuff like that. "Is everything all right?" she asked.

"Course," I said automatically, with a big smile to show I meant it.

Mum didn't look convinced. "You don't usually just come round for an afternoon visit." She frowned slightly. "I suppose your, er, Phil is working?"

"Er, yeah. Busy lad, he is." Not that I actually had a bloody clue what Phil was doing right now, but it seemed like a fair bet.

"I suppose that's something."

I stood up. "Mum, what are those flowers down the end of the garden? Those blue ones."

"Those? Nigella. Love-in-a-mist."

"Want to show them to me?" I sent a significant glance at Dad, who had his mouth open and certainly *seemed* to be asleep, but I wasn't willing to chance it.

Mum looked unhappy about it, but she stood up, and we wandered down past the roses towards the flowerbed at the bottom of the garden.

I took a deep breath. "Mum, I need to talk to you. About my real dad."

CHAPTER TWENTY

Mum frowned at the flowerbeds. "I'm going to have to talk to Gerald about these slugs. We'll need to put more pellets down."

"Mum. Please? I need to know."

She sighed. "It was all so long ago."

I tried to smile at her. "Yeah, I know. Thirty years this week. Well, plus nine months, I s'pose."

"Have you made any plans for your birthday? We'd be very happy to have you round here—"

"*Mum.*"

She sighed. "I didn't set out to have an affair, you know."

"Course not," I said loyally. "Hey, you want to sit down?"

There was a wooden bench at the end of the lawn that rarely got used, since it was in the shade of the apple tree in the afternoons. I brushed off a few old leaves and bits of moss, and we sat, Mum smoothing her skirt primly over her knees.

"So how did it happen?" I encouraged her after a short silence.

Mum stared back up the garden. I wasn't sure if she was seeing Dad, the house, or something else entirely. "I know it doesn't excuse it, but I was so lonely in those days. Richard and Cherry weren't little children—Richard was practically a teenager. They had their own friends, they took themselves to school . . . They didn't seem to need *me* anymore. And your father—" Mum stumbled a bit on the word "—Gerald, I mean, just seemed to live for his work."

It was a bit hard to imagine. He'd never seemed that focussed on his career when I'd been old enough to remember. More like just marking time until retirement.

"How did you meet him? Mike, I mean." God, it'd better not be some cheesy porno setup—something goes wrong in the house, bloke comes round to see to it, ends up seeing to the missus.

"He came round with some letters that had been wrongly delivered. You see, he lived at number forty-four Stoneyhill Road, which I suppose looks a *little* like number forty-four Stonecroft Gardens." That'd been the house we'd lived in, in Edgware, back when I was born. "But really, there was no excuse for the post office to get it so wrong."

"Yeah? Nice of him to bring 'em round in person." I'd occasionally had the wrong mail delivered to mine, but I'd usually just bunged it back in a post box with the words *Delivered to wrong house* scrawled across.

Mum sort of smiled, in a not-very-happy, faraway sort of way. "It was the name, I think. Paretski. There weren't nearly so many Polish people in the country back then, because it was still behind the Iron Curtain in those days, so he thought it was a funny coincidence he'd got our post. And I suppose he'd have been glad to get to know some fellow expatriates."

"Hang about," I said slowly as the little wheels in my head turned and the tumblers clicked into place so bloody loud I was surprised Mum didn't hiss at me to pipe down, I'd wake Dad. "You mean to tell me . . . all those bloody times I've told people I'm not Polish—"

"But you're not. You're British." Mum took a deep breath and glanced up the lawn at Dad, snoring with his mouth open like a geriatric Venus flytrap. "But yes, he . . . Your father was from Poland. Mike Novak was his name. Mike was short for Mikolaj."

It was like the continental divide had just opened up under my size nines. I was Polish. Well, half Polish. And all I knew about Poland was they were keen on solidarity and had a consonant fetish. "Wait a minute . . . *Was*? Is he, well . . ." Pushing up daisies? Did they even have them in Poland?

"I don't know. I'm sorry. We didn't keep in touch, not after . . ." She sighed. "You were just a baby. You didn't know any different, but I couldn't take Richard and Cherry away from their father. And I couldn't *leave* them."

Bloody hell. This Mike had asked Mum to run off with him? And me? I gazed out at the neatly pruned rose bushes and closely mown lawn, and tried to imagine what my life might have been like—no big brother and sister too busy with exams and teenage lives to be anything but annoyed by a much younger kid; no amiably distant Dad who'd always seemed twice as old as my mates' dads. Had Mike been younger? *Much* younger? Another thought struck. "He wasn't a plumber, was he?"

Mum gave me a weird look. "No. He worked in a restaurant. As a sous chef." She blushed beetroot red. "He cooked a meal for me once. It was very nice. A bit, well, *fussy*. But nice."

Huh. A chef. I supposed working the antisocial hours made it handy for carrying on with women whose husbands weren't around during office hours. "What, um, what kind of restaurant was it?" Mum frowned, and I carried on hastily. "I mean, I didn't reckon Polish cuisine had really caught on around here back then." Or now, come to that. Funny, really. Every neighbourhood seemed to have its own *Polski Sklep* these days flogging imported groceries to the expats, but I could count the number of times I'd passed a Polish restaurant in Hertfordshire on the fingers of, well, one finger.

"They just called it Baltic." Mum shrugged. "It wasn't really my kind of thing."

No, but the chef was, I didn't say. God. All the what-ifs and might-have-beens were starting to give me a headache.

"Did I ever meet him?"

Mum looked even less happy. "Only once. It was an accident. I took you out in your pram, and we just bumped into each other."

I wanted to ask where she'd taken me, and how much of an accident it'd been—on either of their parts. I mean, shit, if I'd had a kid, I'd want to at least see it once. Actually, that was bollocks. I couldn't imagine having a kid and not wanting to be involved. It hurt that Mike hadn't felt the same way.

It hurt even more, knowing he'd met me and still decided not to bother.

I mean, Christ, I could understand him rejecting me now. But kids are cute, for fuck's sake. Even the ugly ones, and I'd seen pictures of me as a baby. I hadn't been *that* hideous.

"Things were different in those days," Mum said. I gave her a sharp look, wondering if the psychic abilities had come from her side of the family after all.

"What was he like?"

Mum went a bit pink. "He was nice. Very easy to talk to."

Yeah, and apparently not that difficult to do other stuff with either. And ye gods, I did *not* want to be thinking about that sort of thing in connection with my mum.

"He had a lovely smile," Mum went on. "You look a lot like him."

I knew. I'd seen the pictures and had a certain private investigator point out all the physical similarities. "How old was he?"

Mum went a lot pink. "In his thirties when I knew him." Whereas she'd been in her midforties, having the classic midlife crisis fling. Maybe that was another reason she hadn't been able to view him as a serious relationship prospect.

Still . . . thirties wasn't so young you'd expect the bloke to have panicked on finding out he was going to be a dad. I mean, it's not nice when any man runs out on a woman he's got up the duff, but at least, if the bloke's in his teens or early twenties, you can sort of understand it. When you've not really grown-up yet yourself, the prospect of having kids of your own must be bloody terrifying.

But thirties . . . He might have been thinking about that sort of stuff anyway. "He didn't have a family already, did he?" I asked.

"No—well, you know. Relatives in Poland. But he wasn't married. Or, well, with anyone. He said it was hard to meet people, working the hours he did."

Apart, of course, from lonely housewives. "And he never got in touch again? You know, to see how I was doing and all that?"

"Mike agreed it would be best if he didn't."

I gave her a sharp look. "You didn't want him hanging around? Even though he was my real dad?"

Mum wouldn't meet my eye. "Children need stability."

And I guessed she'd wanted Dad—Gerald—whatever the hell I was supposed to call him now—to forgive and forget about the affair, and it'd have been a bit hard with the other party popping up every weekend to take me to McDonald's or whatever noncustodial fathers did with their kids in those days.

Well, maybe not McDonald's, with him being a chef and all. Maybe he'd have shown me where he worked, got me helping him out in the kitchen . . . Nah, restaurant kitchens are manic places where tempers run hotter than the ovens. Mum wouldn't have been chuffed if I'd come home talking like Gordon effing Ramsay. Or with third-degree burns from accidentally getting myself flambéed.

I jumped when Mum touched my arm. "Tom?"

"Sorry, did I zone out a bit there?"

"I was just asking if you wanted another slice of tea loaf."

"Nah, I'm good, thanks." I stood up, and Mum followed suit. "I'd probably better get going, anyhow."

It wasn't that I'd run out of questions. There was still a shedload of stuff I wanted to ask.

I just wasn't sure I was up to any more answers right now.

Mum nodded. "I'll wrap up some cake for you to take with you."

We wandered back up the garden to where Dad was still snoring in his chair beside his now-cold tea.

"Gerald? *Gerald.*" Mum gave him a sharp prod in the ribs. "Tom's leaving now."

Dad woke up with a snort and a splutter. "Who? Ah, yes." He heaved himself to his feet despite my protests and patted me weakly on the shoulder. "It's been good to see you, Tom."

"Er, yeah. You too, Dad." Was it just me seeing things, or did he startle slightly when I called him that?

Nah, it was just my imagination. I was positive it was.

Dad was smiling in that vaguely adrift way old people have, and I felt a bit bad leaving without actually talking to him at all. "You keeping all right?"

"Ah, well, you know. Can't complain, not at my age."

I was waiting for Mum to chip in with a minilecture on the terrible state of Dad's knees, not to mention the National Health Service, but she was just hovering, looking from one to the other of us with a worried look on her face.

There was only so much of that I could take. "Yeah, well, it's been great. You two look after yourselves, yeah? And I'll—I'll be around, okay? You know. Call me if you need anything."

I gave Mum a hug and a peck on the cheek, then turned to say my usual no-touchy-no-feely goodbye to Dad, who nearly made me jump a mile when he thrust out a hand for me to shake. I swallowed and shook it. He gave me that lost smile again, and Christ, were his eyes a bit watery?

Just how asleep had he been, while Mum and me were talking?

I didn't even know, I realised, if he'd always known I wasn't his—or if he'd spent the first few years in presumably blissful ignorance. I'd always assumed, from what Cherry told me about the kerfuffle when I was four, that that was when he found out. Had he known all along? Had he suspected?

I felt like a total selfish bastard. All this time, ever since I'd found Auntie Lol's secret letter stash, all I'd been worrying about was what it meant for me. I'd barely spared a thought for what Dad must be going through. Must have been going through my entire life.

"Tom?" Mum's voice cut in on the self-flagellation. "Are you all right?"

"Er, yeah. Sorry." Oops. Maybe I ought to try to make sure I was on my own for the next emotional revelation, at least until I'd learned to multitask while it was going on. "Right. Just on my way. You take care, okay?"

I thought, *Sod it*, and pulled Dad in for a hug.

He went a bit red and muttered, "Steady on," but I think he was chuffed, really. Mum looked like she was going to cry.

I legged it before it could all turn into an episode of *Jeremy Kyle*. Mum and Dad hated all that emotional stuff.

CHAPTER TWENTY-ONE

I drove home feeling . . . weird. Sort of like someone had offered me a seat, and then whipped the rug out from under it, leaving me hanging on for dear life as the chair teetered on one leg.

I hadn't realised, before I spoke to Mum, just how much the prospect had been weighing on my mind all these months. I mean, if anyone had asked me a couple of days ago if I was even *planning* to talk to her about it, I'd have asked them if they were having a laugh. Now I'd done it, though, I realised I'd always known I couldn't simply let it rest. And now I'd done it, it was like I'd finally put down a whole rucksack full of baggage I'd been carrying around with me.

On the other hand, though . . . Fuck me.

Another thing I hadn't realised was that part of me had just been hoping Mum would turn around and say *Don't be silly, dear, of course Dad's your father.* Because that was what mothers did, wasn't it? Stick a plaster on it, give the kid a kiss, and everything would be all better.

Apparently they didn't make Band-Aids this big.

And then there was the Polish thing. Someone up there was definitely having a good old snigger at my expense. Couldn't he—my real father, and bloody hell, just thinking about that was tying my guts up in knots—have been Romanian or Slovenian or something? I mean, Jesus, there had been a time when I'd been a nipper when I'd seriously thought the family surname, in its full version, was Paretski-But-We're-Not-Polish. Suddenly finding out that was only fifty percent true in my particular case was . . . Well. Doing my head in.

Back home, I was just leaning back on the sofa, trying to ease the headache that'd set in, when there was a knock on the front door.

I heaved myself up to answer it.

And stared in surprise. It was Phil, smelling of posh shampoo and looking fresh and fucking wholesome in a plain white T-shirt and cargo shorts.

"What happened—lose your key?" It came out a bit more of a challenge than I meant it to.

He smoothed a hand over his hair, which was curling a bit where it was damp at the ends. The action showed off his triceps nicely, not that I was looking. "Didn't feel right, just walking in. But we need to talk."

"Sure that's a good idea? Didn't seem to go all that well last time we tried it." I was already standing back to let him in, though. Apparently it wasn't my brain my body was taking orders from right now.

"I meant about the case," he said, walking on past me and into the living room. The cats went wild to see him—well, maybe not wild, but even Arthur deigned to jump off the sofa cushion and pad over to decorate his trousers with a bit of cat hair.

I was feeling a lot less enthusiastic myself now I knew he'd come on business. "What case?" I countered. "Harry hired you to find a way of getting Carey out of her and Marianne's hair. I'd say that job's pretty much done."

Phil's expression turned ugly, and I took a step back from him before I'd even consciously noticed his hand had clenched into a fist. "That's what you think, is it?"

"For fuck's sake, I didn't say I thought you'd bloody offed him!" I stared at him, knocked right off-kilter by his overreaction. Examined more closely—and with a bit more attention to detail above the neck—he wasn't looking quite so fresh. There were dark smudges under his eyes, and a tense line to his jaw. And he'd missed a bit when he'd shaved. "Phil—"

"Jesus fucking Christ." He leaned back against the wall and rubbed both hands over his face. Merlin milled around his ankles and miaowed in concern. "Don't do this to me. Not you as well."

So everything was my fault, was it? Anger buzzed through me. "What the fuck have I done?"

"I just spent five hours with your mate Dave and his chums putting on the thumbscrews, all right? Only got out of there half an hour ago." He looked up. "And before you ask what they were after, they weren't fussy, all right? They want me to either tell 'em I did it, or drop Harry in it. So you can get off your fucking high horse, all right?"

Shit. He looked . . . Well. Pretty much how you'd expect him to look after that. There was a painful tightness in the region of my chest, which might or might not have been where my conscience was hanging out these days.

"You want a beer?" I asked. Seeing as I was fresh out of actual olive branches.

Phil sort of huffed, almost a laugh. It didn't sound very happy, though. "Yeah."

I grabbed a couple of beers from the fridge, opened them, and brought them back into the living room. Phil was slumped on the sofa, Merlin already occupying the prime real estate of his lap.

"Cheers," I said, handing him a bottle.

He nodded his thanks and took a long draught of beer. "Christ, I needed that."

I could tell that just by looking at him. I was definitely starting to feel ashamed of myself for getting the hump with him like that. "You eaten?"

Phil blinked at me, his eyes a lot less focussed than they usually were. "Had a sandwich at the nick."

"Yeah? How long ago?"

"God knows. Tasted like cardboard."

I nodded. "Egg on toast? Bit of bacon as well?"

Phil's eyes closed, and he smiled. "You're a lifesaver."

I plodded into the kitchen and lit the hob. When I opened the fridge, the usual furry strike team didn't materialise, and I was left to bung the bacon under the grill in peace. It seemed the cats really had missed Phil.

And, yeah, all right, if I was held at knifepoint and forced to be honest, they weren't the only ones. Lucky there were no cutlery-wielding inquisitors around here.

Whistling a bit to break the silence while I flipped hot butter over the eggs in the pan—there's nothing worse than runny bits of uncooked egg white on top of your fried egg—I almost jumped out of my skin when Phil slid his arms around me from behind. "Oi, careful! You nearly made me break a yolk."

"God, I've missed you," was all he said, his voice a low rumble in my ear that seemed to vibrate right through me, like laid-back thunder over distant mountains.

I swallowed. "Thought this visit was purely business?"

Shit. Not a good thing to say. I chanced a glance at Phil's expression, and the storm was definitely nearer now.

"You're fucking joking, right?"

No, but I was willing to pretend if it'd get me off the hook. I was glad when a loud miaow made me look round again. Phil had brought a couple of furry minders in here with him, and now they wanted feeding too. "Should've known that was too good to last."

Phil backed off a step. "Meaning?"

Okay, *now* it looked like I was in imminent danger of lightning strike. And I didn't even know why.

"*Meaning* I was enjoying getting to cook for once without being pestered for food by a couple of moggy muggers. That a problem for you?"

"Shit. Sorry." Phil sighed. "Fuck it, I ought to go."

He looked tireder than ever.

"No, you ought to rescue that bread from the toaster before it turns to charcoal, and bung on a bit of butter while I get on with not burning the bacon. *Then* you ought to sit down and eat, all right?"

I made a couple of mugs of tea and carried everything out to the living room. Phil sank down on the sofa, leaned back, and closed his eyes for so long I thought he'd fallen asleep. I was just wondering if I should prod him and remind him the food was getting cold, or if I should simply scoff it myself—I hadn't been hungry when I'd started cooking, but there's something about the smell of eggs and bacon that just flips the appetite switch—when he opened his eyes again, leaned forward, and set to like he'd been starving for a week.

I slurped my tea and told my stomach not to rumble.

We didn't talk while he ate, and after around five minutes or so, Phil pushed his empty plate away, drank the last of his tea, and turned to face me with a serious expression. "Look, all that stuff about me leaving the force. If I explain how it was, are you going to listen?"

I took a deep breath. "All right. Want another beer before we start?" Because I bloody well did.

Phil nodded, and I headed back into the kitchen with the empty mugs and grabbed a couple more bottles out of the fridge. They were the last two, so I shoved a couple more in from the cupboard, then bunged the cups in the dishwasher.

That done, there really wasn't any further excuse to put it off.

Phil nodded his thanks when I handed him his beer. He put it down on the coffee table but didn't speak immediately, just looked at me a moment longer.

I took a swig of beer and waited.

"It was a bad time for me, all right?" Phil said eventually. "Mark had just died, and the bastard whose fault it was didn't even get charged with reckless driving. Insufficient *fucking* evidence. I was sick to bloody death of people shoving two fingers up at the justice system already, and when it happened again with this domestic case . . ."

He'd lost it. "So you thought you'd go all vigilante? With your fists?" Anger had flared again, and I couldn't seem to keep it out of my voice.

"Tom. Listen to me. Please." Phil breathed deeply. "You didn't see her. The wife. He broke her fucking jaw. She was a fucking mess, all right? And there he was, giving us the whole wide-eyed innocent act. 'No, Officer, course I'd never hit my wife.' All that shit. Just like every other bastard we dragged in for domestics. 'She'll back me up, she just fell down the stairs. Had a couple of glasses of wine too many, you know what women are like.' And sure enough, next thing I know, she comes in, jaw wired up and her face so swollen she can only see out of one eye, and she's telling us it's all a big misunderstanding. Nothing to do with him at all. All her own fault. So we had to let him go."

He paused.

"Then what happened?" I tried not to make it sound like a challenge. Wasn't sure I succeeded.

"I lost it, didn't I? There he was, sauntering off home with the missus like he hadn't got a care in the world, and he turns and says something to her. Didn't catch what he said, but I saw her flinch. And I lost it." Phil stood up jerkily, nearly making me spill my beer.

I put the bottle down on the table, next to his, and rested my elbows on my knees. "That's not what Dave said. He reckoned you

followed the bloke home. Went round his house and beat him up."
Ding dong, assault-and-battery calling. And yeah, it definitely came
out sounding like a challenge this time.

"What? Bollocks." Phil paced the room, his hands clenched into
fists and his face twisted in a snarl. If he was trying to convince me he
was harmless, he was doing a piss-poor job of it. I just about managed
not to jump when he wheeled suddenly to face me. "That's not how it
was, all right? Yeah, I followed him out the station and grabbed him
in the street. For fuck's sake, we were only a couple of yards away. It
wasn't . . . Jesus, it wasn't fucking premeditated. I swear it wasn't."

He sank down on one knee in front of me, his hands grabbing
mine. His touch was so gentle it hurt. "I didn't set out to do it, all
right? It just happened. Tom. It just happened. Don't leave me over
this. For fuck's sake, don't leave me."

I couldn't take it. Not anymore.

Couldn't look into his eyes and still keep my distance. And yeah,
I knew nothing much had changed. I knew he'd beaten this bloke
up—he'd admitted that, and all the rest was just one person's word
against another. He'd—well, if not lied, he'd kept secrets from me.
Secrets I might have been expected to want to know, seeing as how
I'd been under the distinct impression he'd left all the bullying crap
behind him when he'd left school.

It hurt. But I'd missed him so *fucking* much.

"I'm not leaving you," I said, my voice rough. And then we were
kissing, and I was so hard all I could think of was him, the way he tasted
of the food I'd cooked him. The way he'd taken the time, shattered as
he was, to have a shower and change before he'd come round. God,
the feel of him against me, on top of me. My T-shirt was bunched up
under my armpits, and his had disappeared entirely, God knows when.
Our skin burned where it touched.

"Christ," Phil grunted, his fingers fumbling to get my jeans open.
When he finally succeeded, I yanked them off so bloody fast it was
a miracle I didn't do myself a mischief. I got his shorts undone and
shoved my hand into his underwear. His prick was like a white-hot
iron bar in there. I needed it like air.

I grabbed both our pricks in one hand and jerked them together,
and it was fucking amazing, but it wasn't *enough.* I just needed to feel
him, and Christ, if he was going to hurt me, I wanted it to be *now.*

I couldn't take waiting any longer.

"Get inside me," I panted. "Now."

"Don't want to . . ." *Hurt me*, I guessed he meant.

"Don't care. Do it." I hitched my legs up with my hands. "Fucking do it."

He spat on his hand, wiped it on his dick and lined up. "You sure?"

"Just do it," I snapped.

It hurt like fuck when he pushed in. We'd done it without prep before, but never without lube, and Christ, the burn was almost too much to take.

God, I needed it.

It was all I could think of for a mo. That long, agonising stretch as he filled me up. When I looked up at Phil, he had this weird expression I couldn't read. I wondered what he saw in mine. If I told him I was hurting, would he stop?

Fuck *that*.

"Move," I said harshly, and he did. Slowly at first, then when I grabbed hold of his arse and pulled it to me, he sped up. He slammed into me, harder and harder. The slap of skin on sweaty skin just fuelled the fire, and I dug my fingers into his arse. Didn't care about leaving bruises. I *wanted* him to bruise me.

Christ, he felt so big. In me. On top of me. I pulled him in closer, gasping for breath. My whole focus was on him, and when I came, it took me by surprise, my orgasm ripping through me like a scab coming off. I made some kind of inhuman noise, and Phil answered with a choking sound as his rhythm faltered and stopped.

My vision went fuzzy for a long, long time.

I blinked and looked around as Phil pulled out of me and got to his feet. "Think we scared the cats off," I joked weakly.

He didn't smile. "Tom?"

"Yeah?" I was starting to get worried.

"Don't . . . don't ask me to do that again." He sounded broken.

Oh, fuck. "Phil, I—"

"It's all right. I'm all right. Just, not again, okay? Not like that."

Shit. *Fuck*. I hadn't meant to hurt him. Had I? Christ, what the hell had I been thinking of? "Phil, I—"

"Anyway," Phil cut me off as he started to pull his clothes back on, seeming to gather himself together. I reached for my jeans. "I did some more digging, like I said. Into your old man. Wasn't easy with only a first name—"

"His full name's Mike Novak. Mikolaj," I blurted, then felt like a bastard. More of a bastard. "I spoke to Mum. Sorry. Didn't know you were still, you know. Digging. He lived in Stoneyhill Road. Number forty-four."

Phil's face closed off, and he looked away. "Right. So you don't need me anymore, then. Right."

Now I felt like a *total* bastard. "I didn't . . . Look, it just happened. Talking to Mum. I was there, and Dad was snoring away, and I just . . . wanted to know, you know? So I asked her. Think she was relieved I'd finally got round to it, actually."

He nodded. "S'pose it's none of my business anyhow."

That fucking stung. "S'pose not," I agreed, not looking at him either.

I felt the draught as he walked away, and then heard the front door shut quietly behind him.

CHAPTER TWENTY-TWO

I got about as much sleep that night as you'd expect and staggered out of bed the next morning feeling worse than I had when I'd got in it.

I'd fucked up. Christ, I'd fucked up.

Hadn't meant to, but then who the hell ever does? I should've known what having sex like that would do to Phil. Especially after I'd told him straight I didn't trust him not to hurt me.

I hadn't even given him a fucking choice, had I?

And the stupid part, the really, pathetically, stupid part, was that I knew he was more vulnerable than he liked to let on. I *knew* it.

I knew *him*.

I couldn't believe I'd managed to lose sight of that fact. I'd been so bloody worked up about the stuff I'd been told about him, I'd completely forgotten I'd spent the last seven or eight months in close contact with the bloke. Seeing how he'd react in any given situation—and Christ, there had been a few.

Finding out about stuff he'd done in the past was like . . . like finding out my dad wasn't who I thought he was. I wasn't a different person now than I had been before I'd known. And neither was Phil. Maybe the hot weather over the last few weeks had fried my brain.

Maybe I hadn't had much of one to start with. God, Phil Morrison was the single best thing that'd happened to me, and I'd done my best to shove him away. If he never came back . . . I didn't want to think about him not coming back. But it'd be no more than I deserved.

I had a couple of jobs booked in for the morning, neither of them too complicated, thank God. I managed to slog my way through, although the customer service was definitely lacking. If I got any repeat business from these two, I'd be very surprised.

I thought about calling Phil at lunchtime, maybe ask him to meet me. But it'd probably be better to give him a bit of time to cool off. Not that he'd been angry with me, but, well. I wouldn't have blamed him if he had been. So I had a lonely cheese sandwich in the van and pretended to read the paper, then went through the motions of work again in the afternoon.

I couldn't muster the energy to cook anything for dinner—just had a sandwich made up of odds and sods from the fridge. And half a pack of choccy biccies.

Then I stared at the telly for a bit, because it was either that or get drunk, and let's face it, I was running pretty low on brain cells already. The last thing I needed was to pickle the few remaining ones in alcohol.

And, yeah, I could have called someone. But then I'd have had to actually talk to them. So no go there.

When my phone rang, I broke all land-speed records dashing into the kitchen where I'd left it on charge. But it wasn't Phil calling.

"Tom?" Marianne sounded even more little-girly on the phone.

I mustered up a vaguely cheerful tone to answer her. "Hullo, love. What can I do you for?"

"Is Phil with you? I been trying to call him, but he ain't answering."

My heart sank, proving I'd been wrong about having hit rock bottom already. "No. Sorry. Not sure where he is."

"Can I ask you something, then?"

"Course you can, love." A thought hit. "Long as it's not investigating any more nasty niffs in the cellar, all right?" I laughed so she'd know I was joking.

Although I really wasn't.

"No, see, it's nothing like that. I just need a bit of advice." She took a deep breath. "It's about Kev, see? He texted me. He wants me to go meet him."

"What, at the Dyke?" I looked at my watch. It was past eleven already, which seemed suspiciously late for a meeting. Still, maybe he didn't know the pub was closed at the mo.

"No. He said to go over to this hotel he's staying at and meet him in the bar. It's in St. Albans. He said he'll give me the taxi fare when I get there. He said we got to talk about stuff. 'Cept, I don't want to go, see? I don't want to talk to him, 'cos he don't listen."

"Men, eh?"

"And if I'm honest, see, there's always the chance 'e might talk me into going back 'ome with him. It's been horrible, since—you know." I knew, all right. "I ain't slept a wink, and I been getting these dreams . . ."

Which was a bit contradictory, but I knew what she meant. "So don't go," I said firmly. "Just 'cos he's asked you, doesn't mean you have to do what he says. Why don't you make yourself a cup of cocoa, bung a bit of rum in it, and turn in for the night? If he wants to talk to you so bad, he can come round and see you. In the daylight, at the pub, with Harry around to keep an eye on him." I wondered why she hadn't asked Harry for advice, but it seemed a bit rude to ask.

"Okay," Marianne said, sounding relieved. "Doctor gave me these pills. Maybe I'll take one of them."

"You do that, love." I tried to sound as encouraging as possible.

"Thanks, Tom. You're a good friend."

I felt a bit better after we'd hung up. It was a good half an hour later before a thought struck. Shit. What if Kev went round causing trouble for Marianne once he realised she wasn't going to turn up like he'd told her to? I reckoned Harry could probably handle him, but what if the reason Marianne hadn't asked her advice was that she wasn't there?

Why the bloody hell hadn't I checked up on that?

Damn it. Should I ring Marianne back and find out where Kev was staying, then go round there myself and give him a talking-to? They were supposed to be meeting in the bar, a public space; chances were Kev wouldn't risk punching my teeth in for sticking my nose into his family's business in front of witnesses. Trouble was, he wasn't likely to pay a blind bit of attention to what I said either.

I hated to admit it, but physically, I was outclassed here. Kev was about twice my size—even on the very slim chance he kept it to a fair fight, I wasn't going to be the one walking away from any little altercations we might have. It was like Carey had said—if you can't beat 'em on strength, you have to choose other tactics . . .

Shit. Carey.

What if they hadn't been on the same side after all? Or what if they had, and had just, I dunno, rubbed each other up the wrong way? Or if Kev had decided it was Carey's fault Marianne had turned queer? Whatever the motivation, it was easy to imagine one punch from Kev being the thing that took Grant Carey out of the equation for good.

And the whole body-in-the-cellar thing—that actually made sense if it was Kev. He'd been a burglar, so he'd know how to get through the odd locked door. And if Harry got done for the murder, well, that'd serve the purpose of getting Marianne away from her . . .

Shit. I froze for a moment, then grabbed my phone and called Phil.

It rang and rang.

"Answer, you bastard," I muttered. Then it occurred to me that if he picked up, it probably wouldn't be a great start if the first words he heard from me were *you bastard*, so I shut my gob.

It didn't make a difference anyway. He still didn't answer.

Damn it. I couldn't leave Marianne and Harry—if she was even there—to deal with a possible murderer on their own. Maybe Harry could take him in a fight, maybe she couldn't, but the trouble was, she wouldn't be expecting any danger. Harry just thought Kev was a waste of space, not the sort who could kill a bloke and then try to frame her for it.

I dialled up Harry's number, but it went straight to voice mail. For fuck's sake, was this national no-phones night? Should I call Marianne back? With my luck, she'd be deep in artificially induced sleep by now. Even if she wasn't, I could imagine how it'd go: *'Ullo, love, I think your brother's a murderer. No, no evidence, just a gut feeling based on something your evil ex told me once . . . Hello? Hello?*

Sod it. I sent Phil a quick text—*Gon to Dyke, danger from Kev*—and added *plz cm* at the end. Then I grabbed my keys and headed for the Fiesta.

Turned out the drive from Fleetville up to Brock's Hollow was easily long enough to have second thoughts. And third and fourth thoughts, come to that. After all, what the hell was I basing all this panic on? A bloke who wanted to talk to his sister, that was all.

Then I had a fifth thought: if Kev wanted to go after Harry in any sort of homicidal fashion, wouldn't he want Marianne out of the way?

I bombed down the country lanes, narrowly missed taking out a fox on the prowl, and took the final corner.

Shit. There was smoke coming from the windows of the Dyke.

And Kev Drinkwater was standing there in the beer garden. Watching the place burn.

CHAPTER Twenty-Three

I screeched to a halt in the car park, one of the furry dice hanging from my mirror nearly taking an eye out on the rebound. Just as I was about to jump out of the car, Phil's Golf rounded the corner and skidded to a stop next to the Fiesta.

He'd come. He'd got my message and he'd come. And that meant... I didn't have time right now to think what that meant.

But I was bloody glad he had.

What with all the stuff going on in my head, Phil got to Kev first. "What the fuck have you done?" he yelled, grabbing him by the front of his shirt and spinning him around in some weird, angry dance.

Looked like Phil had noticed the smoke too, then.

"Burnin's too good for this place. She'll 'ave to come 'ome now," Kev said mulishly.

Jesus Christ. Didn't he *get* it? "Marianne? Where is she?" I snapped out.

"She's safe. I sent 'er to St. Albans."

"She didn't go!" I stepped up to him and shook him by the shoulder, yelling up into his thuggish, stupid face. His breath was sour and reeked of alcohol. "Jesus, is she still in there? Did you even fucking check? And Harry? What about her? Christ." I let go of him, fumbled out my phone, and jabbed 999.

I gave the bloke on the other end the address, but he kept fucking talking, so I thrust the phone at Kev, who was still standing there, slack-jawed. "You talk to him. Do something useful for once in your life. I'm going in."

Phil grabbed my arm. "Are you out of your mind?"

"Look, I can't see any flames yet. That's good, right? Means it's not taken hold." But smoke could kill too, couldn't it? Shit, when a pub went up, did barrels and stuff explode? I mean, it did when the pub in *EastEnders* burnt down, but that was just telly, wasn't it? God, I wished I knew where the bloody hell Harry was. Had this bastard killed her already? "Marianne's in there—she's in there because *I* bloody well *told* her not to go out. I'm not just going to leave her in there."

"I'll get her," Phil said. "You stay here."

"Fuck that."

"Then we're going in together."

There wasn't time to argue and anyway, if Harry was in there too, maybe passed out from the smoke—maybe worse, but God, I didn't want to think about that—I'd need Phil to help me get them both out.

The door to the public bar wouldn't open, but Kev had to have got in somehow to torch the place. I ran round to the kitchen door and sure enough, it was unlocked. When I pushed it open, smoke billowed out and the heat hit me like a cricket ball to the head. I flung up my arm in front of my eyes and wished I'd thought to do the whole wet-rag-over-the-face thing. Too late now. Needed to find out who was in here and get them out, pronto.

I blinked rapidly, and my vision cleared. I almost wished it hadn't.

The old wooden staircase leading up to the bedrooms from the private area behind the bar was crackling away furiously—in fact, it seemed to be the centre of the fire. Kev, you *bastard*. The ceiling was cracked and mottled black.

There was a loud *pop*, and I jumped a mile. "Jesus!"

"Light bulb." Phil's voice was almost drowned out at the end by a crash as debris started to fall, and I jumped again.

Bloody hell, this place was turning into a death trap. Even if we managed to get to the stairs without cremating ourselves, what were the chances they'd hold our weight?

"Any ideas?" Phil yelled.

Think, Paretski. Then I remembered. What had Harry said was the only other way to get to Marianne's room? The not-so-secret passageway in the fireplace, right over the other side in the lounge bar. It was so perfect I almost laughed. In an old building like this, what could be more fireproof than the bloody chimney?

I grabbed Phil's arm. "This way," I managed to gasp out before a coughing fit hit me.

I backed out of the bar, keeping hold of Phil to make sure he followed, heaved in lungfuls of air and legged it around the building. If Kev was still around, I didn't notice him. Didn't care.

"What's the plan?" Phil panted.

"Secret passageway."

He stared at me. "What?" I'd forgotten he didn't know this place as well as I did.

"Seriously. In the fireplace. There's a staircase. Goes up to the bedrooms. Fuck. Door's locked." I rattled the handle of the door to the lounge bar furiously, as if I'd be able to shake it loose somehow.

"Not a problem." Phil picked up one of the heavy stone urns that stood by the door and heaved it through the window, flowers and all.

I stared for a moment at the massive hole in what had, until thirty seconds ago, been a nice, Olde-Worlde, diamond-paned window. "Yeah, that'll do it."

Phil used his elbow to knock out the last of the glass, then squeezed himself through the window and into the lounge bar. I was hard on his heels. The fire hadn't got through the internal doors to reach this half of the building, thank God, and there was way less smoke, although that'd probably change pretty quick now we'd taken out a window and created a cross-draught. "Fireplace?" Phil yelled.

I nodded. The door to the passageway was locked, but a swift bit of vandalism with the fire irons soon sorted that. I opened the door and looked into darkness. Well, it was better than flames, but I had a nasty feeling they might be along any minute now.

Phil's hand was on my arm. "Look, about last night..."

I spun around. "Forget it. Shouldn't have happened."

Christ, the pain in his eyes. I realised what it must have sounded like.

"I mean, not like that," I said quickly. "I shouldn't have made you ... I'm sorry. I love you, all right?" I turned again, blinking a bit, and my heart thumping, blundered up the stairs. I couldn't see a bloody thing—but there was only one way to go. Phil was close behind me, a guilty comfort.

The door at the top was only held by a flimsy little bolt, thank God. We found that out after Phil squeezed past me to shoulder it open a bit more explosively than I reckon either of us was expecting. The passageway opened straight into Marianne's bedroom, and I groped around the wall until I found a light switch.

The room was plainer than you'd think, but with a few girly frills. There was a surreal feeling of normality in the room—no sign of fire, and it wasn't even all that warm. For a moment, I felt daft for breaking in like that. Like I might have made a mistake, and there wasn't a fire after all.

Then my breath caught in my throat, and I realised there was a soft-focus look to everything. Smoke was already seeping into the room—under the door, maybe, or even through the floorboards for all I knew.

Bloody hell, Marianne hadn't even woken up.

Her curls spilling over the pillow, she lay in bed under a duvet with a unicorn on it, looking like a prepubescent Sleeping Beauty waiting for her ten-year-old prince. I started in her direction. Phil barged past me to open the far door, and hot air and smoke billowed in from what must be Harry's bedroom.

"Christ!" Hand over his mouth, he disappeared.

I froze, paralysed with the fear I was going to lose him here.

Before I'd even made things right with him.

I went weak with relief when Phil slammed back through the door and shut it behind him, an acrid waft of smoke coming with him and rolling across the ceiling.

"No sign of Harry in there," he rasped. Then he shot ice water straight in my veins with his next sentence. "Going to need to go look for her. You get Marianne out."

"You can't go out there!" I yelped.

"What about Harry?"

Oh God. "Wait here a mo, I want to try something."

He gave me a frankly doubtful look.

Shit. Harry wasn't exactly hidden. Maybe the spidey-senses wouldn't work. But maybe they would. I stood there, and *listened*.

Fucking.

Hell.

The vertigo was so sudden, I nearly fell over. Everything was painfully sharp and bright. It was like I was standing at the edge of a black hole, with Phil a burning white furnace in front of me and Marianne a brave little toaster off to one side.

"What?" Phil said above the roaring of the fire—unless it was just the blood rushing in my ears. He grabbed my arm. "What is it?"

"Nothing," I gasped out, struggling to close the door on the vast emptiness I was looking into in my head. "I mean, literally, nothing. She's not there. Trust me."

He still didn't look convinced. "You're sure?"

"Positive. Come on, we're wasting time." I ran to Marianne, still, unbelievably, asleep in the midst of chaos. For a heart-stopping moment I thought she wasn't breathing. Then an eyelid flickered.

"Marianne! Wake up! The pub's on fire." I shook her roughly, but only got a sleepy mumble in reply. Her eyes half opened, but didn't seem to focus on me. Whatever she'd taken to help her sleep was working far too bloody well. I dragged her out of bed. Thank God she didn't weigh much.

Phil came to help, and we managed to get her upright between us.

"Where's Harry?" I yelled at her, my voice breaking on the end as smoke caught in my throat.

She blinked at me woozily. "Out. Flossie."

Harry had taken Flossie out for walkies at gone midnight? Seriously? Right now, though, I didn't give a monkey's if she'd gone to dance naked round a ring of toadstools. She wasn't here—that was all that counted.

There was a muted crash from downstairs. Firemen breaking in? Or the building breaking down?

Christ, that could have been Phil with the floor collapsing under him.

"I'll carry her. You first." Phil coughed.

There wasn't time to argue, and I didn't have a lot of breath to spare anyway. I led the way.

God knows how we got down that staircase so fast without ending up in a big heap at the bottom. We piled out into the fireplace—thankfully still not lit—and half carried Marianne to the door. We didn't bother faffing around trying to unlock it—I climbed out the window first, then Phil posted a still-woozy Marianne out to me. The cooler air outside seemed to wake her up a bit, and she sat on the grass and started *Oh-my-God*-ing like a stuck record, staring at her home going up in smoke.

Flames were clearly visible now, tearing through the roof of the pub, and a thick plume of smoke showed grey-white against the night sky. There was an extended crash—upstairs floor falling in, maybe?

Christ. That could have been Phil in the middle of all that, if I'd let him go looking for Harry. I sat down heavily on the grass next to Marianne.

Dunno how long it was before the fire brigade got there. Minutes, I reckon, if that—we'd already heard the sirens when we first got outside. Phil went around to the road to flag them down and tell them what was what, and came back with a couple of big firemen. One scoped out this side of the building while the other came over to where I was sitting with Marianne. I had my arm around her—she was shivering in the skimpy little shorts-and-vest combo she'd worn to bed. He draped a blanket around her skinny shoulders, and she clutched it in white-knuckled hands.

"Cheers, mate," I said on her behalf, and started coughing again.

An ambulance arrived three minutes later, and paramedics took off the fireman's grey blanket and wrapped her in a flame-coloured shock blanket, which seemed a bit unnecessary, but there you go. We all got shepherded over to the ambulance to be poked and prodded while we got a grandstand view of the firemen doing their stuff. God, between the fire itself and all the water they were pumping in, was there going to be anything left of the Dyke?

Various scrapes and grazes I hadn't even noticed myself getting were starting to make themselves felt, and my hip was telling me straight it wasn't a fan of all this action-man stuff.

"You all right?" Eerie shadows danced over Phil's face as he peered at me. He'd just finished being treated for a glass cut and had been looking at the dressing with a frown, like he hadn't noticed when he'd got it any more than I had.

"Yeah, 'm okay." I tried to say more, but all I got out were wheezes and coughs and then the ambulance bloke shoved a mask over my face. I shoved it away again.

Phil grabbed it and yanked it back into position. Seeing as I was already coughing from the effort, I thought, *Sod it*, and let him win.

"Stop being a bloody hero," he said and promptly had a coughing fit of his own.

I gave him as smug a look as I could manage over the oxygen mask, which probably wasn't very.

We'd done it. We'd saved Marianne.

And we'd done it together.

CHAPTER Twenty-Four

B y the time we got let out of hospital for good behaviour and were allowed to go home, it was well past dawn. We'd had to give lengthy statements to our boys in blue too, which hadn't helped my throat any.

Kev had done a runner sometime after Phil and me had gone inside the pub to get Marianne—taking my phone with him, to add insult to injury—but at least they were looking for him now. I couldn't believe he hadn't even waited to see if she was okay, the bastard.

On the plus side, the police told us they'd managed to track down Harry—where, they didn't bother to say—and it was a relief to have it confirmed she and Flossie were okay. I mean, I'd *been* certain they hadn't been in the Dyke when it was burning, but the more time had passed, the more the nagging doubts had crept in until I'd half convinced myself I'd left them to die.

"Coming back to mine?" I asked Phil tiredly. There was an unexpected flutter of nerves in my stomach.

Phil hesitated. He had a weird look on his face—if I'd had to put a name to it, I'd have said he looked vulnerable. "Sure?"

"Yeah, I'm sure." Funny how every inch of me felt like it weighed a ton, but smiling at him took no effort at all.

Some of the tense lines eased out of his face. "How about we go to mine instead? The cats can cope with a late breakfast."

"You say that, but don't blame me if they go for the throat next time we walk in my door." I yawned, too bloody knackered to ask how come he was bothered where we crashed. "Yeah, whatever." Then I roused myself. There was something I'd been meaning to say. "Look, we should book that holiday, yeah? Go climb a mountain somewhere. Visit Pompeii. Dig up the lost city of Atlantis, whatever."

Phil looked at me a moment, then he nodded.

I thought he was going to say something, but then our ride turned up to take us home. The taxi driver wasn't chatty, which suited me fine, and I was almost asleep on Phil's shoulder by the time we pulled up in front of his flat.

"Shower?" I was desperate to lie down and not get up for a week, but we both stank of smoke and so would Phil's bed, probably forevermore, if we didn't do something about it. We stumbled into the bathroom and shared a pathetically chaste shower. Then we made a half-hearted effort at drying off, mutually gave it up as a bad job, and tumbled into bed, damp as we were.

Just before everything went black, I heard Phil say something. "Whassat?" I muttered.

Phil's voice was fond. "I said happy birthday."

Oh right.

I'd forgotten all about that. Happy thirtieth, me. "Where's m'presn'?" I mumbled.

"Tomorrow," he said, and that was it. I was off to the Land of Nod.

It was almost noon before I woke. My throat felt dry and sore, and not for any of the good reasons.

Then I remembered we'd quite possibly saved Marianne's life, me and Phil, and decided it *was* for a good reason after all.

Sunlight was streaming in through the skylight, but somehow I wasn't getting the greenhouse effect like last time I was here. The air coming in through the open window felt fresh and cool, the bed was just the right side of soft, and I was pretty convinced I could happily lie here all day.

Well, apart from attending to one or two basic needs, obviously. The *other* basic needs, I was confident my bedmate could handle. Phil was dozing beside me, his blond hair sticking up in places where he'd gone to bed with it damp and his chin rough with stubble like a farmer's field after the combine harvesters had been.

God, I loved him.

He made a sort of snuffly sound, and then his eyes opened, blinked a bit, then stayed open. He smiled. "Morning."

"Just about." I was grinning so widely my cheeks ached. I reached over and grabbed him, decided that wasn't enough, and climbed on top. Various bits rubbed against other bits, causing a couple of said bits to perk up noticeably.

Phil huffed a laugh. "What's got into you this morning?"

"Nothing yet, and I'm seriously considering complaining to the management."

"Expect better service round here, do you? I'll see what I can do." He rolled us over suddenly, leaving me underneath him, which was already going a fair way to addressing my complaints.

I arched up, grinding our hard cocks together. "God, that feels good."

Which, obviously, was Phil's cue to pull away from me. I really should learn to keep my big gob shut.

Then again, there are worse things than having Phil Morrison slither down your body and get his lips around your cock. *Lots* of worse things. His tongue got into play, teasing around the head and sending sparks fizzing right up my spine. I groaned.

Phil lifted his head, the bastard. "Sorry. Didn't catch that."

"Fucker. I am *definitely* putting in a complai— Oh, Jesus. Don't stop." He was back on my cock and fingering my arse as well. "Oh yeah. Yeah, that's good."

He went on for a few more moments of blinding ecstasy. Then he stopped again, and pulled off to look up at me. "Want me to bring you off like this?"

I took a breath. Wasn't sure if I should ask or not, but I did anyway. "Do you want to get inside me? 'S okay if not," I added quickly. "We can do anything. Anything you want."

I meant it. This time . . . This time was for him.

Phil's gaze didn't waver, but something seemed to soften in his eyes. He half smiled, then reached into the bedside drawer for a couple of necessary items. "Better warn you, I'm not in the mood for taking it quick."

"Good," I said, and I meant that too. "C'mere." I reached for him, drawing him in for a kiss.

I could taste myself in his mouth, salty with a hint of musk. I kept kissing him, wanting to get past that, to taste *Phil*, not me. He moaned softly into my mouth and pressed our bodies together.

It wasn't urgent, desire-driven rutting. It was *way* better than that. We kissed for what seemed like hours, but it still wasn't long enough, and when he moved away I tried to pull him back.

Phil smirked. "All things come to him who waits." He opened up the lube and slicked himself up.

"Only thing I want right now is you." I was surprised how husky my voice sounded. Last night's smoke, it had to be.

That was definitely why I had to blink back moisture too.

He took it slow this time, and I didn't try to make him hurry it up. This was him and me, reconnecting—no pun intended. I wanted him to know how much he meant to me. When he finally pushed inside me, I let out a long, heartfelt groan.

"All right?" he asked, his voice a bit strained.

"God, yeah. 'S good. Don't stop."

God, having him inside me . . . It was *nothing* like the last time we'd done this. He filled me up, chased away the shadows, and when he moved . . . Christ. It was like every nerve ending in my body had somehow migrated down to where he was touching me inside, and every single one of them was connected to my balls and my dick. He pulled sensation out of me like a flint sparking on stone.

Then he changed the angle, got even closer, and my legs tightened around his back as my prick rubbed between our bellies. It was too fucking much and perfect at the same time. I wanted him so much, needed him so much. Loved him so much. Christ, he was everything to me. I was babbling, I knew I was, and I didn't even know what I was saying, but I couldn't seem to stop.

Phil's face above me was so fucking open, the tense lines around his eyes all gone. Then he closed his eyes and gasped my name, and that was it. I was flying, way up high, and it felt like I was never coming down. I groaned so loud my throat hurt, and I didn't give a monkey's because my whole body was burning in ecstasy. I swear I felt Phil come inside me, his strokes stuttering as he lost control.

We held each other for a long time after that.

Eventually, though, reality always has to kick in. In my particular case, it decided to kick me in the bladder. I kissed Phil and rolled out of bed. "Gotta see a man about a dog."

I whistled half-heartedly as I peed, and winced when I caught a glimpse of the time. No wonder my stomach was starting to complain it hadn't had enough attention this morning. Probably time to see about some breakfast before it got too late to even have lunch. Casting a wistful glance in the direction of the bedroom, I padded into the kitchen and filled the kettle. Coffee was definitely called for.

"Christ, what a night," I muttered to the jar of instant. Mugs, needed mugs.

"You said it." Phil slung a warm arm around my waist from behind. "You know, not that I'm complaining, but I'm pretty sure you've got a clean pair of jeans here. Not to mention underwear."

I leaned back into his—sadly—now clothed chest. Apparently he had ninja dressing skills to add to his sneaking-up-on-me skills. "I'm rebelling."

"What, against the tyranny of trousers?"

"Yep. And the fascist dictatorship of shirts."

"After last night, I'd have thought you'd be all for protective clothing." Phil's arm tightened around me.

"Protective, yes. Cock-blocking, no." I twisted in his grip. "Come on, let me go, I can't get to the milk here."

Phil stepped back, then reached around me to get some mugs out of the cupboard while I raided the fridge. By the time I'd spooned out the coffee, the kettle had boiled.

We leaned on the counters with our mugs of coffee slowly clearing away the cobwebs, and it was just like any other morning we'd spent together. Relaxed. Cosy, even. It'd have been pretty easy to pretend all the crap had never happened and carry on from here.

But I didn't want to do that. Didn't think it'd be fair. There was stuff that needed to be said. That *I* needed to say.

"So, um . . ." I rubbed the back of my neck, realised it was a gesture I'd caught from Phil, and put my hand down rapidly. "I did some thinking, after . . . you know. The other night. And, well, Kev Drinkwater, last night. I couldn't help noticing you didn't go ballistic on him." A bit of dancing around the car park, maybe, but that wasn't exactly grievous bodily harm.

Phil looked at me. "No. I didn't." He was silent a mo. "Reckon he killed Carey?"

"Yeah. Yeah, I do. Not entirely clear on the *why*, mind."

Phil nodded. "Not got the longest fuse around, has he? And from what you told me, he's pretty homophobic. Maybe he blamed Carey for turning her off men?"

"Yeah, maybe." We were getting away from the important stuff here, though. I put my mug down and briefly wished I'd bothered to put some clothes on. Then again, would I feel any less naked with my kit on? Somehow I didn't think so. I took a deep breath. "So . . . Anyway. What I wanted to say is, I reckon I overreacted big-time about all that stuff Dave told me." My face was all screwed up by the time I got it out.

Phil wasn't looking at me. Apparently his feet were much more interesting right now. "I should've told you about it."

"No, you shouldn't. It's all in the past, innit? Done and dusted. Nothing to do with me."

"Course it's to do with you," he said, then stopped. "I don't mean . . . Shit." He scrubbed at his face with both hands, then looked up. His gaze was scarily sincere. "I know I've done things I shouldn't have. And, Christ, no matter what I do, I can't promise I never will again. But I will *never* hurt you." He didn't add, *not unless you ask me to*. I knew that part already. "You've got to believe that. And the other stuff . . . I'm trying to be better, okay? I'm trying."

My heart felt like a wet rag someone was wringing out to dry. "Phil . . ." My voice cracked. I cleared my throat and gave him a wonky smile. "You don't have to be better for me, all right? Don't want *new and improved*. I'm fine with *original and best*. More than fine." I stepped forward and cupped his face in my hands. "I love you, you prick."

Phil blinked at me. In his shorts and T-shirt, with his hair all fluffed up, he looked like an overgrown kid who was worried his mum was about to wallop him. "Still?" His voice was hoarse.

Could have been last night's smoke, mind. But I didn't think so.

"Always, you plonker." I sank against his chest, feeling all warm and fuzzy, and was more than mildly miffed when, after a sec, he pushed me away. "Oi, I thought we were having a moment?"

Halfway across the room, Phil turned, looking jittery. "It's your birthday, right? And I promised you a present. So just . . . just wait there, all right?"

I folded my arms and leaned back against the counter.

Turned out my birthday present *was* in the bloody kitchen cupboard. Phil rummaged for a mo, then came out holding something in one hand.

It was pretty small—fitted easily in the palm of his hand. We already had each other's keys, so it wasn't that—cuff links, maybe? For that formal shirt he'd made me buy for Gary and Darren's wedding? Or—

I stopped with the guesses as the whole world tilted sideways. Well, metaphorically speaking, Hertfordshire not being known as the earthquake capital of the world.

Then again, this measured about ten on any scale you could mention.

Here, in the middle of the kitchen, Phil had gone down on one knee.

He held out a little box, opened to show a medium chunky band of gold. "Tom Paretski, would you do me the very great honour of becoming my husband?"

In the circs, it was probably unfortunate that the first thing that came to mind was a heartfelt "Fuck me!"

Phil huffed a laugh. "That's generally part of the deal, but you probably ought to give me an answer first." Then his expression changed, got all vulnerable. "You don't have to say right away."

Something twisted inside me. I sank down on both knees in front of him. Mostly because my legs had gone wobbly. "Yeah, I do." I smiled at him, probably a bit soppily. Well, probably a lot soppily. "And, well, yeah. I do. Want to marry you, that is."

Phil closed his eyes for a moment. Just long enough for me to take his face in my hands and kiss him. He kissed back feverishly, one arm going around my neck and almost pulling me off-balance. Then he drew back. "God, I love you."

We moved to the sofa after that. The wood flooring at Phil's wasn't exactly easy on the knees, and let's face it, we were both the wrong side of thirty now. I popped back into the bedroom to grab a spare pair of shorts and a T-shirt first, seeing as I was apparently going to be all respectable from now on.

Phil patted the cushion, and I sank down beside him. "I can't believe you just proposed to me when I was starkers. Think we might have to edit that part out when we're telling the grandkids."

He laughed and pulled me in close. "Have you seen what kids are like these days already? In thirty years' time, nothing'll shock them."

"God, that's a weird thought. One day we're going to be just a couple of boring old farts, and nobody'll think twice about gay marriage." I hoped so, anyhow. "Actually, I can't believe you proposed to me at all. After all the crap I've put you through . . ."

"No, you haven't."

"I sodding well have. Um. You do realise we're going to have to invite my mum and dad, yeah? I mean, if you want to change your mind, I won't hold it against you." It was half-true.

All right, no it wasn't.

"Don't worry. Your mum's got way too much class to make a scene at a wedding." Phil huffed a short laugh. "It's my family we're going to have to watch out for."

Bloody hell. "Hey, you know it's traditional to have the two families on opposite sides of the church or whatever? Maybe we could erect some kind of riot shield between 'em."

He grinned. "I was thinking separate services myself. Or, as last resort, I hear Gretna Green is nice this time of year."

"Too easy for 'em to follow us to. How about a beach wedding in St. Lucia?"

"You and your sodding beaches. No, we can have the honeymoon anywhere you like, but if we're doing this, I want to stand up and do it in front of a congregation of our family and friends."

"Well, I'm in." I snuggled in closer to him. "Long as you're still talking about getting married, that is. Hey, you thought about when we'd do it?"

Phil didn't answer.

"Phil?"

"Sorry. It's just . . ." He took a deep breath. "Didn't want to make any plans. You know, tempting fate and all that bollocks. Thought my chances were dodgy enough already. But, yeah, what do you reckon? Next summer? Let the dust settle from Cherry and Greg's bash first?"

It was my turn to make him wait for an answer, seeing as I was a bit preoccupied with the way my heart was turning into mush and, apparently, taking all my brain cells with it. "Dodgy chances? Are you serious? That's just . . . I'm not even going to say what that is, you muppet. And yeah, next summer sounds good. Really good."

It'd give us time to do things properly. Get a good venue and all that stuff.

Maybe even find a certain Mike Novak and slip him an invite, although I wasn't sure how Mum and Dad would feel about that.

Come to that, I wasn't sure how *I* felt about it.

CHAPTER TWENTY-FIVE

The wedding of the century took place the following week, on Midsummer Eve, giving rise to not a few gags about short wedding nights.

And no, I don't mean Phil and me decided to elope to Las Vegas. I'm talking about Gary and Darren's do. They got spliced in St. Albans Registry Office, a pretty impressive, Gothicky red brick building that apparently used to house the governor of an old Victorian prison. There were some surprisingly nice gardens out the back, with an even more surprising old cannon—I assumed it hadn't been got in for target practice on uppity prisoners, but you never know with Victorians—that Gary and his newly wedded husband made *full* use of in the photos.

Don't ask. No, really, don't ask. I'm not going to repeat my best man's speech here, but let me tell you, with a venue like that, I wasn't short of gag material.

The sun was shining, but the temperature had dropped at least ten degrees. It wasn't cold, exactly—pretty much normal for the time of year, as the weather man on the telly kept reminding us—but I'd just started getting used to Mediterranean temperatures, so I was actually glad of my posh Italian wool suit.

The grooms looked, as Gary himself modestly admitted, fabulous, dressed in matching dark-blue tuxedos and crimson bow ties, each with a perfectly matched rose as a buttonhole. Phil and me, as best men, were in dark-grey suits that looked pretty similar but were actually subtly different.

He'd insisted weeks ago that we should buy them instead of hiring. I'd thought it was a waste of money at the time, but, heh, it looked like I was going to get at least one more wear out of mine. I had to keep reminding myself not to tell anyone that, though. We'd decided to keep the engagement quiet until after Gary and Darren had jetted off to their not-so-secret honeymoon hideaway in the Seychelles—no way was I going to steal any part of my mate's thunder on his big day.

Gary, being Gary, had insisted me and him set off half an hour early, presumably in case a sinkhole opened up and swallowed the road or something and we had to hike there. So I was expecting the place to be empty, or possibly even still full of the previous wedding's guests. As it happened, though, we walked into the foyer to find the party already in full swing. Darren was standing on a chair and handing out champagne like a king dispensing largess to a rowdy crowd.

I'd been looking forward to seeing what Darren's family were like—all right, I'd been looking forward to seeing how many of them, if any, were also of the dwarfish persuasion—but actual blood relatives of his seemed to be pretty thin on the ground.

His mum was there, all five feet nothing of her, which still made her a good six inches taller than her son. She looked a lot like Darren, actually, all except the goatee—although she did have the makings of a pretty impressive 'tache. Hefty arm muscles too, presumably from lugging crates of fruit and veg around. The bloke with her, though, who was around Phil's height and had a permanent stoop from bending down to speak to his better half, turned out to be Darren's stepdad. His real father had apparently copped it twenty years ago in a tragic market accident. I didn't ask.

They were currently making stilted conversation with Gary's mum and dad—or Mumsy and Pops, as Gary liked to dub them. Both were dressed up to the nines, for them—Mumsy in a sort of shapeless kaftan thing the wardrobe department on *Joseph and the Amazing Technicolor Dreamcoat* would have rejected for being too garish, and Pops in an antique dinner jacket and with braids in his beard. I caught a snatch of Gary's mum, whose accent is posher than the Queen's (pun not intended), getting all poetical about the mystical energies of the solstice. It was clear Darren's folks didn't have a clue what to make of them.

There was also a whole barrowload of market traders, most of them still in their everyday clothes but one or two in their posh frocks. One bloke was even in a top hat, but seeing as I recognised him as the bloke who ran the hat stall, I didn't reckon he deserved any special credit for that.

Darren yelled out to Gary over the crowd. "Angel! Light of my life! Come and get some of this inside you!"

A middle-aged lady with a deeply lined face gave a raucous cackle. "Oi! You can wait till after the wedding for that!"

The crowd parted genially, and we trooped up for an audience with the Champagne King. Phil, standing at Darren's side like a mafia enforcer, sent me a smile that was mostly in his eyes, and I felt like I'd been at the champers already.

"Sweetie pie," Gary cooed, making grabby hands at the glass Darren had filled for him. "A man after my own heart."

"And the rest of you," Darren said with a wink and a leer.

"Some bits more than others," Mrs. Raucous suggested and nudged the hat man so hard in the ribs, he spilled his champagne.

I gave Phil a helpless grin, but he seemed to be enjoying himself anyway.

Marianne was standing off to one side, all on her lonesome. She was looking summery in a floral sundress that was a bit see-through in the sunlight streaming in through the foyer window.

Her eyes were pretty bright already, but I swear they lit up even more when they spotted me. "Tom!" she called, waving so hard her boobs jiggled. I was worried her strappy frock might not be up to the task of keeping them in check.

I grabbed a glass for her and walked over for a natter, having already run out of prewedding duties. There's only so many times you can check you've remembered (a) the ring, (b) the speech notes, and (c) the groom. And if I drank too much bubbly, I'd be bound to belch embarrassingly halfway through the ceremony. "All right, love? Here on your own?"

"No, I'm here with Cas—remember I told you about her? She's just gone to the ladies'. She'll be along in a mo."

"Uh . . . remind me. It's been a rough few weeks."

Marianne's hundred-watt smiled dimmed a little. "You're not wrong there. I told you and Phil about her, back before everything? Cas. My ex, well, sort of. From London, see?"

"Cas! Right. Gotcha." So the girl off powdering her nose must be the one she'd tried to dump Carey for, back in London. "So are you and her getting back together now?"

Marianne bit her lip, looking shy but happy. "Maybe." All at once, she gave a sunny smile. "This is Cas," she said unnecessarily as I turned to see who'd put the light in her eyes.

I blinked. Cas was . . . Well. Not what I expected at all.

For one thing, she was *tiny*. And for another . . . You know those dolls they make in Russia? Where you open one up, and there's an identical one inside, only smaller? That was Marianne and Cas. Both blonde, both bubbly, both pretty and busty.

"Hi!" Cas said, flashing me a perky smile and sliding an arm around Marianne's waist. *Her* dress went partly see-through in the sunlight too.

"Cas, this here is Tom," Marianne said.

Cas's eyes widened, and she literally launched herself from Marianne's side and threw her arms around my neck. "Oh my God!" She squealed it right in my ear, which started ringing a bit. "You saved her *life*! Thank you *so much*!"

I wasn't quite sure what to say to that. *It was nothing* didn't seem like it'd be very complimentary to Marianne. "Er, yeah, anytime," I muttered, patting her arm and hoping she'd take it as a hint to let go.

She did, but not before she'd given me a big, cherry-lip-gloss-flavoured kiss, which got us a wolf whistle from somewhere in the foyer and a shout of "Get a room!"

Still deafened from all the squealing, I wasn't positive, but I reckoned at least one of the two had come from Gary.

"Is it just me, or is that a bit weird?" I whispered to him after I'd disentangled myself from Cas's arms and left the girls to it.

"Barbie's little sister wanting to kiss you? Well, it takes all sorts, as I always say. Now, are you sure you've got the ring?"

"Positive. And no, you muppet, that wasn't what I was on about. I meant, Marianne going out with someone who looks exactly like her."

"Well, I suppose it is a tad narcissississ . . ." Gary frowned at his champagne. "What *are* they putting in this stuff these days? Vain."

"What, Marianne? She hasn't got a vain bone in her body. Nah, must be something else."

"The urge," Gary said solemnly, tapping a finger on the side of his nose, "to merge."

I shook my head. "Nah. They wouldn't get up to anything like that in public."

Marianne and Cas promptly proved me wrong by engaging in a passionate smooch.

Nobody told *them* to get a room.

I *would* say the ceremony went off without a hitch but, heh, that might send the wrong message in the circs. The vows were surprisingly traditional, Gary and Darren promising to love, honour, and cherish till death did them part. They didn't even put in any risqué stuff about worshipping each other's bodies. It was all really moving, actually. Mrs. Raucous snuffled into her hanky, and even I felt a bit moist around the eye area.

'Specially when Phil slipped his hand in mine and squeezed tight.

The reception was down the road at mine and Dave's hangout of choice, the White Hart. It's an actual old Tudor inn with a hole in the middle to drive your coach through, a suit of armour in the lounge, and ghosties in the walls. Allegedly.

The place was packed—a lot of people who hadn't wanted to come to the registry office or hadn't been invited had been happy enough to toddle along to celebrate once Darren had mentioned the magic words, "free bar." There was going to be a sit-down meal in the restaurant in an hour or so for what Gary liked to call his *intimate inner circle* of around fifty people, but for now, anyone was welcome.

"Tommy!" Gary cooed as I elbowed my way into the place. "Do be a darling and fetch me a drinkie. I'm *gasping*."

I grinned. True to form, him and Darren were sitting in state in the two red plush thrones the management liked to keep in the main bar for some unknown reason. "All you need is a couple of crowns, and you'd be the perfect king and queen."

"Don't be ridiculous, darling. I'm already the perfect queen. Now, chop-chop, or it'll be off with your head!" He giggled, and Darren sent him a besotted look.

"Anything for His Majesty?" I asked.

Darren held up his half-full pint. "Nah, but your faithful service has been noted, vassal. Could be a knighthood in it if you play your cards right."

Behind me, Phil laughed. "If you think I'm letting my bloke get down on his knees so you can tap him with your sword... No, nothing for me either, ta," he added at my questioning look.

I fought my way to the bar, where I ordered a martini for Gary and a pint for me, then looked around while I waited. Harry was sitting on her own at the far end of the bar, looking a bit lost without any glasses to polish. She nodded at me, and I ambled on over. "All right, there?" I sort of felt like I should say something along the lines of *Sorry your pub burned down*, but I wasn't quite sure how to put it.

"Not so bad," Harry rumbled. "Going to be opening a pop-up in the Granary next week. Keep the regulars happy till we get the old place up and running again."

"Yeah?" I wasn't sure what a pop-up was supposed to be, but she sounded pleased about it.

Harry nodded. "Be serving drinks in their downstairs room, evenings six till eleven. Going to have to be bottled ales, but some of it's all right." She raised her bottle of Fanny Ebbs in illustration and took a swig.

"Sounds great." It was a weight off my mind to know Harry wasn't going to be stuck twiddling her thumbs wherever she was staying for now—actually, where *was* she staying now?—gloomily waiting for the insurers to give the thumbs-up to rebuilding the Dyke.

Harry put her bottle down on the bar and put a hand on my arm, which was so unusual for her, I looked at her sharply. "I'm sorry you got dragged into that business with Carey's body," she said.

I shrugged. "Yeah, well. Not like you put him there, was it?"

"I wouldn't have got you involved, but Marianne panicked. Wanted him out of there. My fault, though. I told her about you finding bodies before, and it must have put the idea in her head."

I stared. "You knew he was down there?" I hissed, darting a look around to make sure no one was in earshot.

"Course I bloody knew," Harry said, her voice equally low. "You think I don't know what's in my own cellars?"

"So why didn't you call the police as soon as you found him? Or Phil, at least?" It wasn't like I'd gone around advertising that me and him weren't on the best of terms at the mo, so it couldn't have been a display of solidarity or anything.

Bugger. Since I'd spoken to Mum, the word *solidarity* just made me think of Mike Novak. Right now, I didn't need the distraction.

"Wanted to talk to a couple of people first. Look at my options. And no offence, but your Phil would've gone straight to the police. Once a copper, always a copper."

I glanced over at Phil, who was laughing at something Gary or Darren had said and looking more relaxed than I'd seen him for weeks. "He's got a lot of ex-colleagues who'd beg to differ with you on that one. These people of yours . . . had a bit of practice dealing with inconvenient dead bodies, have they?"

"Met all sorts when I was boxing," Harry said, which, if it was an answer, wasn't a reassuring one.

"Surprised you didn't call them in to deal with him in the first place, then."

"If I'd been after that kind of solution, I wouldn't have called in your Phil, would I?"

I couldn't help smiling at the thought. Yeah, he was my Phil all right. Then I gave her a hard look. "So it definitely wasn't you who threw that cricket ball at my head?"

"Swear to God. No, my money'd be on Carey for that one. Malicious little shit."

"Yeah, you're probably right. Him or Kev, anyway. Though Dave tells me Kev swears blind it wasn't him. And seeing as how they're doing him for murder and arson already, one little count of assault wouldn't up the sentence much, so you wouldn't think he'd make such a fuss about it if it wasn't true."

Harry nodded. "Kev's more the up-close-and-personal kind of violent. Carey's the one who didn't like getting his hands dirty."

To be honest, I'd have been happier if it'd been Kev. I was still having trouble reconciling the way Carey had been last time I'd seen him, with him having at that point already put me in the hospital.

I hesitated, not sure if I should tell her the next bit, but sod it, she was a mate, and she'd just told me something pretty bloody incriminating herself. "Look, keep this to yourself, yeah, but Dave told me Kev's admitted killing Carey. Though he says he never meant to, obviously. Carey went to see him, tried to get him on side to help him get Marianne back—but he reckoned without Kev's dodgy logic that someone must've turned Marianne off blokes. So when Carey lays it on thick about how happy they'd been until she left him for a woman, all he hears is 'I turned her gay.' Couldn't have helped, either, that Carey had zero interest in her going back to Bristol or anywhere else he wouldn't be able to keep his beady eye on her. Things got heated, Kev lost his rag and hit the bloke."

Harry shrugged. "Well, we've all wanted to do that to the slimy little bastard."

So much for not speaking ill of the dead. And wasn't it ironic that with all his clever, manipulative scheming, Carey got brought down in the end by a bloke running on beer and bigotry?

"Course, once Kev had a dead body on his hands, he wasn't above trying to use it to his advantage. He's confessed to stashing the body in your cellar—he was hoping even if the frame-up didn't work, the pub'd be closed down." I hesitated, then thought *in for a penny* and all that. "Oh, and he said a few uncomplimentary things about your door locks."

It'd turned out Kev was actually fairly knowledgeable about housebreaking. His late mum must have been so proud. He'd even managed to find the override key and disable Harry's smoke alarms before he'd started, the bastard. Evading police pursuit, though, had turned out to be another matter. It hadn't taken long for them to track him down at a mate's house in Somerset and haul him back here for questioning.

I was still waiting to get my phone back, mind.

Harry snorted. "Not going to be a worry for a while, now, is it?" She took a long swallow from her Fanny Ebbs and put the bottle back down on the bar with an *ahh* of satisfaction. "I'll be able to get some new ones on the insurance."

"Yeah, well, it's an ill wind." I was glad she was being philosophical about it. "Listen, are you all right in the meantime? Got a place to stay?"

"Cheers, Tom, but I'm fine. You enjoy the party."

I picked up the drinks and headed back to the happy couple.

"Somebody was a long time," Gary said reprovingly. "That's you off the New Year's Honours List."

I handed him his martini with as much of a bow and flourish as I could manage without spilling it or my beer. "Yeah, well, I got talking, didn't I? Don't suppose you know where Harry's staying, while the Dyke's out of bounds?"

"Well, far be it from me to spread salacious gossip—"

Darren choked overdramatically on his pint. Gary mock-glared at him and continued, "But the word amongst the bell-ringing fraternity is that she is currently residing at the vicarage."

"Yeah? What's she doing there?" I perched on the arm of his throne so I could hear him better over the hubbub.

Darren gave me a pitying look. "You mean *who's* she doing? And there's only one other person what lives there. *And* who Harry's been seeing on the sly, sneaking her in and out the pub at all hours. Told you before, them church types, they're all at it."

I goggled at him. "You mean . . . Harry and the Rev? Seriously? I mean, Christ, what the bloody hell have they got in common?"

Gary tittered. "Apart from the obvious, you mean?"

Phil huffed a laugh. "I don't know. Maybe Harry's got deep religious beliefs she never talks about. Or maybe Lillian's a boxing fan. Maybe they just get on well, you ever thought of that?"

"Yeah, but . . . Is it even allowed? I mean, I know vicars are allowed to be gay these days, but are they allowed to have, you know, relationships?" I shied away from saying *have sex*. Some pictures I *did* not want in my head, and the mental image of Harry *in flagrante* was definitely among them.

Phil shrugged. "Current line is, it's fine as long as they're celibate. Some of 'em are even married, civil partnered, whatever."

"Seems a bit hard. Pun not intended." I tried to imagine living with Phil and not, well, shagging him. I'd have permanent wrinkles from all the cold showers I'd have to take. Then I frowned. "When you say 'celibate,' what does that mean, exactly?"

I got patronizing looks from all three of them.

"Well," Gary said slowly. "When a vicar and a landlady love each other very much, sometimes they like to have a special kind of cuddle—" He broke off, cackling, when I jabbed him in the ribs.

"I meant, where do you draw the line? Is kissing all right? Is it all right as long as you don't slip 'em some tongue? Are there parts of the body that are no-go areas, or is it all good as long as there's no actual penetrative—hang on a mo, how does that even apply here? Seeing as neither of them's got a dick." I was getting a headache. "Do strap-ons count?"

"Tell you what, why don't you go and ask Harry about it?" Phil asked with a smirk.

"I'll tell you why. Because Harry'd have *my* bloody dick as a trophy."

"So what does that tell you? That it's your own potential lack of a sex life—and mine, come to that—you should be worrying about, not Harry's. What those two get up to in private is between the two of them."

"And God," I added piously. Then I sent a quick mental apology skywards in case anyone up there might think I was taking the piss.

"Yeah," Phil went on. "And last I checked, His name wasn't Tom Paretski."

I fluttered my eyelashes at him. "Shame, that. Does that mean you won't be getting on your knees to worship me later?"

"Oh, *please*," Gary broke into me and Phil's little tête-à-tête, and I noticed Darren was making gagging motions. "Anyone would think you two were the newlyweds, not my sweetie pie and me."

Phil and me shared a glance, then he started talking to Darren about the plans for the honeymoon quick before we could give the game away.

"You know, your Phil's starting to grow on me," Gary said after a while, in full earshot of the man himself.

"Like a fungal infection?" I suggested before Gary could do it himself.

Phil sent me a glare that promised retribution later. I was looking forward to it.

"Mm, no, actually," Gary continued thoughtfully. "More like bindweed. You know if you don't uproot it ruthlessly, it'll take over the whole garden, but it does look rather pretty when it blooms."

"Nah, he's all right, Phil is," Darren butted in. "Just 'cos he ain't all touchy-feely don't mean he don't care." He fixed me with a stern look. "Like an apple, he is. Hard on the outside, looks tough, but bruises easy. You want to watch you don't bruise him."

"That's it," Phil said. "Anyone coming up with any more vegetable metaphors for me has to keep 'em to themselves or put a quid in the tip jar."

"Similes," Darren corrected. "They ain't metaphors, they're similes." He caught us all staring. "What? So Spanish ain't the only evening course I took."

"Isn't he just *too* perfect?" Gary sighed.

The meal was great—lots of plain English food washed down with fancy French plonk—and by the time I started getting nervous about my best man's speech, which was when I stood up to make it, I realised everyone was too pleasantly sloshed to give a monkey's what I said as long as I kept it short and didn't eat into valuable drinking time.

They laughed at the funny bits, anyhow, so that was a win.

Phil's speech was even shorter and went straight for the heart. It didn't have any laughs, but it did have me tearing up again. Must have been all that wine. Or something. When he invited everyone to raise their glasses and themselves to the happy couple, the cheers almost drowned out the hideous scrape of fifty chairs being pushed back as one.

Sitting back down, I groped for Phil's hand. We'd been seated next to each other—well, your usual wedding seating plan doesn't really cater for having two grooms and two best men, although I bet someone somewhere was busy writing out a new book of etiquette to cover the situation.

"Great speech," I whispered.

Phil looked uncomfortable. "You don't think it was too much?"

"Nope," I said. "Perfect."

Gary and Darren left for their honeymoon soon after the end of the meal, to a chorus of catcalls and cheers and not a few thrown condoms. My face was starting to ache from smiling all day, so God knows how Gary was managing. I'd never seen him look so happy, bless him.

Phil and me stayed at the White Hart for another round of drinks, finally catching up a bit with Greg and Cherry. Sis was looking pretty in a summer frock (*not* see-through) and one of those weird feathery things women wear instead of hats. Greg had somehow managed to find a dog-collar shirt in pride pink, which I thought was pretty decent of him.

After a bit, Phil stood up. "Right. Got something I need to do."

"It's through the door and on the left," I told him helpfully.

He made an exasperated noise. "Not *that*." Then he hesitated and looked at his watch. "See you back at yours in about an hour and a half?"

"Yeah, all right." We hadn't made any plans for the rest of the day, and it was still fairly early. And while I'd have been quite happy to support our local enterprise until closing time, a bit of couple time had definite attractions.

"You'll be there?"

"Course."

Phil nodded, and I watched him walk away.

Well, failing to do so would have been a criminal waste.

CHAPTER TWENTY-SIX

I made sure I got back to mine good and early, seeing as it seemed to be important to Phil for some reason. I thought about using the time to give the place a quick tidy. Then I thought, nah, no point, it was only Phil coming round, and he'd helped make the mess in the first place.

I wondered what this was all about. I had a nasty feeling it might be to do with my spidey-senses—Phil's eyes had lit up like Blackpool Illuminations when I'd told him about the effect the fire had had. He'd gone on about stuff like *focus* and *need* that made me think he'd actually clicked some of the links at the end of the Wikipedia article on dowsing this time.

The internet's got a lot to answer for, in my view.

I had a quick cup of coffee—the walk back had cleared my head a bit, but I was still feeling the effects of midday drinking—then sat down with the cats. And promptly had to stand up again when the doorbell rang. If that was Phil, I was going to have words with him about using his key.

Whatever I'd been about to say died on my lips when I opened the door.

Standing on the doorstep with Phil was an old bloke about my height, maybe an inch or so shorter, with thick grey hair and clear green eyes with deep crow's-feet etched into the corners. He must have been in his sixties or so, but he was still pretty straight-backed, although he had a walking stick in his hand and Phil was hovering a bit, as if the bloke might have been a bit unsteady on his feet on his way to the front door.

"Phil?" I asked, gobsmacked, meaning *Is this who it looks like, and do you realise I'll sodding kill you if it's just some random bloke off the street?*

He gave me a crooked half smile. "Happy belated birthday. Here's the other half of your present."

I just stared at the old bloke.

"You're Tom Paretski?" he asked, in a voice with a touch of the West Country about it—and a touch of the Old Country too, even after all these years.

"Yeah," I managed, my throat dry.

Jesus Christ.

Leaning on the stick with his left hand, the bloke held out his right. It felt dry and crepey but warm when I took it. He smiled, and the crow's-feet deepened. "It's good to finally meet you."

"Tom?" Phil said, staring intently at me, his gorgeous face unreadable as ever and not looking remotely like a flower or a fruit or anything else from the vegetable kingdom. "This is Mike Novak. Your dad."

Explore more of *The Plumber's Mate Mysteries*:
riptidepublishing.com/titles/series/plumbers-mate-mysteries

Dear Reader,

Thank you for reading JL Merrow's *Heat Trap*!

We know your time is precious and you have many, many entertainment options, so it means a lot that you've chosen to spend your time reading. We really hope you enjoyed it.

We'd be honored if you'd consider posting a review—good or bad—on sites like **Amazon, Barnes & Noble, Kobo, Goodreads, Twitter, Facebook, Tumblr,** and your blog or website. We'd also be honored if you told your friends and family about this book. Word of mouth is a book's lifeblood!

For more information on upcoming releases, author interviews, blog tours, contests, giveaways, and more, please sign up for our weekly, spam-free newsletter and visit us around the web:

> **Newsletter**: tinyurl.com/RiptideSignup
> **Twitter**: twitter.com/RiptideBooks
> **Facebook**: facebook.com/RiptidePublishing
> **Goodreads**: tinyurl.com/RiptideOnGoodreads
> **Tumblr**: riptidepublishing.tumblr.com

Thank you so much for Reading the Rainbow!

RiptidePublishing.com

ALSO BY JL MERROW

The Plumber's Mate Mysteries
Pressure Head
Relief Valve
Blow Down
Lock Nut (coming May 2018)

Porthkennack
Wake Up Call
One Under

The Shamwell Tales
Caught!
Played!
Out!
Spun!

The Midwinter Manor Series
Poacher's Fall
Keeper's Pledge

Southampton Stories
Pricks and Pragmatism
Hard Tail

Lovers Leap
It's All Geek to Me
Damned If You Do
Camwolf
Muscling Through
Wight Mischief
Midnight in Berlin
Slam!
Fall Hard
Raising the Rent
To Love a Traitor
Trick of Time
Snared
A Flirty Dozen

ABOUT THE AUTHOR

JL Merrow is that rare beast, an English person who refuses to drink tea. She read Natural Sciences at Cambridge, where she learned many things, chief amongst which was that she never wanted to see the inside of a lab ever again. Her one regret is that she never mastered the ability of punting one-handed whilst holding a glass of champagne.

She writes across genres, with a preference for contemporary gay romance and mysteries, and is frequently accused of humour. Her novel *Slam!* won the 2013 Rainbow Award for Best LGBT Romantic Comedy, and her novella *Muscling Through* and novel *Relief Valve* were both EPIC Awards finalists.

JL Merrow is a member of the Romantic Novelists' Association, International Thriller Writers, Verulam Writers and the UK GLBTQ Fiction Meet organising team.

Find JL Merrow on Twitter as @jlmerrow, and on Facebook at facebook.com/jl.merrow

For a full list of books available, see: jlmerrow.com/ or JL Merrow's Amazon author page: viewauthor.at/JLMerrow

9 781626 497245